From One Night to Forever
Henderson Family Book 4

SYNITHIA WILLIAMS

Copyright © 2024 Synithia Williams
ISBN: 978-0-9975729-6-4

Originally Published by Crimson Romance
November 2025

Cover Art by: Mae Phillips at Cover Fresh Designs

Synithia Williams
Columbia, SC

ACKNOWLEDGEMENTS

I've had so much fun writing the Henderson Family Series! Thank you to all of the readers who contacted me about Janiyah, David, Kareem, and Aaron Henderson. I appreciate you taking the ride to bring happily-ever-after to this family. Many thanks to the fantastic team at Crimson Romance who originally helped me with this series: Tara, Jess, and Julie! I also have to thank my two sons for reigniting my enthusiasm for professional wrestling (which you saw in this novel). I've been a fan all my life, but now I have an excuse to watch again and slip my guilty pleasure into my novels. Finally, as always, thank you to my fantastic husband, who supports me every time I slip away to my writing cave.

CHAPTER 1

Aaron Henderson's stomach kept up the angry growl it had started twenty miles down the road as he walked across the packed parking lot of Momma's Kitchen. The hotel clerk had recommended the restaurant after Aaron had parked his big rig, Bertha, and checked in. The lively sounds of a band filtered from the restaurant's closed door. The name *Momma's Kitchen* in pink neon letters glowed from a sign over a front porch. When the clerk had mentioned the place, Aaron remembered his friend Reggie Holmes saying something about the restaurant and the good food.

Reggie was the reason Aaron was in Resilient, Tennessee. After two years of talking about merging their trucking companies, Aaron and his old college friend were actually taking the steps to do it. Both successful in their own right, the merger would make their company a leading contender for transportation in the Southeast.

Not bad for a college dropout. A grin spread across Aaron's lips. Many people had sneered and thought he was crazy when he'd sold all his belongings, cashed out the savings account his parents had set up for him, dropped out of Appalachian State, and bought Bertha ten years ago. Hell, he hadn't thought his spur-of-the-moment decision to drive big rigs and see the country would turn into running his own business, and four years ago when he'd hired his first driver he hadn't imagined he'd be on the verge of doubling the size of his company. Henderson and Holmes Trucking would one day be a powerhouse in the freight industry. He not only believed that; he was certain. Things always worked out for him.

A couple came through the front door, increasing the sound of the music and bringing out the savory smells of good food. Aaron's stomach growled in appreciation, and he jogged up the stairs and through the front door. He quickly scanned the busy seating area. Tables covered the black-and-white-checkered floor and were filled with couples, some families, and groups of guys. A young woman belted out Tina Turner's "What's Love Got to Do With It," accompanied by a band in the far right corner. A long wooden bar with silver and black stools ran along the left wall.

Aaron turned to the hostess standing behind a podium right near the door. "How long is the wait?"

The hostess smiled, emphasizing a pair of cute dimples. Her ponytail swung to the side as she checked the list. "Umm...about twenty minutes. Unless you want to sit at the bar."

She met his eye and the corner of her friendly smile went up a little more with interest. Aaron grinned and his eyes flicked down to the abundance of cleavage in the white button-up shirt straining to contain her blessings. Cute, definitely, with golden tan skin and shiny dark hair, but he guessed she was in her early twenties. Not too young for him, since he was only thirty, but the early twenties came with drama and he didn't need more drama.

"I'll wait at the bar, sweetie, thanks." He winked and the hostess licked her full lips.

Aaron chuckled to himself and rubbed the stubble on his chin. He strolled to the bar and grabbed an empty seat in the middle. The female bartender scrambled from the back holding a tray filled with glasses in her arms. She dropped the tray with a rattle on the shelf behind the bar, wiped her forehead with the back of her hand, and then waved his way.

"I'll be with you in just a second," she said and hurried to fill two of the new glasses with beer from the tap and gave them to two men sitting at the end. After chatting and laughing with them, she made her way down the bar to him.

"What can I get you?" She looked up from her notebook and her friendly smile tilted up with interest.

She was another cutie, more his age, and with enough curves to cushion a man for days. She wore the same tight white button-up and black pants as the hostess and other waitresses he'd spotted. No wonder Reggie told him to check out this place. The women were beautiful.

"I'll start with a Budweiser and a menu." He glanced at the name tag on her chest. "Monique."

"You got it, handsome." She winked and handed him a menu from beneath the bar, then sashayed over to fix his drink.

The woman on stage finished her song and the place erupted in cheers. The guy next to him whistled. "Another one, Kacey!"

The rest of the place joined in whistling and asking for more. Aaron raised a brow and watched as the performer waved a hand and shook her head.

"Come on, this is my night off." The smile on her face said she was loving the call for encores despite her words.

"One more. One more!" someone chanted.

"Fine, one more, then I'm going back to the bar. I'm supposed to be celebrating," she said with a laugh. "Not working."

The guy next to Aaron bumped him with his elbow. "She can celebrate with me, know what I'm saying?" The guy chuckled.

Aaron grinned and let out a light laugh. "I guess she's a local favorite."

"Oh, yes. Everyone loves Kacey. Good girl, but that doesn't mean I wouldn't mind being her surfboard for the night." He elbowed Aaron again. "Know what I'm saying?"

Aaron nodded. "Yeah, I get you."

The cute bartender came back with his beer. "Ready to order?"

Aaron barely glimpsed at the menu. "Just bring me the best thing in the place."

She flipped her waist-length hair over her shoulder and batted her long lashes. "I'm not on the menu."

Aha, so it was like that. Aaron checked her out again, appreciating the smooth brown skin and voluptuous curves. Her thick makeup wasn't his thing, nor the extra-long lashes, but that wasn't enough to make him not take interest.

You're here on business, not to get laid, he reminded himself. That could wait until he got things settled with the merger. But it didn't mean he couldn't lay the foundation for a future hookup with a little harmless flirting.

"That's too bad," he said with a smile. "I guess I'll have to compensate with a burger and fries."

She slid the notebook into the pocket of her apron and gave him another flirtatious look. "Coming right up." Her full hips swung suggestively as she sauntered over to put in his order. She gave another glance at him over her shoulder.

Business, man, business. He had enough female drama in his life right now. Too many glasses of champagne at his sister Janiyah's wedding to his best friend, Fred, had contributed to Aaron making the monumental mistake of sleeping with

Janiyah's best friend, Liz. The sex was good; the two—or three—hookups the organ below his belt agreed on later weren't bad, either. On the way up his oldest brother, Kareem, had called to say that Aaron's hookup with Liz had led Janiyah to believe Aaron and Liz were becoming serious.

At least the misinterpretation wasn't on Liz's end. They'd been on the same page with their friends-with-benefits relationship. He and Liz hadn't hooked up in the last three months. He hadn't been in town much, and she'd gotten back together with her ex-boyfriend, an architect she had an off-again, on-again relationship with.

The band revved up and the sounds of "Lady Marmalade" filled the place. The guy next to him drummed his hands on the bar. "I love it when she sings this," he said to Aaron.

Aaron nodded at the guy's enthusiasm. "Number-one fan" would be an understatement of the man's excitement. Aaron focused back on the woman who had the poor guy so enthralled.

His first thought was she was a little too skinny. He liked them like the bartender, but the songstress had perfect curves in just the right locations. Her face immediately drew him in. She wasn't classically beautiful—some would say her lips were too full or her cheeks too sharp—but that didn't prevent Aaron's heart from starting a crazy rhythm.

She swayed from side to side with the music. Her slim hips hypnotized him and the rest of the men in the crowd with their easy flow in dark jeans and tall black heels. A red tank top with a white heart with wings spread across her perfect rack, and dark straight hair brushed her russet brown shoulders. With each word and graceful movement she commanded the stage. Her voice belted out to perfection the suggestive lyrics with enough passion to have Aaron shifting in his seat.

Aaron tapped the guy next to him. "Hey, what's her name again?"

"Kacey," the guy said almost with idolization.

Kacey? He would've expected something more elaborate or flamboyant. Something more suited to the goddess onstage.

"Me and her used to hang out," the guy said. "I think I may try to rekindle that flame tonight. Know what I'm saying?" Another elbow to Aaron. "Show her why breaking up with me wasn't such a good idea."

Aaron shook his head. The guy's overuse of the elbow and "know what I'm saying" made Aaron think Kacey was smart for breaking things off.

Aaron picked up his beer without taking his attention off the woman onstage, the curvy bartender forgotten. Aaron brought the bottle to his lips and watched the seductive sway of Kacey's hips as she sang the Creole words every man wanted to hear from a beautiful woman. "Do you want to go to bed with me tonight?" Heat rose slowly up his body, an affirmative answer to her lyrical question.

No complications, remember?

Aaron pushed the thought aside. Talking to her a little wasn't the same as going home with her.

"Can I get you another drink?" Monique asked.

Aaron shook his head. "No, but you can send one over to her on my tab when she's done." He pointed to his stage goddess.

Monique cocked a brow and chuckled. "No offense, but you're the sixth person who's ordered my sister a drink tonight."

Aaron leaned on the bar. "Sister, huh? One of these guys in here special to her?"

Monique shook her head and leaned a hand on her hip. "Nope."

"And there are five guys ahead of me interested in getting her attention tonight?"

A smirk crossed Monique's features. "Yep."

Aaron raised a brow. "None of us stand a chance, huh?" He took another sip of the beer.

"She's the good sister. If you want some fun tonight, you might want to look elsewhere." Monique winked again, then went down the bar to tend to the other customers.

A smart man would follow the path of least resistance. One night stands and easy hookups were more his thing. Anything else lead to feelings, which lead to serious relationships followed soon after by the bad break up. Aaron was very familiar with bad breakups having been through one before. Bad because he'd chosen to walk away rather than accept at twenty-two he was ready for a long-term commitment. He'd broken up with Denise, the only woman he'd come close to loving, and lived his life since having fun and being free.

Aaron glanced back at the goddess onstage. Her gaze swept the room, caught his, jerked away, and then snuck back. An electric sizzle zoomed across his skin from the brief contact. Aaron smiled and brought the beer to his lips. One night of fun didn't mean a relationship. And he wasn't interested in the path of least resistance. He always preferred a challenge.

CHAPTER 2

Twelve years of working and singing in her momma's restaurant made Kacey Randal pretty good at avoiding distractions during her set. But tonight she wasn't supposed to be working and only sang because some of the locals had begged her to. According to her sister, Monique, tonight should be epic. The last night of her break from classes. The last night she could relax and have fun before diving in to the final semester of graduate school. The last night she'd have no really good reason to ignore the very big distraction of the sexy guy at the bar watching her every move with dark, soulful eyes.

He was just her type of distraction too: tall and slim with just enough muscle to show he was all man. Wild curly Afro begging for her fingers to dig into and a five o'clock shadow he wore better than any other man she knew. The second he'd strolled into the building with that laid-back, looking-for-a-good-time swagger, her radar went off and her libido—ignored far too long because of school—perked up. A sexy Casanova here to tempt her on her last free night.

She finished the song with her usual flourish. "Thank you!" she called to the cheering crowd, some she'd known all of her life, some strangers like the guy at the bar, and others the usual guys who hung around to drool down the cleavage of the waitresses in the sexy uniform her mother had picked specifically to appeal to the male clientele. If there was one thing Kacey's momma knew, it was how to make a man drool and spend his money.

Kacey grinned and waved at some of the regulars as she skipped off stage and walked to the bar. On the way she noted if any tables needed drink refills, noticed table forty-two hadn't gotten their food yet, and scanned the wait staff to make sure they were smiling and happy when talking to the patrons. She couldn't help herself. She loved this place. Loved that her momma had worked her fingers to the bone to open Momma's Kitchen after people wrote her off for popping out four kids in the five years after she turned twenty. Her momma's sacrifice to build her restaurant was ten times more than Kacey's sacrifice of fun and excitement while completing her MBA. After this last semester, she would graduate with a hard earned 4.0. Then she could help take the next step and finally open their second restaurant in Chattanooga. She wanted Momma's Kitchen to go from local favorite to a well-known franchise.

The source of Kacey's pride, her momma, Sabrina Holmes, stood at the end of the bar, one hip propped against the worn wood and a big smile on her slim face. At forty-five, people often mistook Sabrina for Kacey's sister. Sabrina's brickhouse figure made Kacey wonder why she hadn't inherited her momma's Marilyn Monroe curves instead of the broomstick skinny she'd gotten from her daddy.

"You sang good tonight, Kacey," Sabrina said. "Even with the trip up."

Kacey grabbed the towel Sabrina held out and wiped her brow. Sabrina didn't miss a thing. "Trip up? What are you talking about?"

The music started and her cousin Natoya got up to sing. The evening singing by the friendly, and flirty, waitresses was one of the biggest draws of Momma's Kitchen, after the food.

"Don't be coy with me, girl. Six guys bought drinks for you during your show, but only one of those guys caught your attention." Sabrina winked. "I see the way you're pretending not to watch him."

Kacey's heart upped the tempo. "I'm not watching anybody."

"Sure you aren't. He's sitting next to Howard."

"I know."

Sabrina chuckled. "But you're not watching him, huh." Sabrina snatched the towel, then hit Kacey on the rear end. "If you weren't my most responsible daughter, I'd tell you what to do with that man."

Kacey shook her head. "Good thing I am."

Her older sister, Monique, hurried over and slid a beer across the bar toward Kacey. "This one is from Howard."

Kacey slid the beer back toward her sister. "I'm not seeing Howard anymore."

Sabrina grabbed the beer and slid it back to Kacey. "Never waste a free drink. Accepting doesn't mean you have to go home with him." She patted Kacey on the back and then went through her nightly routine of talking to the various customers at the tables.

Kacey leaned on the bar and raised a brow toward Monique. "How's it going?"

"Everything is absolutely fine, Ms. Worrywart." Monique pointed a hot pink nail at Kacey. "You are supposed to be making tonight epic. Not singing. Which is a backdoor way of working."

The waitress for table forty-two, Jamelah, came from the kitchen, and Kacey waved her down. "What's going on with the food for forty-two?"

Jamelah glanced at Monique. "I thought she was off tonight."

Monique shrugged. "She is off."

"I am off," Kacey said.

"You're never off," Jamelah said with a chuckle. "They didn't want mushrooms with their steak and Bobby messed up their order. Don't worry, I've already let them know and your momma is giving them a free dessert."

Kacey nodded, satisfied that what she'd noticed was already being handled by the staff. Not that she should be surprised. Jamelah was one of their best waitresses, and her momma wouldn't let any customer leave unhappy.

Jamelah leaned in. "Now go have some fun and quit worrying about table forty-two. You can bark orders at us tomorrow."

Kacey flicked the towel at Jamelah, who scooted out of the way and chuckled. "You worry about your table."

Jamelah shook her head and sauntered off. She grabbed a pitcher of tea and water and started going through the tables, giving refills.

"Jamelah's right, you don't have to be here. The restaurant will survive when you're away."

"I know that," Kacey said, turning back to her sister, who was rolling her eyes.

"If you know that, then why aren't you grabbing a hottie and having your way with him instead of coming here, singing, and asking about wait times?"

"I'm not looking for a hottie," Kacey said. "I don't need any distractions right before school starts. I barely started my last semester on time after the weekend I spent with you in Nashville during my last break."

Monique laughed and slapped the bar. "That weekend was awesome!"

"My hangover wasn't," Kacey said with a laugh. The only time she let loose was in her breaks between semesters, and only because Monique usually dragged her out to have fun. With Monique working, Kacey's ideas of ways to have fun became limited.

"Fine, if you're only interested in hanging out here with me and momma, then don't talk about work, or complain when I leave with the hottie at the bar instead of going to hang out with you."

"What hottie?"

"The one on the end, with the hair and eyes that say *let me screw you so hard you'll speak in tongues*." Monique bit her lower lip and grinned. "I'm taking him home tonight."

Damn it! She should have known Monique would have noticed the same guy. Their weakness in men ran along similar lines. Usually she let her sister be the more daring, then fill her in on the details of her fun time. But something about this guy made Kacey want to be the daring sister. She still probably wouldn't do it, but she also didn't want to hear about how awesome he was in bed if Monique went home with him.

"Come on, Monique, you don't even know the guy."

"Yeah, but I know my body. And right now..." She looked around Kacey and wiggled her fingers. "My body says go home with him."

Casanova returned Monique's wave. Then his gaze connected with Kacey's and he gave a smile that made her heart trip all over itself. Heat flashed up her cheeks and a tickle started in her midsection.

The thought of the bedroom eyes that had watched her entire performance landing on her sister made Kacey's stomach clench. "How do you know you're leaving with him?"

Monique shrugged. "Because I'm the path of least resistance. He also bought you a drink, but you'll pretend all night like you're not interested because of some old-fashioned sense of good behavior. I, on the other hand, want to get laid." Monique rapped her long nails on the bar, then went back to helping customers.

Of course Monique had inherited the Coke bottle figure from their mother. Didn't hurt that Monique's father had a little extra meat on his bones. If given a choice, Kacey was pretty darn sure Casanova would go home with the thick sister. Guys usually preferred thick over thin.

Kacey tried not to be jealous. Except she hadn't had good sex in over a year and refused to have another mediocre—beggars can't be choosers—hookup with her ex-boyfriend Howard. Her lady parts needed tending to and had snapped to immediate attention the minute Casanova walked through the door.

Honestly, she wanted to get laid, and it wasn't as if she couldn't easily get laid. The women in her family had no problem attracting men. The problem was, they attracted men who were experts in drama, heartbreak, or potential scandal. Kacey's momma and her married-to-someone-else father were the perfect example. Kacey wanted to get laid without complications or distractions, and sex with Howard, or one of the other regulars, would come with one or the other. School started on Monday, and she'd be forced to go without for another twelve weeks. Her options were either to continue to be the grown woman afraid of a one-night stand, or take the hot guy at the bar home.

She picked up the beer and took a long sip. She'd start by thanking him. That wouldn't hurt, and if it turned out he was a complete jerk, then she'd go home and give her vibrator another round of action. Even though that was getting old.

She took another sip and made her way down the bar. Howard immediately sat up straight and grinned the knowing, hopeful grin of a guy who knew where he fit into her life. Howard was a decent enough fellow, but she knew he hadn't been lonely since she'd broken things off with him last summer.

"You did great, Kacey." Howard bounced like a seven-year-old at a professional wrestling match.

Casanova turned in his bar seat next to Howard to stare at her. Yep, his eyes were just as sexy up close as they were far away. His *sexy comes naturally* five o'clock shadow perfectly framed smiling full lips.

"Thanks, Howard." Kacey lifted the beer in her hand.

"Is that the beer I bought you?"

Kacey shrugged. "I'm not sure. Monique mentioned that it came from this end of the bar." She looked back at her distraction. His gaze was taking the long route across her body. Kacey's body sizzled in response. "I came to thank both of you."

Howard frowned. "Huh."

Her distraction slowly lifted his gaze to hers. Her heart hitched and her stomach clenched. Deep in her bones...well, deep in another heated part of her body, she felt more stirrings of desire. How long had it been since she'd felt stirrings not related to the *it's been too long, I guess I'll have sex* feelings that normally came after finishing a semester in school?

"Finally decided to meet my eyes," she said in a voice that hid her inner yearning. He still had time to screw up the very crazy thought budding in her brain.

He leaned his elbows on the back of the bar and tilted up kissable lips. "Just saving the best for last. You have beautiful eyes."

The line was older than eight tracks, but the corner of her mouth flexed. "Is that tired line an indication of what you're all about?"

"That was no line. You do have beautiful eyes." He winked and lifted the beer to his lips. "But to be clear, it's also no indication of what I'm about. I'm not easily tired."

She perked up at the double meaning, and was surprised by how much she didn't mind. "Then are you one of those bouncing-around jackrabbit types?"

"Not at all. I'm nice and easy. Things are so much better when you take your time." His dark eyes stared deep into hers, caressing the long-dormant part of her personality that wanted to witness his definition of nice and easy.

Howard cleared his throat and coughed next to them. Kacey blinked and focused her attention back on him.

"Are you okay, Howard?" she asked.

Howard looked from her to the guy next to him. His shoulders slumped just a little, and he pulled money out of his wallet. "Nah. You sang really well tonight, Kacey."

"Thanks, Howard."

Howard tossed the money on the bar. He looked back at the guy, then met Kacey's eyes. "Be careful tonight, okay?"

She nodded. "I will."

Howard squeezed her arm, then walked away from the bar.

"Don't tell me I chased off your number-one fan," his hotness said.

Kacey slid into the seat Howard abandoned. "He's probably on his way to his girlfriend's place."

The guy raised his brows and chuckled. "And here I thought his heart belonged to you."

"I'm not trying to own any man's heart right now." She met his gaze. "I don't have time to take on any new complications."

His eyes widened slightly, and he leaned a little bit closer to her. "Good thing I'm not complicated." He took another sip from the beer and his tongue did a quick sweep afterward.

Kacey's nipples tightened and visions of the tip of his tongue gliding across the tips of her breasts had her sucking in air. "Really? The way I see it, most men do have some complications."

He held his arms out to the side. "What you see is what you get. I like to have a good time and meet new people." He dropped his arms. "But that doesn't come with any extra demands."

Monique strolled over and placed a burger and fries in front of him. Another button was loose at the top of her fitted white button-up shirt. A red bra and an abundance of cleavage peeked from the deep V.

"You need anything else, cutie?" Monique asked.

His scorching gaze remained on Kacey, which was unheard of when her sister's bosom was in the vicinity. "Nah, I'm good."

Monique slowly stood straight. Kacey met her sister's eyes and looked for any signs of disappointment that her plan for the night had ignored her. She grinned at Kacey and winked before walking away.

"So, mister *I don't come with any demands*, what do you come with when you're meeting new people and making new friends?"

He grinned. His lips weren't overly full but plump enough to make her wonder how soft they might be.

"I come with the promise of a good time."

"And how do you know the *friends* you've made had a good time? Please don't give me another line about people begging for more of your time." She sipped her beer.

"Number one, that wouldn't be a line. But before you roll your eyes and walk away—"

"Who said I'm an eye roller?"

"You've got that look. As if you've heard all the lines a man could possibly throw your way and you've perfected the not-interested eye roll."

Kacey grinned at his adept evaluation. She'd been hit on nightly in her twelve years working here. "Fine, I've been known to occasionally roll my eyes."

He picked up a fry and nodded. "I was correct in my assessment."

Her brows lifted and she leaned back. "Oh, so you're assessing me now."

"I always assess people. Can't help it."

"And do you spend most of your time assessing women?"

"Only the ones as captivating as you are," he said in a low, deep voice, those dark, soulful eyes staring straight into hers.

She almost wanted to believe him. Kacey blinked and looked away. "Another tired line. I'm beginning to think you're mistaken about those friends who've had a good time with you."

"And yet you're still here talking to me."

"I can't help it. I like to look out for other people, and I couldn't possibly let you subject a non-eye-rolling woman to those lines."

He let out a deep chuckle. "Oh, really now?"

Kacey lifted her shoulder flippantly. "Part of my civic duty, you see."

He leaned close again and his arm brushed against hers resting on the bar. A light brush, but enough to jolt her awareness.

"What other civic duties do you have?"

"Well, for one I can't have you promising people a good time and then not following through."

"I wouldn't expect you to," he said with mock seriousness. "Here's what I propose."

"What's that?"

"I show you a very good time and then you can verify that my tired lines, as you call them, are not tired but in fact the truth."

She'd seen enough guys come through Momma's Kitchen looking for a one-night stand to know that was exactly what Casanova was about. But that was all she needed tonight, if she went through with being the daring sister. "Finish your burger and fries while I consider that offer."

CHAPTER 3

Aaron was almost done with his burger, which was delicious, but he hadn't enjoyed it nearly as much as he had his conversation with Kacey. Not once had she asked him his name. He wasn't sure if that boded well for the vibe he felt humming between them.

Her sister had left the bar to sing onstage, and the woman who'd sung before was now at the bar. She too was young, busty, and flirty. Aaron again noticed the appeal of the place.

He looked back at Kacey, and when her wide, dark eyes met his, he forgot what he was going to say. A woman hadn't struck him speechless since he was in middle school.

"Your singing voice. It's beautiful, by the way," he blurted out.

"It's a family thing," she said with a shrug.

Aaron glanced at the new bartender and then her sister. "Are you all related?"

"Most of us who work here are in some fashion or another. But not everyone."

He pointed toward Monique. "After talking to you, I wouldn't have pegged you two as sisters."

"Most people don't, but why do you say that?"

"Most sisters have similar vibes. You're more intense than her. It hit me the moment we made eye contact."

Kacey's brows drew together. Aaron couldn't believe he'd let that slip out. He'd spoken the truth, but knowing she liked to call him on his "tired" lines, he doubted she'd believe him. In that case, he might as well voice all the expressive thoughts she conjured up in him.

"What's that supposed to mean?"

He sipped his drink. "I'll have to work a little bit harder to get to know you better."

Her brows relaxed, and she slowly lifted her head up and down. "Aha, I see." She lifted her shoulder. "Maybe you should go the easy route."

He leaned his elbow on the bar and met her eye. "I like a challenge."

"Most men do, but that doesn't mean having a good time with you tonight includes me sleeping with you."

He liked that she dropped the innuendo and put the idea out there, even though he didn't believe she wasn't considering taking him home.

"I don't think I have a chance in hell to get you in bed. But I never refuse a conversation with a beautiful woman."

She smiled. She had the thickest, sexiest lips, which, like her eyes, made him lose his train of thought when he focused on them. Aaron cleared his throat and glanced around. If he stared too long his body would give an adolescent reaction to her sexiness. "So, tell me, what do you do when you're not working here?"

"What do I do?"

"Yeah, tell me." He leaned forward and took another sip of his drink.

She raised a brow. "What do you do when you're not trying to pick up women in bars?"

"I'm driving Bertha."

"Bertha?"

"My truck."

She frowned. "You're a trucker?"

He heard the distaste in her voice and disappointment filled him. "You disapprove?"

Her face cleared and she shook her head. "No, truckers come through here all the time. I'm just surprised. So, why Bertha?"

He shrugged, but felt as if he'd lost some points with her. No problem, he'd encountered that with women before, and he usually overcame any doubts they had about his success.

"She just felt like a Bertha." Kacey's chuckle made him grin. "When I'm not driving, I'm hanging with my family. I'm the youngest of three boys with one sister after me. I like playing video games, baseball, and sometimes still think about pursuing my childhood dream to hold professional wrestling's intercontinental championship."

Kacey cocked her head to the side. "Why not the world heavyweight champion? I mean, that's a title worth holding."

Aaron leaned back and his eyes widened. "What do you know about world heavyweight championships?"

She shrugged and smirked. "I know the heavyweight champion is pretty much the face of wrestling. And they have the bigger belt."

So she knew a little bit about wrestling. "Bigger isn't better."

"Is your insecurity showing?"

He was really starting to like her sassy mouth. He wagged a finger at her. "Aha-ha, you've got jokes."

"Just an observation." She dragged out the last word before taking another sip of her beer.

Aaron's thoughts fled, chased away by the sight of those luscious lips wrapped around the long neck of the bottle. He blinked and shook his head. "Who's your favorite heavyweight champion?"

Kacey refilled his glass. "Easy. The Mountain."

Aaron slapped the bar and shook his head. Most women liked that guy because of his looks and the successful acting career he'd started after leaving wresting. "No! Are you serious? You have to go back to when wrestling was great. That's when Hardy Boy Ricky Mable held the title."

"Hey, I'm not hating on Ricky, but the Mountain was awesome. He is still awesome!"

"I can't believe this." He tapped the shoulder of the guy next to him. "Can you believe this?"

The guy looked from him to Kacey and shrugged. Aaron turned back to her. "Tell me why you think he's so awesome."

That started a debate of the best and worst champions and tag-team duos in wresting history. Kacey proved she knew more than a little bit about wrestling, and impressed the hell out of him. The bartender brought his check, and Aaron paid after Kacey challenged his ranking of the Wild Hawaiians in the place of all-time best tag-team champions.

"I give it to you," Aaron said as he signed his credit card receipt. "You know your wrestling."

"I've watched since I was a kid." She leaned in close. "It's my guilty pleasure."

"Nothing wrong with that." He slid the signed receipt across the bar, then turned to Kacey. "So, are you ready to go have a good time?"

Her easy smile faltered. Bluntness normally worked easier than being sly.

"Are you sure you don't want to take the easy route?" she asked.

"Positive."

She swallowed and he followed the movement of the muscles in her neck. Everything about her drew his attention. Crazy, he'd never been this into a woman he'd just met before.

"Go on out and give me a second to wrap things up with my sister."

"Don't want to be seen leaving the bar with a man you just met?"

"Something like that."

He nodded and stood. "I'll see you outside." He ran a finger down her arm. Not to be seductive, but because he'd been dying to touch her all night. Her skin was soft, and the simple touch thrilled him more than he'd expected. Aaron knew that even if she didn't meet him, he'd never forget his reaction to her.

CHAPTER 4

Kacey walked out onto the wooden deck of Momma's Kitchen, her heart pounding in her chest. She hadn't told Monique she was taking the hot guy from the bar home. Just said she was tired and would catch up with her later. Monique had caught the eye of another guy and waved Kacey off.

What am I doing? The straitlaced side of her brain said to ignore the crazy rush going on inside of her body, go home, and get ready for her last semester in school. The long-neglected side argued that backing out meant going home to a bowl of popcorn and Netflix. Or, more likely, getting online to go over the course description for her final class and then doing some online research.

Neither of which were what she really wanted to do. What she really wanted to do was live out the fantasy of being daring enough to go home with the hot guy at the bar. To forget all the lectures about not letting loose and actually do just that. So what if the last time had ended in heartbreak and disaster? She'd been seventeen and stupid. Now she was twenty-seven and smarter.

Theoretically anyway.

"Changing your mind?"

Kacey blinked and turned to her left, where Casanova stood leaning against one of the beams in the porch. She still hadn't asked him for his real name. She didn't want to know his name. If she went through with this, it would be to have a little fun, a no-strings-attached kind of thing.

His sexy gaze never left hers, and Kacey's blood heated. She definitely was not going home to Netflix and Google.

"Why would you say that?" She strolled down the steps toward the parking lot, trying to appear as if she was as sure of herself as she pretended to be.

Casanova pushed away from the beam and followed. He got close enough for his arm to brush against hers as they walked, sending sparks across her skin. "The way you burst out of the door then stopped and chewed your lower lip screamed you were reconsidering."

Kacey chuckled and shook her head. The evening breeze was a welcome refresher to the heat in her body. "You've got lots of experience in this arena."

"What arena?"

"This whole hookup thing." Kacey stopped and faced him. He took a step back, giving her space but not enough to prevent the crisp smell of his cologne from toying with her hormones. "So tell me, how does this usually work?"

Casanova's brows drew together over dark eyes. "How does what work?"

"You know, your mack routine. Do you sweep into town and panties drop as soon as you give that smile?"

The smile in question lifted the corner of his mouth and he ran a hand across the bristly shadow of a beard. "You like my smile, huh?"

She rolled her eyes though her heart did a little flip. "It's all right. I'll admit you've got the sexy lip lift mastered." She grinned and pointed toward his absolutely kissable mouth. "Did you practice to get it so perfect?"

"No practice. I guess I'm just a natural."

She bet he was. He chuckled and shook his head. "I'm just kidding. There are no expectations behind my smile."

Kacey raised a brow. "Oh, really? So, when you offered to show me a good time, you didn't expect leaving meant *let's go have sex*?"

He brought a hand to his chest and his eyes widened. "Not at all. I just thought we could leave and get to know each other. Maybe see where the night takes us."

She raised a brow. "Really?"

His brows drew together, and his head tilted to the side. The smile on his face slowly morphed into a look of surprise. "You really do have beautiful eyes."

He sounded like a hero from an epic romance. And like a love-struck heroine, her cheeks flushed and she returned his appreciative look with a grin. So what if he probably spouted that line a hundred times? Tonight, she wanted the flowery words, the buildup of anticipation, and—hopefully—an explosive ending. Her life of schoolbooks and work rarely afforded those moments. All the more reason to seize this one.

"And you really do have a nice smile," she said. With that his smile returned. "So, how do you propose we get to know each other?"

He pointed across the street. "We'll start over there."

Kacey turned in the direction he pointed. Lights flashed on a mini-windmill that slowly turned at the miniature golf course next to the Hampton Inn across the street. She frowned with her confusion. "Are you serious?"

"Very."

"Miniature golf?"

"Of course. It's fun, and I get the feeling that you're slightly competitive."

"Another observation?" she asked with a laugh.

"Just a guess. Come on, let's play."

He took her hand in his. His hand was surprisingly warm and his skin smooth. Long fingers entwined with hers, and a gentle tug had her right against the side of his body. He might be tall and slim, but there wasn't anything lightweight or frail about the hard muscles pressed against her side. Nor were there any further doubts about leaving the bar with her fun fling.

• • •

Kacey held up the miniature golf club and twisted her lip. "Two things. I am competitive, but I'm terrible at miniature golf."

They stood before the first hole. Casanova had paid for the game and handed her a club with an enthusiastic look on his face. She hadn't lied; she sucked at miniature golf. She knew customer service, singing, and running a business, but not hand-eye coordination.

"Lucky for you, I'm an expert. I'll help you out." He held out his hand to indicate the starting point. "Ladies first."

She blew out a breath and pulled her lower lip between her teeth. "Don't say I didn't warn you."

By the fifth hole, Kacey was having fun, if not playing well. He, on the other hand, always handled the course easily. She would have been annoyed by how easy he made the game look, except he kept her laughing, mostly with his random questions to test her knowledge of wrestling. With every one she answered correctly, the admiration in his eyes grew.

She approached the fifth hole and hit the ball directly into the course's green lagoon. A muffled sound came from behind and she spun to face him. He placed his fist over his mouth and pretended to cough. Kacey lifted her chin and suppressed her own laughter. "Are you laughing at me?"

He dropped his hand and grinned. "Yes. You're terrible."

"I'm not terrible. I'm just not...good," she said with a smile.

"It's your swing. You're swinging too hard and you're not looking at the ball."

"I am looking at the ball." She looked down at the fake green grass.

"No, you glance at the ball, then you look at the hole and swing as if you're trying to hit a baseball." Aaron dropped his club and came up behind her. "Here, let me help you out."

He turned her to the side and wrapped his long arms around her body. She let out a silent gasp and fought not to groan. His lean body didn't quite press into hers, making her want to eradicate the distance and rub her back against his front.

His agile fingers wrapped around her wrists, the tips directly over her fluttering pulse. Easing his fingers past her wrist, he fully engulfed her hands around the thin club. Kacey's body hummed. She shifted from foot to foot, but the vibrations of desire didn't lessen.

He stepped forward, their bodies touching. "Stop fidgeting," he said close to her ear. His lips didn't touch and that made her want to shift so they could.

She sucked in a breath. Her body tightened, but she didn't move away.

"Relax," he whispered into her ear and ran his hands up her bare arms. His palms were slightly calloused, but not enough to detract from the pleasure of having his hands on her body. She didn't like men with soft hands; she worked hard and loved men who worked equally as hard.

Even if he's a trucker?

She blinked and pushed away that thought. He was a trucker, but he wasn't Dewayne. The older guy who'd taken advantage of her romantic teenage heart for his own pleasure. Since Dewayne had forced her to grow up the hard way, she'd avoided dating truckers who only came into Momma's Kitchen to eat and hook up. But this time was different. She was older. Wiser. In control. *This* wasn't dating. *This* was one night of fun, *not* the start of a lifetime of love.

"You're tense," he said. "You can't hit the ball if you're stiff."

"I'm relaxed," she said in a low and strained voice.

Once again he clasped her hands on the club. "You've got the club in a stranglehold. It's not a bat. Hold it gently. Caress it." His fingers massaged her stiff fingers. "Stroke it." His lips brushed her ear.

A shiver went through her body before she let out a light chuckle. "Stroke the golf club?"

His fingers continued the slow massage. "Yes." He kept his mouth close to her ear.

Kacey pushed her hips backward just slightly. He pressed forward and the hard rod of his erection met her backside. "Stroke it."

Another tremble went through her body and a vision of the hardness pressing into her filled her brain. She lowered her lids, blocking out the sights and sounds of the course, then slowly ran her fingers up and down the smooth silver pole. Her mind went there: imagining taking another long, hard object into her hands. Watching his body swell as the soft skin slid over the rigid flesh beneath. The pressure of his erection against her backside grew.

Kacey pressed her hips back further. "Hmm, you must like the way I stroke it."

He cleared his throat. "How can you tell?"

Her heart leapt at the low, grumbling sound of his voice. She'd never known she liked playing the seductress. She rubbed her backside against the lump in his pants. "Just a feeling."

His hands lifted to gently squeeze her biceps. "Yes, ma'am, I definitely like the way you stroke it."

If she didn't stop, she'd be thinking of finding a dark spot out here on the mini golf course they could slip away to. "Good to know."

She stepped away. Cool air replaced his heated body, but the imprint of how great he felt lingered. She strolled, on wobbly legs, to the next hole.

"You just gonna walk away like that?"

"Don't you want to finish the game?" She peeked at him over her shoulder and caught him rearranging his hard-on. Her breath got stuck somewhere in her chest and her breasts became heavy.

He caught her looking and gave her a cocky grin. "Let's finish the game."

The rest of the game was both pleasurable and agonizing. They still kept up the playful debate on wrestling, but Kacey made sure to stroke the club before every hit and added an extra swing to her hips. It was a poor imitation of her more-endowed female family members, but the way his eyes always popped when they landed on her small behind made her not care. She wouldn't have been so daring if he hadn't turned up the heat, getting her to stroke the club followed by the slight touches while they played. Brushing against her. Running his fingers down her arm. Whispering instructions in her ear, his lips gracing the outer shell a few times. By the last hole, Kacey's breathing was shallow, her nipples hard and aching, and her panties wet.

He watched her as she set up to hit the ball. This time she was determined, despite the heat running through her body, to try to get the ball in the hole. Too bad she'd have to get the darn thing through a waterfall cascading over plastic rocks. She leaned forward and her ponytail fell over her shoulder. He leaned in and ran his finger over the back of her neck. She knew what he touched—the small birthmark there.

Kacey gasped, then spun to face him. His dark, hypnotizing eyes burned with desire. He took another step forward and gently cupped her face in his hands. She shifted toward him and lifted her chin. Slowly he lowered his mouth to hers. He didn't kiss hard or clumsily. Instead his lips and tongue made a slow, detailed exploration of her mouth, getting bolder when she sighed or switching the pressure if she hesitated. This man knew how to kiss a woman. The golf club had long since fallen from her hand; she gripped his shirt and pulled him closer. His heart crashed against his ribs like the miniature waterfall.

He pulled back. "Let's get out of here."

"Dinner and a movie now?" she asked in a breathless voice.

Casanova smiled, but shook his head. "My hotel room."

She bit her lower lip. Now or never. She had no uncertainty; she wanted tonight with this man. "Lead the way."

CHAPTER 5

Casanova held her hand as they walked through the lobby, into the elevator, and down the hall to his room. Kacey almost wanted to know his name. But every time she started to ask she stopped herself. This was a one-night fling, not the start of forever. Still, walking hand in hand with him felt natural. His long, sure strides and the steady pressure of his hand against hers guided her exactly where she wanted to go.

She appreciated the view of jeans against his long legs, and toned arms revealed by the short sleeves of his green T-shirt. Sleek and powerful were the two adjectives that jumped to mind when she looked at him.

He didn't hesitate when they got to the door of his room. No stopping to ask whether she was still sure. No need. She was sure. He crossed the threshold and led her inside, wrapping an arm around her shoulders and drawing her into his embrace. Kacey pushed the door closed with her foot and stared into the sexiest pair of eyes she'd ever seen.

The corner of his mouth tilted up. Her heart did a crazy shiver. This was right.

Digging her fingers into the springy curls on his head, Kacey pulled him down. His pliant lips touched hers and shivers of desire ignited through her body. He grasped her butt with one hand, pulling her tight against his firm body and the long, stiff rod growing between them. The other hand gently removed the band holding her hair back. The pressure of the ponytail gave way. Kacey sighed and pressed her tongue against his lips. His mouth opened and his firm tongue slid across hers while his long fingers gently pressed against her scalp.

The kiss was slow, unhurried, as if he wasn't just interested in getting into her pants, but actually wanted to savor and explore the time they had together. Kacey wasn't as patient. She slid her leg between his until the wet ache between her thighs pressed tightly into his strong leg. A long, low moan rumbled through his chest and the hand on her behind drifted up and under her tank top. His palms, warm and eager against her back, caressed as he lifted the tank top.

Kacey pulled back enough for him to remove the shirt, then grabbed his hair again for another kiss. His hand traveled across her back and then her bra loosened. The guy had obvious skills to unhook it with one hand. Breaking the kiss, his burning gaze locked with hers and he eased the straps off her shoulders and down her arms. The pads of his fingers made featherlight touches against her heated skin. Touches that left a trail of fire in their wake. His eyes lowered to her breasts and his lips parted before his tongue did a quick sweep across the swollen lower one. Her breasts were a decent B cup, not enough to garner envy or lustful looks. But he stared as if he'd just revealed perfection.

He grasped her breasts, kneading the soft flesh and then pushing them up from beneath. A second later his warm lips closed over one hard tip.

"Mmmm, yes," Kacey moaned, her hand once again plunged into his hair.

He sucked deep, then slowly ran his tongue across her aching nipple. Sure fingers gently massaged the other breast while his mouth did deep, slow sucks of the sensitive nub. Each pull created an answering twitch of the muscles of her sex. Desire soaked her panties, and Kacey pressed forward and twisted for more. Switching sides, he started the same delicious tug on her other breast.

Both of Kacey's hands were in his hair, and she held his head in place. She could stand here, let him do this to her forever, but she wanted more. She lifted his head away from her breasts. He released her swollen nipple with a long, slow pop that made the tips harden even more.

He raised a brow. "I thought you were enjoying that?"

"I am." She opened the button of his jeans and jerked down the zipper. "But I'm impatient for more." Her hand pushed into his underwear and wrapped around the stiff length of his erection.

His lips curled into a sexy grin and her stomach trembled. "A woman who knows what she wants is always sexy."

"I know exactly what I want." And for once she wasn't afraid to go for what she wanted. Kacey pushed his jeans down his slim hips. She lowered to her knees and came face-to-face with his erection. Long and lean, like the rest of him, with a slight curve to the left. An organ that appeared designed with female pleasure in mind. She glanced up at him, saw the hopeful glow in his eyes. Her lips kissed the thick tip, and his body jumped. She slowly rose to her feet.

Wrapping her hand around his erection again, with steady pressure she slid her hand up and down. She leaned in to kiss his ear. "I want this." Her hand squeezed slightly, then her thumb ran across the wet tip.

His hand grabbed the back of her head and he kissed her with more urgency than before. His body shifted from side to side as he kicked off his shoes and used his feet to pull his legs out of his pants. Kacey kicked off her heels, and with the same expert efficiency as before, he got her jeans unbuttoned and down her hips. His fingers extended into the wetness between her thighs. Kacey's head fell back as pleasure radiated from where his fingers touched her most sensitive spot.

"You are ready." A long finger pushed deep into her. When he slid out, she clenched around him, trying to hold on to the pleasure. A breath hissed out between his teeth. "Do that again." His eager finger dipped back in and she clenched harder. His head dropped to her neck, where he moaned. "You're going to feel so damn good."

Kacey's feet entangled with his as they kissed and moved to the bed. Their tight embrace was the only thing keeping them from falling to the floor. Kacey pulled out of his addictive embrace to lie on the bed. He pulled a box of condoms from his overnight bag beside the bed. The bag was a reminder he was only in town briefly. A pang of longing went through her chest, but she pushed the silly emotion aside. That was the way of one-night stands. Right now was only about pleasure.

Her eyes were glued to his fingers as they easily slid the thin condom over his curved erection. It was a sight she wouldn't soon forget. Nor would she forget the way his gaze roamed over her body with an unhurried pace, taking in every curve with a look of wonder. Both were heated memories that would get her through the long nights of school ahead.

Kacey leaned back on her elbows, raised her knees until her feet pressed flat against the fluffy white comforter, and spread her legs wide. Dark and excited desire flashed in his penetrating eyes. Pulling his lower lip between straight white teeth, her sexy one night stand came back to the bed.

She expected him to jump on her, push in deep, and screw her brains out. Instead he slid his lean naked body against hers. The curly hairs on his chest tickled her stomach and breasts on the way up. Long legs entwined with hers, and gentle fingers pressed into her hair. He lifted her head and kissed her with the same slow thoroughness as before. Her body rose from the bed, and her arms wrapped around his muscled torso. Without breaking the kiss, he lowered a hand between them, took the heavy length of his arousal in his fingers, and ran the blunt thickness over her swollen clit.

Her nails dug into his back. Kacey's knees spread further apart. Her hips rocked back and forth, twisting beneath him, increasing the slick waves of pleasure of his body rubbing hers so intimately. He pressed the blunt tip of his penis against her wet opening. Kacey lifted her hips, trying to get him all the way in, but again he was slow, deliberate. With steady, short strokes, he slowly filled her to the hilt.

Kacey's head pressed back. His lips lowered to kiss her chin, then her neck and he started a steady rhythm. Strokes that resonated deep inside her body. Waves of pleasure traveled to every nerve ending she possessed. A strong hand gripped her thigh. He lifted her left leg higher and pushed even deeper.

"Ooh, yes, like that," she moaned.

"Do it again," he said in a low, thick voice. "Tighten around me." Kacey grinned and squeezed her internal muscles around him. The friction increased, and she sighed with pleasure.

A long, rugged groan ripped through him. "God, yes."

His strokes continued, and with each one she clenched him tighter. Their movements quickened as their pleasure grew. Until his body jerked deep inside of her. "Oh, shit, I can't..."

She didn't care that he came because as soon as his body shook then jerked, her own orgasm crashed through her. Her legs locked around his hips, and her arms seized against his chest. The world exploded in a rainbow of colors, and her lungs refused to accept air. If having him buried so deep didn't feel so good she'd be afraid of the violent reaction of her body. But he did feel good. Good enough for her to risk the lack of oxygen again and again to relive the best orgasm of her life.

CHAPTER 6

Fifteen minutes after the best sex of his life, Aaron was almost ready to leave the bathroom. They'd lain on the bed, both breathless and stunned, before embarrassment drove him to hide in the bathroom under the pretense of getting cleaned up. The same guy he'd seen all his life stared back at him in the mirror, but that guy usually didn't get turned out the first time he had sex with a woman. That guy definitely didn't come *before* the woman he was with.

You gotta do better, Aaron! He would do better the second round. Because he damn sure wasn't letting his sexy goddess go without another taste of ecstasy!

He opened the door and froze, his brows drawing together. Kacey was frantically picking her clothes up from the floor and dumping them into a pile on the bed. Her back was to him, and she hadn't noticed him leaving the bathroom. She reached for her beige underwear and bent to put them on. Aaron hurried across the room and wrapped his arms around her from behind. She straightened and dropped the underwear. Her body stiffened, but she didn't jerk away.

"Sneaking out on me?" He couldn't get over how much he enjoyed her skin pressed so tightly against his.

"I thought the long stint in the bathroom was my cue to leave."

Aaron pushed her hair aside and kissed the birthmark on her neck. The little star-shaped mark was his favorite thing about her, because kissing that mark had led to their first real kiss.

"Definitely not a cue. It just took that long for me to put together the remains of my broken ego."

She chuckled and twisted in his arms to face him. "Broken ego?" Head tilted to the side, she wrapped her arms around his neck.

"I've always been a guy who believes in ladies first. But you, goddess, sapped out my usual ability to hold back." Gripping her cute ass in one of his hands, he gave a squeeze. "I must redeem myself."

"Oh, really?" Her brow lifted. "What makes you think I'm interested in a rematch?"

Aaron's hand left her behind to slip between the front of her thighs and deep into her body. When she tightened around his finger, Aaron's eyes lifted heavenward. Memories of how good she'd felt around him, and how quickly she'd brought him to his knees, surfaced. He needed to calm down or the second show would be a repeat of the first.

"I think you're interested." He slowly slid his finger out of her slick channel.

A sexy grin lifted her thick, full lips, and she leaned in to kiss him. Aaron pulled his head back. "But first, I've got a few more questions."

A cute line appeared between her brows, and she pulled the corner of her bottom lip between her teeth. "You know we're past that point in the night."

"I can't help myself. You've got me intrigued." He stepped back and pulled back the covers on the bed. "I want to know more about you." Slipping between the covers, Aaron gave a soft tug on her hand, but she didn't get back in the bed.

Instead she crossed her arms over her chest and glanced around the room. "You really don't have to do this. Tonight is just about having fun."

"Well, I think it's fun to get to know more about you." He gave her the smile she'd complimented him on earlier and tugged on her arm. The confusion on her face finally cleared up, and she slipped into bed beside him.

His actions confused him. They were past the point where he had to try and be the suave guy she wanted to go to bed with. Still, something in him couldn't let her go without knowing more. Hell, he honestly wouldn't mind spending *a lot* more time with her in the few days he spent in Resilient, both now and in the future, working on the collaboration.

So much for "no complications."

Aaron shook aside that thought. "Favorite color?"

She lifted a shoulder. "Green."

His brows drew together. "Green?"

Her chuckle sent a pleasant thrill through his chest. "Yes, green. What did you expect? Pink, or yellow or lavender?"

He nodded. "Okay, you got me. But why green?"

"I don't know, I just like it." She turned on her side to face him, her head propped up on her hand. "It's the color of spring, rebirth, all things new in a year."

"So spring is your favorite season?"

"It is. Everything starts over in spring. It's nature's reminder that no matter what happened before, there's always hope to start again." Her eyes drifted off, and something was reflected in her voice. She'd been hurt before. Which made him want to never hurt her.

Aaron brushed her cheek with the back of his hand. She blinked several times, and the coy smile from earlier returned.

"Okay, your turn. What's your favorite color?"

"Orange."

"Orange?" Disbelief filled her voice.

"Yes, orange. It's bright, funky, fun. And I'm all about having fun." She grinned, and his lips raised automatically. Her smiles were contagious. "My favorite season is summer."

"It's so hot in summer."

"I know, but it was always the best time growing up. My dad is all about family. Down to routine family meetings, Sunday dinners, and heartfelt lectures. So of course every summer he dragged the entire family out on some weeklong vacation. The beach, the mountains, the lake."

"Sounds fun."

"It was great." He frowned. "Then one year my oldest brother started sulking and kinda sapped a lot of the joy out of things. He'd start arguments and then disappear. My parents tried to pretend as if things were okay, and even force fun on the rest of us, but we knew Kareem, that's my brother, wasn't making it easy. Pretty soon the vacations stopped."

"I'd think that would make you hate summer."

"Nah, there're still good memories there. And I can't help but long for the beach vacations to return."

She lifted her hand and smoothed the line that had formed between his brows. He hadn't thought about the end of his family vacations in years, nor had he considered the strain that had started in his family around that time. He'd been too young to understand, and thankfully his family had overcome all their hardships, but that young, happy time was forever lost.

Aaron took her wrist between his fingers and brought her hand to his mouth, where he lightly kissed the soft flesh of her palm. "Favorite meal?" His tongue traced over the spot he kissed, and she shifted closer in the bed.

"Hmm, that has to be the country fried steak and gravy we make at Momma's Kitchen. You?"

"Spaghetti. Mostly because my mom always makes it when we're all there." He kissed her wrist and caught a hint of a sweet-smelling perfume.

"That's nice," she murmured. He wasn't sure if she meant the kiss or his reference to his mom's spaghetti.

"What's your favorite song?"

He frowned. "I've never thought about that."

"Well, think."

"Sisqo, 'Thong Song,'" he said with a grin. "What man doesn't love a thong?"

She rolled her eyes but laughed, and they spent the next few minutes trading favorites. He'd lain around with women he picked up and asked them questions before, got to know them a little better—all to kill a little time before the second or third round of sex. But he'd become so interested in learning more about Kacey that he forgot all about this being a time filler.

"You know my mom met Ricky Mable several years ago," she said when their conversation traveled back to wrestling.

Aaron's eyes widened. "Really? How?"

"She ran into him in a deli in New York years ago."

"You're joking?"

"She has the Polaroid photo to prove it."

"I would love to see that."

Her smile tightened, and her eyes shifted away. "Yeah, sure. So have you been to a wrestling match before?"

He nodded. "Yeah, I took a friend when I was in Phoenix and they were in town for a live broadcast. She wasn't into it, though."

The rest of her body tightened. Aaron wanted to curse. Bringing up other women wasn't very smart. Normally he left out conversations of the female friends he kept. He'd let his guard down, since he felt as if he were talking to a friend. Aaron pushed the hair away from her face and held the back of her head. "You know, I'm in town for a few weeks. I'd like to see you again."

She shook her head. "Let's not start making promises or anything. Tonight was fun."

"And we could have more fun."

Her brow quirked up then down. "Yeah, sure."

Aaron admitted he wasn't looking for a relationship. And he definitely didn't want a repeat of the situation with Denise. He hated to think of his ex, but the easy feeling he got with Kacey was how things had started with Denise. He wasn't any more ready to settle into anything serious now than he had been back then.

He pulled her head closer. "You're right. Let's not talk about tomorrow when we still have the rest of tonight to enjoy each other." He pressed his lips to hers. Kissing her was addictive.

He leaned in for more, but she pushed him onto his back and straddled his waist. She sat up with a wickedly delicious grin on her face.

"Ready to redeem yourself?" She reached over for one of the condoms on the nightstand.

"Redeem myself, huh? I thought you enjoyed the act?"

"I did." She opened the foil packet with her teeth. "But I'd wager I can get the same result out of you."

Aaron's heart revved like an overheated engine. "Oh, really?"

She slowly slid the condom over his dick. "Really." Her voice became a throaty whisper.

"Give me your best?"

The decadent smile returned before she slowly impaled herself. Her mouth fell open in a silent sigh, and Aaron's hands gripped her waist. *Damn, she feels so good.*

Her hips twisted, and her miraculous body squeezed him tight, bringing to mind those Chinese finger handcuffs he used to play with as a kid. He'd never be able to look at the toy again without thinking of her.

"Get ready to get it." Her body moved up and down, her slick sex squeezed him hard, and her small breasts bounced beautifully. The intense pleasure made his toes curl and his eyes cross. She was likely to win this round as well.

CHAPTER 7

Kacey woke slowly, contentment flowing through every pore of her being. Bright sunlight created a red glow behind her closed eyelids. Her body sank into the soft mattress, the thick, fluffy comforter cocooning her in warmth. She liked mornings like this. No rush to get up. Just lying in bed, enjoying a slow wake up. Satisfied and content with a man's arm around her waist.

Her eyes popped open. The events of the night before hit her with an *oh shit* intensity. She was slowly and happily waking up with a stranger in a hotel room.

She eased toward the edge of the bed. The strong arm around her tightened and pulled her closer. Crap, how had she ended up with a cuddler for a one-night stand? He settled back down and softly snored. The stiff length of his morning erection pressed into her behind. Desire twisted low in her stomach. The memory of one of the best nights of sex she'd ever had replaced the *oh shit* feeling. That definitely meant it was time for her to get the hell out of the hotel room.

Kacey twisted her head to better see the clock on the nightstand. Eight forty-seven, damn! She was supposed to be at her momma's at nine to help her go over the layout for the new menu and then meet with her professor at ten to go over her thesis proposal. This was not the time for a lazy awakening in the arms of a stranger, no matter how nice and comforting having his muscled arm wrapped around her midsection felt.

Kacey held her breath and eased his arm from around her waist. He sighed and rolled over onto his back. She peeked over her shoulder and softly exhaled when he didn't wake. He did a little twist of his nose, the movement reminding her of a rabbit, before his lips parted and he let out another soft snore. She smiled. He was very cute. His curly fro was messed up, and the shadow of a beard from the night before had thickened even more. The sheets covered most of his chest, but she remembered the strong, lean muscles covering his entire body. Definitely a one-night stand worth remembering. After she escaped without any awkward good-byes.

She sucked in another breath and slid toward the edge of the bed, hoping he didn't wake up and ask where she was sneaking off to again. Or give her the cold, morning-after *it was fun, I promise I'll call* speech. She'd been there and done that before. Back when she was too young to realize that most truckers were only interested in quick hookups and not long-term relationships.

Thankfully, he didn't stir. Kacey found and slipped on her bra and panties in less than a minute. He didn't move and she congratulated herself of her ninja-like abilities to dress undetected. She found her pants on the floor at the foot of the bed and bent over to grab them. She'd just slipped in one leg when a pair of strong hands gripped her hips and gently pulled her back against the firm chest she'd kissed several times the night before.

"Trying to slip out on me again?" He pulled her hair aside and pressed his lips against the back of her neck.

Desire shivered down her spine, and she had to force herself not to close her eyes and lean back for more. "I didn't want to disturb you."

"Where are you going?"

"I have a lot of things to do today. I'm actually running late." She tried to pull away, but he followed the movement.

His hand spread across her belly. "There's a lot I have to do today too, but I'd really love to start my day with you...in the shower."

He kissed her neck again and softly massaged her breast with his hand. Her eyes fluttered. A picture of how good he'd look covered in soapsuds while they washed each other's backs formed in her mind.

No! Last night was last night—and that was all it was.

Today she had to face reality. Her last, and most important, semester of school was starting, and she was working at the restaurant that night, intent on making the family business a success. Making moves to open a second restaurant. She didn't have time to go another round with him. The rounds last night had been too good, and slightly addictive. Her life was busy enough without the added distraction of a guy who'd just breeze out of town in a few days.

"I wish, but I really should go." She stepped quickly out of his embrace, instantly missing his body. She faced him as he stood gloriously naked and amazingly tempting. So not helping her determination.

Eyes on face. Must keep eyes on his face.

He placed his hands on his lean hips, not bothering to hide his nakedness or his long, hard cock. God, this man would look awesome on an erotic postcard.

"Give me your number," he said. "Maybe we can hook up later?"

Kacey snorted and smirked. His lame attempt quickly distracted her from his naked body. Almost.

He crossed his arms, the lean muscles in his arms flexing with the movement. "What was that for?"

"Nothing," she said, grabbing her shirt off the floor. "It's just, you know, you don't have to pretend as if you're going to call."

"Pretend?"

"Yeah. I know what last night was. And really, I appreciate the attempt to make it seem like you want me to hang around, but let's just admit that things were fun and move on like the adults that we are."

She slipped on the tank top and pulled her hair out from the back of the shirt. She had no clue where the band that held her ponytail was and she wouldn't waste her time trying to find it before leaving.

He took a step forward. "Well, if we're going to be adults about this, how about you admit that you enjoyed last night as much as I did, and that you would love to give me your number so we can do this again sometime."

His cockiness made her laugh. "Sometime, like when? The next time you breeze through Resilient? Six months from now, I'll get a call from you and we'll hook up again in this hotel?"

"I was thinking more like tonight we hook up again in this hotel, but I'm good with adding six months from now, as well." His lips rose into a sexy, confident smile.

She shook her head. "I don't think so. I know how you truckers are."

He frowned. "'You truckers'?"

"Yeah, you breeze into town, grab a bite to eat and a willing female to screw. I agreed to be that willing female last night, but I'm not signing on to be your regular hookup in the town of Resilient."

He took another step forward and took her hand, slipping his fingers through hers. His eyes stared into hers, looking both innocent and tempting. "Maybe I really like you and want to spend more time with you. Come on, last night was great. There's no reason we can't enjoy each other."

This guy was good. And obviously used to getting what he wanted from women. She noticed he didn't deny her assumptions. And he'd said, "Enjoy each other." Translation: "Have a bunch of sex until I hit the road." They'd hook up one more night and then he would call her six months to a year from now when he was in the area and needed an easy lay. Not today. She'd gotten what she wanted and she refused to be his easy plaything.

Kacey took a step back, slipping her hand out of his. "I can think of a few reasons why we can't." She lifted a shoulder. "Thanks for the orgasms."

His brows rose. She tried to walk around him, but he took her hand. "Give me your number."

Kacey sighed. "Why?"

"Because I want it?"

"You don't need it."

He let go of her arm. "Yes, I do. I want to call you, even if it doesn't include outstanding orgasms."

"Oh, really? Why?"

He scratched his stomach, right below his belly button, drawing her eyes down, and once again reminding Kacey he was gloriously naked. And hard.

"Because I like you," he said.

Her eyes flew up. Distracted from his nakedness, kinda sorta, once again. Casanova's brows lowered, and confusion lined his sexy eyes. She'd bet the restaurant he hadn't meant to say he liked her.

The damn problem was that she liked him too. Or at least the version of him she'd spent the night with. The real him couldn't possibly be that great.

Her heart fluttered, the excited, happy fluttering she usually got before singing on the stage at her momma's restaurant. The one she used to get back when she thought meeting a guy and falling in love was the best thing that could happen in her life. The older, wiser Kacey wanted to believe he was just delivering a line. The younger, innocent Kacey sighed all happy-like. Thankfully she knew how to shut the younger Kacey up. She'd had to after her "relationship" with Dewayne had blown up in her face. He'd chuckled when she said she loved him, and said she was just in love with the sex. Then he'd told her about his wife and kids. Kids who were around her age. Even after that revelation, she'd still thought she could make him love her. Make him leave his family and marry her, only to have her heart broken later when he'd unloaded her as casually as one of his trucking hauls.

Don't be a fool again, Kacey. She stepped around him again and looked for her purse. "Yeah...I'm gonna go."

"You're really not going to give me your number?"

She found her small beige bag and slid the long strap crossways over her body. Instead of confusion, he wore the look of sexy amusement that had hovered around him the night before.

"Nope, I'm really not."

He opened his mouth but then his cell phone rang, cutting off whatever he was about to say. "Wait just a moment."

He backed up toward the bed, eyes trained on her as if she'd disappear if he turned his back. She forced her gaze to remain on his face. Not his gloriously naked body. He picked up the phone, and after a quick glance, his brows rose. He pressed the screen and brought the phone to his face but met Kacey's gaze.

"Janiyah, what's up?"

The sound of a frantic female voice filtered across the room, and his brows drew together. His gaze dropped to the floor. "Pregnant! You're pregnant? Seriously?"

He spun away from Kacey. And just like that, reality hit. The surprise and disbelief in his voice told her all she needed to know. He'd gotten someone pregnant. Pain from her own past mistakes landed heavily in her womb. Her mind flashed back to making a similar call, hearing the same surprise...disbelief...anger. Finally Dewayne's cold words. *Prove it's mine. You've probably slept with half the guys who come into that restaurant.* Kacey's throat closed up, and the pain she'd long ago come to terms with tried to rise.

After Sabrina had found out about Kacey being in love with a thirty-six-year-old man, her advice was, *"Tell him you're pregnant. Nothing shows how much a man doesn't love you faster than blurting out that you're pregnant."* Her momma would know that.

Sabrina hadn't known that Kacey had actually thought she was pregnant. Had hoped for it, the final thing that would force Dewayne to be with her. Instead he'd brushed her off. Kacey had cried all night. Her period came the next morning.

Unwilling to hear another woman get the same cold treatment she'd gotten, Kacey spun on her heels and hurried out the door.

• • •

Aaron pulled Bertha into the truck parking area of Reggie's business, R.H. Transportation. He parked at the end of a line of blue and white trucks parked before a loading dock next to the brick warehouse. He hopped out and looked around the well-organized yard. Bertha's bright yellow and black paint was like the exclamation point at the end of the line of vehicles. He made his way to the entrance. The same blue and white theme on the trucks adorned the interior of the polished reception area. Aaron was impressed. Reggie's place was nice. He grinned at the lady behind the receptionist desk.

"Good morning, I'm here to see Reggie Holmes," he said.

"You must be Mr. Henderson." She made a few clicks on her computer keyboard, a calendar displayed on her screen.

"That would be me."

"Mr. Holmes is expecting you." She stood and batted her long lashes. "Right this way."

Aaron followed her down the hall to an office. She peeked at him over her shoulder, and her hips swayed a little more after he smiled. He would have followed up on her invitation to flirt if his brain wasn't still trying to recover from the simultaneous shock of learning his baby sister was pregnant and that the woman who'd entranced him the night before had slipped out without giving him her phone number. He was happy for his sister. And forcing himself to be happy with the situation with Kacey. She reminded him too much of his ex. Specifically the thoughts she'd stirred up in him. The thoughts that said this woman could be *the* woman. Not good for him.

Aaron believed in love. His own family was proof the emotion existed. What he didn't believe in was his ability to settle down with one woman. Forever. No other women. Forever. That might work for millions of others, but he wasn't quite sure it would work for him. He was selfish, and he liked his life the way it was. Better for her to recognize that and walk out first than have him get commitment cold feet and hurt her later. Yep, this was all for the best.

Maybe I'll stop by Momma's Kitchen for dinner and try to see her again.

The receptionist stopped at a door. She knocked before opening it and announced Aaron. She stepped back and motioned for Aaron to enter the office. One glance at his old friend and Aaron grinned.

Reggie hadn't changed much. Tall, dark, and big. The three words to best describe his friend. But beneath all the brawn Reggie was just a puppy. The combination drew in the ladies.

"Yo, Aaron, I'm glad you made it," Reggie said. His long legs got him across the office in only a few strides, where he took Aaron's hands in one of his large ones and pulled him in for a one-armed hug. "How's it going, boy?"

Aaron would've chuckled, but Reggie's half hug nearly knocked the wind out of him.

"Damn, Reggie, I see you're still eating bricks for breakfast," Aaron said.

Reggie stepped back and gave Aaron a firm pat on the shoulder that made Aaron tilt to the side. "And you're still as scrawny as ever."

Aaron chuckled. "Hey, I'm sleek and slender."

"Sleek and slender, huh? I never did understand why women fall over themselves to be with you."

"And I couldn't understand why they'd go for you. I'd think having sex with a grizzly bear would be easier."

Reggie laughed and walked back over to his desk. "I do miss you and your smart mouth. We had some good times for the second we were in college."

"Good times is an understatement." Reggie sat behind his desk and Aaron slid into the chair across from it. "Remember spring break?"

Reggie's thick brows went up. "Remember it? You know I remember it. Bahamas, the booze cruise, those twins from Texas."

Aaron ran a hand over his chin and grinned. "You're never going to let me live that down."

"Hell, no. It was the one time I stole a woman from right under your nose."

Aaron laughed at the memory. Aaron had worked every last one of his seduction and charm skills to convince the twins to spend the night with him. Only to have Reggie snag one away before the end of the night. Though Aaron had had a great night with one sister, he'd given Reggie hell for thwarting his attempt to have his first threesome.

He and Reggie had both loved the ladies, and their pursuits had earned them a reputation envied by other guys during their short stint in college. After one year, Aaron purchased his first big rig and hit the road. Traveling across the United States to places not always on a tourist map seemed infinitely more appealing than sitting in lecture halls for the next three years. Soon after, Reggie did the same. Though they hadn't seen each other in two years, they kept up with each other via social media and occasional phone calls.

"The one and only time, let's not forget that," Aaron said.

"Hey, I'll talk about that for the rest of our lives. You were the man, and I rarely bested you. Baseball hero and ladies' man extraordinaire." Reggie chuckled and shook his head. "I can only imagine the number of women you would've bagged if you'd signed that baseball contract."

Back in college a minor league team had approached Aaron and offered him a contract to play. Aaron liked playing baseball, even competitively, but he hadn't wanted to make baseball his career. He liked his freedom. A contract felt like signing his life over to the league. No money was worth that. When he'd turned down the offer, his brother David had said he was crazy.

Maybe he had been, but not playing baseball wasn't on his list of regrets. "I didn't need a contract to pull in the ladies. Still don't," Aaron said with a grin. He glanced around. "You've got a nice office, and I like the layout of your place. Hard to believe you only got this place a year ago."

Reggie nodded. "Yes, sir, it is hard to believe. Sometimes I have to pinch myself to think my following you on a whim led to all this." Reggie encompassed the room with a broad sweep of his large hand. "I hate to admit it, but seeing your setup was what convinced me to make my trucking business more official. Not just randomly hiring extra guys to haul for me."

Aaron popped up from the seat and separated a section of blinds on the window to look out over the spacious loading bay. "But you've got more room to grow. My space in Columbia is limited. Honestly, if you hadn't mentioned a merger, I wouldn't have even considered going larger than I am now."

"Maybe not right off hand, but eventually. You always had big ideas, they just come spur of the moment and then you dive in. I have to plan things out."

"You're right about that." Aaron turned back to Reggie. "Before we get down into details, why don't you show me around the place?"

"Not much else to see, but come on."

Reggie's "not much else" was an understatement. Not only did the warehouse have room to expand for loading and unloading, but there was also a decent amount of storage space that would allow Reggie to provide temporary storage between hauls. The drivers who came in and out wore blue golf shirts with *R.H. Transportation* on the right breast pocket and khaki shorts or pants—the same outfit Reggie wore. Aaron felt underdressed in his jeans and casual blue button-up shirt. Even the company logo and mission statement were emblazoned in the unloading bay.

The attention to detail and coordination impressed Aaron. He would be the first to admit that he wasn't the guy to come to with long-range, big-picture ideas. He lived in the moment and went with his gut instincts. Buying his first truck, and later hiring drivers to handle hauls for him, were all spur-of-the-moment ideas that came with necessity, not from an overall master plan to grow his business. But now he was thirty, and the time for spur-of-the-moment decisions was over. Hell, his brothers were all settled down, and even his baby sister had turned her part-time job into a thriving business. It was time for Aaron to make some type of long-term plans.

"This is nice, Reggie," Aaron said as they made their way back into Reggie's office. "You've gotten things laid out perfectly."

"Maybe too perfectly. You know me, I spend so much time planning it makes me hesitant to take a step. I need a guy like you to push me when I'm toeing the line too much."

"You need me to be your wingman."

"More or less. I can plan it out, but you're the action guy. That's the way things always worked with us. If I put the plan in place, I know you'll make it happen. If we merge our companies together, we'll go far."

"I can't argue with you on that, but I haven't changed much. I'm still not the guy who sits around waiting for things to happen. I'll drag you along kicking and screaming. Are you sure you're ready for me to be your partner?"

Reggie laughed, but some of the old concern he'd once shown whenever Aaron dragged him into things in college shadowed the sound. "I'm not saying I'm going into this partnership lightly either. I'd like for us to work together for a few weeks. See if we can do it without killing each other. Running a business is a lot different than partying and sharing classwork."

Aaron nodded. "A hell of a lot different."

"How long can you stay in town?" Reggie asked.

"I let the drivers know I wouldn't be in Columbia for at least two weeks. I can handle arranging things from here. Go home and check in, then come back while we work things out. So if you need me to stay longer, I can."

Reggie's broad grin returned. "Good deal. Hey, where are you staying?"

"At the Hampton Inn."

Reggie shook his head. "No way am I going to let you stay at a hotel. I've got a rental house. My sister's living there, but the apartment over the garage is empty. You can stay there."

Aaron raised a brow. "A rental house?"

"Yeah, man, got it right after I started the business when it came up for sale in the neighborhood. Camila pretty much manages that, which is easy since my sister's in the main house."

"How is Camila?" Aaron had never met Reggie's wife, only heard about her through his conversations with Reggie and seen a few pictures on social media when Camila tagged Reggie, who rarely posted anything. From the pictures, he'd discovered his friend's wife was a knockout.

"Man, she's great. Pregnant, seven months."

"Wow, pregnant. That's great." The third person he knew who was thrilled to be having kids. First his older brother David, then his baby sister, and now Reggie. Aaron shuddered at the thought. Wife, kids, houses, all things that would tie him down to one place and turn his spur-of-the-moment lifestyle into a daily monotonous grind.

"She's hoping for a girl, I'm praying for a boy. We're trying to wait it out, but I don't know if I'll make it till her due date."

Aaron leaned back on the small round conference table in the office and crossed his arms. He studied his friend, the one women always called sweet but who was just as much of a commitment-phobe as Aaron was. "I don't get it, Reggie. You were quiet about it, but you had a woman in every town. Now you're married. Not one but two houses. What changed?"

Reggie shrugged. "Nothing. I still love the ladies; just now I have to look without touching."

"But what made you settle down with just one?"

Reggie sat in the chair behind his desk and leaned back. "It just happened. We were just fooling around. I made it clear that was all I wanted. Camila was cool with that. It worked for a few months, then one day while I was out on a date with someone else, I saw *her* out on a date. Right then it hit me, I didn't want to be out with that other woman, and I didn't want Camila to be out with that guy. I called the next day and told her I wanted us to be exclusive. Two months later I proposed." He shrugged. "Love snuck up on me."

"I'm happy for you." Aaron meant it. Though he had no immediate plans, wants, or desire to get married and have kids, he was truly happy to see other people in love.

"One day it'll hit you too."

"I doubt it. I haven't met a woman yet who made me want her bed to be the only one I sleep in forever."

"Liar," Reggie said. He leaned forward and pointed at Aaron. "You thought about it with Denise."

Aaron shrugged, when he really wanted to flinch. He'd wondered what would have happened if he'd followed up on what he'd felt for Denise back then. Then he'd see some post online from a friend who'd married young announcing a divorce and got his answer. "Thought about it, then broke things off. I liked her, a lot, but I wasn't ready to marry her."

Denise was the one woman he didn't regularly keep in contact with. Most of the women he hooked up with he'd call and check in on when he was in town. After hurting Denise when he'd walked away with a "Sorry, I can't do this" excuse, he couldn't toy with her like that. They were connected via social media, but he didn't check her updates, and if she checked his he had no clue because he never got a like, comment, or anything. Often he'd wondered why they'd even bothered with that.

"You were young. When you're older that feeling is harder to ignore."

Aaron smirked and scratched the back of his head. "It's hard to ignore other beautiful women."

"It's not just about the sex. It's more than that."

Aaron chuckled. "Spoken like a married man."

"Maybe if you saw Denise again you'd feel differently. Or maybe it'll be someone new."

He thought of Kacey. Definitely the best one-night stand of his life. No matter that her walking away without giving him her number was for the best. He knew he'd be right back at Momma's Kitchen tonight to try to bring her back to the hotel again. And Reggie's words were very close to what Aaron was thinking: Seeing her was about more than just the sex. He wanted the sex, but he'd also enjoyed her company, the conversation, the sound of her laugh, those eyes. But forever? Eventually the early infatuation would wear off the way it always did.

"Who are you thinking about?"

Aaron blinked and focused on Reggie. "What?"

"That look, you're thinking about a woman. One I'd say is likely to snare you based on the smile on your face."

Aaron shook his head. "Not likely. It's just this woman I hooked up with last night."

Reggie's eyes went wide. "You hooked up with someone already? Damn, Aaron, you've still got the touch."

"It wasn't even like that. I wasn't trying to hook up with someone. It just happened."

"Funny how sex with beautiful women always just happens with you." Reggie leaned in. "How was it?"

"I thought it wasn't about the sex, married man."

Reggie frowned and waved a hand. "Don't give me that. Every man I hang out with now is married. You're my only single friend, so indulge me a little."

"Fine, I went to the restaurant across from the hotel. Momma's Kitchen. You been there?"

Reggie's eager smile quickly hardened into an angry scowl. "My momma owns that place, and my sisters and my wife work there, along with half of my female cousins."

Motherfu— Aaron worked to keep the easy smile on his face. If there was anything that fired up his otherwise gentle friend, it was the thought of someone screwing around with the females in his family. All through college Reggie had told Aaron stories about the men who'd played his mom and tried to seduce his sisters. He vaguely remembered Reggie going home to confront some older guy who'd slept with his baby sister. Having a little sister of his own, Aaron understood Reggie's protectiveness. But sometimes Reggie was nearly medieval when it came to the women in his family.

A sinking feeling started in Aaron's midsection. The bartender, Monique, and Kacey were sisters. What would be the chances that he'd come into town and slept with his friend's sister? *Son of a bitch!* This partnership would be over before it started if that was the case.

Aaron straightened. "No one working there. I'm just saying, I started out there."

Reggie relaxed. "Good. Sorry, Aaron, it's just that truckers always go through and try to get in the pants of every woman in my family. As if my momma's reputation belongs to all of them."

Aaron looked away from Reggie's tight expression. Aaron knew Reggie loved his mom, but he also knew her reputation was a sore spot. Four kids by four different men in less than five years. Aaron knew it embarrassed Reggie more than he'd admit. And it was the reason Reggie was so *medieval* when it came to his sisters.

"But, hey, finish your story," Reggie said, with renewed enthusiasm. "What happened last night?"

"I don't want to get into all the details." And he wouldn't until he verified that there was still some slim chance he hadn't spent the night having sex with one of Reggie's sisters.

"Just give me the good details."

"The good details are all the details. Nothing about this woman wasn't good."

Reggie rubbed his hands together. "Aww, damn. Now I really want to hear the details."

Aaron's laughter caught and his throat constricted. He covered it with a cough and tight chuckle. He always gave Reggie every single dirty detail. Usually with precise clarity. But he couldn't this time, not if he was talking about the guy's sister.

Reggie's eager eyes met Aaron's. The desperate look of a married guy waiting to hear about the type of wild one-night stands he could no longer have. "What did she look like?"

"Umm, she was cute."

Reggie frowned. "Cute?"

"Yeah...and sexy." Aaron thought about Kacey's slim figure with its perfect curves. "Definitely sexy."

"Was she wild? I mean, did she do *everything* or did she hold back?"

She'd made him come twice before he was ready to, and ridden him like an expert. Aaron's dick twitched at the memory.

Reggie chuckled. "You're grinning again. She must have been good."

Aaron rubbed his chest and nodded. "She was great."

"Whoa, wait, hey!" A frantic female voice came from the door. "Umm, my bad, didn't know you had company."

Aaron recognized the voice and inwardly cursed. *Why, fate, why!* He and Reggie both turned, and Aaron's heart plummeted to his feet. Kacey stood at the door, looking even more beautiful and desirable—in a green tank top and black shorts that stopped mid-thigh—than she had naked and in the bed with him that morning.

She smiled at Reggie. A stiff, brittle smile that meant she'd probably overheard some of their conversation. Damn! Now she'd think he'd spilled all her sexual secrets to her brother.

She held up a white plastic bag. "I brought you lunch."

"Just in time." Reggie stood and crossed the room.

Aaron coughed again and her dark eyes turned to him. Her eyes were cold. *Ah, damn, why does this shit happen to me?*

"Kacey, come in and meet my friend Aaron Henderson." Reggie pulled her into the office.

"Aaron, this is my sister, Peanut."

"This is Peanut?" Aaron pointed to Kacey.

"Yep, all grown up, and she doesn't like to go by Peanut anymore."

Kacey grunted. "I never liked that nickname."

"*Kacey*, this is my homeboy, Aaron."

Aaron met her gaze. Her eyes widened slightly. A clear indication to keep his mouth shut. No problem there. *Kacey is Peanut?* The little sister Reggie was so proud of. The one in college, the one who was the polar opposite of his momma, the one Reggie bragged about constantly. Reggie's favorite. The sister Reggie would break Aaron's arms and legs over if he learned Aaron had spent the night before making love to her over and over again.

CHAPTER 8

With a quick flip of her wrist, Kacey snapped the blue cotton sheet over the bed in the above garage apartment. The force of the snap caused a notepad to fly off the nightstand on the opposite side. If only she could snap the sheet and make her brother fly away. Somewhere far, far away. How could he offer up the apartment without saying anything to her? And to his panties-collecting, got-a-girl-in-every-city, eyes-are-too-sexy-for-words college friend! Oh, she'd heard the stories of Aaron Henderson, in all their debauched details.

This was why she didn't do one-night stands. Reckless behavior always came with a price.

She snapped the sheet again, and a low whistle followed the crisp snap. Swinging around, her body went into overdrive when her eyes met Casanova's...er, Aaron's.

"Are you trying to knock the lamp off the table too?" he asked, a cocky grin on his full lips.

"How long have you been watching me?"

"Long enough to tell something's got you pissed." He pushed away from the door and strolled over to the other side of the bed. "I'm curious to know what."

She scoffed. "As if you didn't know."

He straightened the other end of the sheet. "Let me guess, you forgot to set the DVR and missed the season finale of your favorite show." He tucked the sheet at the bottom of the bed.

Kacey cocked her head to the side and pulled on her end of the sheet. "No."

"Okay, then maybe it's because you finally came to terms with the fact that I was right about my calls on the best wrestlers of all time and you don't want to admit it."

"Hardly." She tucked the end of the sheet. "And FYI, you're still wrong on that."

"Hmm, neither of those. Then it must be..." He hopped onto the bed and lay on his side facing her. Leaning his head on his hand, he grinned at her. "You've realized that a handsome, irresistible man is now living in the apartment right above you, and you have to keep your hands off of him."

"Excuse me?"

"Am I getting closer?"

She crossed her arms and glared. "No, you're way off base."

"So you're not upset that I'll be your neighbor for the next few weeks?"

"Yes...but not because I have to keep my hands off of you."

"Then your brother won't mind if we continue what we started last night."

"Are you crazy? Reggie will go ballistic if we continue what we started. Starting by removing your arms and legs."

He sat up and flipped his legs around to her side. "Good, we're in agreement."

Kacey stumbled back and frowned. "On what?"

"That your very large brother will remove my arms and legs if he knows what happened. So we can't have sex again. Even though we both really want to."

She narrowed her eyes and smirked. "Yes to the first part, no to the second. I told you this morning we weren't having sex again."

He wiggled his brows. "But you want to."

His dark eyes sparked with amusement and desire. His lips slanted up in a jump-your-bones smile. Hell yes, her body wanted him again. That was the problem with bad-for-you men, they were always so damn tempting.

She cocked her head to the side. "Shouldn't you be worrying about the soon-to-be mother of your child instead of flirting with me?"

Aaron's brows drew together. "What are you talking about?"

"The woman on the phone this morning. Janiyah I think is her name. The pregnant woman?"

His face cleared up before he broke into a laugh. "Janiyah is my baby sister. She and her husband, who happens to be my best friend, are expecting. As far as I know, I haven't gotten any woman pregnant." His face became all seriousness. "If I *had* gotten someone pregnant, I wouldn't walk away from her or my child. I don't see kids in my future, but that doesn't mean I'd abandon a child or its mother if the situation arose. I'm not that kind of guy."

"Your sister." He nodded, and relief relaxed her shoulders. What the hell? She shouldn't be relieved. So he hadn't gotten a woman pregnant; it didn't mean her eggs needed to celebrate. "Oh, well, congratulations."

He cocked a brow. "Is that why you bolted?"

"I didn't bolt."

"Yes, you did."

"Well, last night was supposed to be a one-night stand. Now you're living in the apartment above the garage. This type of stuff only happens to me." She rolled her eyes.

He leaned his arms on his knees and narrowed his eyes. "Your one-night stands always end up living next door?"

She chuckled and shook her head. "No, but impulsive decisions always blow up in my face. Going to your hotel room was a mistake."

"It sure didn't feel like a mistake."

Not at all. Kacey crossed her arms again. "But you're right, we can't do that again. You're working with Reggie, and I don't have time for distractions."

"Because of school. It's your last semester, right?"

"How do you know that?"

He shrugged. "Reggie talks about you. He's proud of you. So much so that I think that, along with removing my arms and legs, he'd burn Bertha to the ground if I so much as touched you."

She stepped away from the bed. "Then we'll be adults and move on. Like we were supposed to do anyway. Reggie is the official landlord, so if you need anything, get with him. I'm in classes during the day and I work at Momma's Kitchen at night, so we probably won't see each other much. That'll make things easier."

"Sounds like a very solid, smart, adult plan." His voice gave her the feeling he found the situation humorous.

She gave a stiff nod. "Good. Well, I'll leave you to it then."

"To what?"

"Unpacking."

He ran his hand over the sheets. "You don't want to help me with the bed?"

Oh, she'd love to help him with the bed. *Stop it, Kacey, this is exactly the type of distraction you don't need.*

"Good-bye." She spun on her heel and hurried out of the bedroom and the apartment.

By the time she ran down the stairs to the main part of the house, she was out of breath and her heart raced. Not entirely because of the brief stint of physical activity. Last night had been good. Too good. If she didn't have a crazy-busy workload at school this final semester, she'd be truly fearful of falling down the Aaron Henderson rabbit hole.

She entered the house from the side door that opened directly to the kitchen. Her momma sat at the kitchen table, flipping through the latest *Essence* magazine. Kacey suppressed a sigh. She'd gone straight to her professor this morning instead of to her momma's house, like she'd said she would.

Sabrina slowly flipped a page in the magazine with one long manicured nail. Kacey's momma always looked good, and this morning wasn't any different. She wore a black tank top with *Momma's Kitchen* set in sequins across her ample breasts. Breasts Kacey hadn't inherited. And a short jean skirt with heels way too high for daylight hours. Sabrina tapped the side of her head with the pads of her fingers, Kacey guessed to avoid scratching. Tomorrow was Sabrina's relaxer day.

Sabrina looked up at Kacey. "What happened to you this morning?"

"Sorry, I overslept. I had a meeting with my professor."

Sabrina closed the magazine on the table. She leaned back in the chair and eyed Kacey with interest. "Really? Because I got up early and decided to come see you instead. But you weren't here."

Damn small towns and her momma's ability to pop in unexpected. "We met at nine. I forgot about that when I said I'd come over this morning."

"Mmm-hmmm. You must have left really early."

Kacey shrugged but avoided eye contact. "I was hungry, so I left early enough to grab something to eat."

"But you overslept."

Kacey crossed the kitchen and leaned against the counter. She crossed her arms and met her momma's stare. "Oversleeping doesn't eliminate hunger."

Sabrina smirked. "'Fess up, Kacey, you hooked up with that guy from the bar last night."

Kacey had never had a problem talking to her momma about sex. If anything, Sabrina was a little *too* open with her kids. She said it was to help them avoid making the same mistakes she had. Which was why Kacey got "*tell him you're pregnant*" when she'd found out about Dewayne instead of "*I forbid you to see him.*"

Normally, she would have confessed to her momma that, yes, she had behaved irrationally and taken home the hottie from the bar. If only the hottie had turned out to be any other guy in America.

"I did not go home with him," Kacey said.

Sabrina held up a hand and shook her head. "I'm not judging, honey. You work hard during school and at the restaurant. It's okay if you decided to walk on the wild side for a night."

"I didn't walk on the wild side, Momma. I didn't do anything."

"Honey, women have needs just as much as men do. We just don't brag about it to everyone who'll listen. It's okay. One night doesn't mean you're a terrible person."

Kacey raised a brow. "So it takes two nights to be terrible."

Sabrina lifted a slim shoulder and smirked. "Even more than that. Believe me, I know."

Kacey shook her head. "You're not terrible and you know it."

Sabrina pushed herself up from the table. "Okay, okay, you don't have to tell me again how great of a mother I am." Sabrina grinned, and Kacey shook her head and chuckled.

"Always digging for a compliment."

"They come so few and far between with you kids."

"Ugh, I swear, when I have kids I won't do the guilt trip. But, yes, you were a great mother."

Sabrina patted Kacey's cheek. "I know. And you know why? Because I never let the narrow minds of this town convince me otherwise. I turned my life around for you, your brother, and your sisters. Not for anyone else."

"I know, Momma."

"And if you want to spend a night with a sexy trucker, fine. Just don't get your mind all wrapped up in happily-ever-after. Go in, scratch that itch, and move on. As long as you keep your heart out of things, you're fine."

A lecture she'd heard repeatedly since her ill-advised teenage stint with love. "Momma, I didn't hook up with that guy. I stayed out late and went out early. That's all." She walked away and flipped the pages of the magazine on the table. Mostly because she couldn't lie and look her momma directly in the eye. "Good thing, too. Turns out he's Reggie's friend Aaron Henderson."

"The guy Reggie is always bragging about?"

Kacey nodded and turned away from the magazine. "One and the same. Reggie's letting him stay in the apartment upstairs while they work out the potential merger."

"That was nice of him."

Nice wasn't the word Kacey would use to describe her brother's actions. *Rash* and *inconsiderate* topped the list. "Yeah."

"Well, if that's the case, then I hope you didn't sleep with him."

"I didn't!" she said with enough emphasis to almost convince herself.

"Good. Reggie will cancel the entire deal if he thought his friend was sleeping with one of his sisters."

Cancel the deal was an understatement. When Reggie found out about her "relationship" at seventeen, he'd come home and beaten Dewayne to a bloody pulp. So much so her momma had almost not called the police to report the guy for having sex with her underage daughter. In the end she did, and the police had ignored the bruises after everything was explained. Reggie had become hypervigilant about Kacey and her sisters' reputations and the guys they dated ever since.

Boyfriend cheating: Reggie handled him. Guy at the bar being too handsy: Reggie handled him. Falling in love but not quite sure the guy felt the same: Reggie would force the confession or get him to break things off. Kacey thanked heaven for Camila every day. She'd kept him busy since they'd gotten married so that his warden-like tendencies hadn't been as bad.

"Reggie can stop defending our honor," Kacey said. "None of us are virgins waiting on marriage."

Sabrina chuckled. "True, but your brother is old enough to remember the way people talked about me after I had your youngest sister. Add to that the fights he got in over you girls, and I guess he has the right to be overprotective."

"Fights he started."

"You'd rather he didn't try to look out for you, Monique, and Ashlei?"

Kacey huffed, but she didn't contradict her momma. Reggie was overbearing and way too protective, but he'd kept a lot of assholes out of her and her sister's lives. "He's not our daddy."

"No, he's not, he's just your big brother. Speaking of daddies, did you call yours?"

"No, is he okay?"

"Yeah, I think Brenda is sick again. Or at least that was the word in the restaurant last night. You might want to call and check on her."

Kacey would rather summon the dead than talk to her dad's wife. Brenda had long stopped blaming Kacey for the brief affair he'd had with Sabrina. Now her momma, dad, and his wife had formed a tentative alliance. Her dad refused to stay out of Kacey's life, something her brother and sisters didn't have. So even though Kacey was uncomfortable with the *friendship*, she wouldn't begrudge what her siblings didn't have.

"Brenda doesn't want me to check on her."

"Then call your daddy and let him know you're checking on her. He'll appreciate that."

"Fine, I'll call Daddy."

"Good." Sabrina handed Kacey a few papers that were on the counter. "I also came by to drop off my answers to your interview questions."

Kacey skimmed through her momma's handwritten answers to Kacey's questions about why she'd started Momma's Kitchen and her ideas for the second restaurant. Kacey's master's thesis involved putting together the plan to open another location in Chattanooga. Though she'd worked at Momma's Kitchen since she was a teenager, and she knew the ins and outs of the place, she hadn't known enough about branching out into a second or possibly third location. That was why she'd gone back to graduate school.

"You could have e-mailed them."

"Then I wouldn't have gotten to see my shining star." Sabrina beamed at Kacey. "I'm so proud of you, Kacey. You're the first one in the family to go so far in school. Don't let nothing stop you."

"I won't, Momma."

"That's my girl. Even though I'm glad you didn't sleep with Reggie's friend, I'm still not sure you didn't spend the night somewhere else." Sabrina clasped Kacey's face between her hands. "You need to get laid, sweetheart." She let Kacey's face go.

"Sorry to disappoint you," Kacey said with sarcasm.

"Never that. What time are you coming in tonight?" Sabrina grabbed her clutch bag off the table.

"I'll be there at seven. I really need to get started on my outline for my project."

"Take your time. Now that school's starting again, you're back on flex scheduling."

"Thanks, Momma."

"No problem, baby." She went to the door, opened it, and peered up at the apartment. "Good thing you didn't take him home. That's a whole lotta temptation up a couple of flights of stairs."

"Tell me about it," Kacey said under her breath.

Sabrina looked back with a raised brow. "What was that?"

Kacey smiled and shook her head. "Nothing."

Sabrina raised a brow. "Sure. See you later, baby."

CHAPTER 9

That evening, Aaron got out of Reggie's shiny burgundy Toyota Tundra into the parking lot of Momma's Kitchen. Much like the night before, there were plenty of cars in the lot, and the sound of music along with the smell of great food drifting from the building. After he'd checked out and moved his stuff into the apartment above Kacey—he still didn't know if that was good or bad—he'd met up with Reggie back at R&H Transportation. Instead of going over business, they'd spent the last two hours just catching up before their growling stomachs had them off in search of food.

Reggie grinned at Aaron. "Hope you don't mind eating at the same place two nights in a row."

"Nah, I'm good. The food was great."

They crossed the threshold. The same cute young woman stood behind the hostess stand. Her eyes lit up when she saw Reggie. She hurried around the podium and flung her arms around him.

"Reggie, what brings you in here tonight?"

Reggie pulled out of the woman's embrace and pointed his thumb at Aaron. "My friend Aaron is in town. Thought I'd show the place off, but he came in here last night."

She looked at Aaron and her smile turned wicked. "Came back for more, cutie?"

Reggie's brows drew together, and Aaron chuckled. He slapped his hands on Reggie's shoulders. "Just for the food."

"Too bad," she said in an inviting voice.

Reggie pushed her shoulder. "Stop it, Ashlei."

Aaron's eyes widened. "This is your baby sister, Ashlei? The last picture I saw of her she was just a little thing." Between Monique, Kacey, and Ashlei, Aaron understood Reggie's need to be protective of his sisters. The three had their own brand of sexy going on.

Ashlei's face, with deep dimples and expressive light brown eyes, eyes that were full of mischief, turned his way. "I'm not so little anymore."

"Just show us to a table and let Momma and Camila know we're here," Reggie grumbled.

She led them to a table close to the stage. She kissed Reggie's cheek and ran her hand across Aaron's shoulders as she walked away. Respect for his friend kept Aaron from watching her walk away—his normal reaction if a cute waitress had done that to him.

"Your sister is funny," Aaron said. Reggie grunted and Aaron laughed. "I feel your pain, dude. I've got a baby sister, too."

"You've got one, I've got three." Reggie looked around the room with a scowl. "And every man in here is trying to get to know them better, if you know what I mean."

"They're all grown women. I'm sure they can handle things."

"Maybe, but I've also made it known to the regulars. Screw with one of my sisters and you have to deal with me." Reggie cracked his knuckles.

Aaron decided against commenting. His baby sister was one of the biggest flirts he knew, and while Aaron definitely tried to avoid knowing everything about her dating history, he'd trusted her judgment. Even when she'd started dating his longtime best friend, instead of getting upset he'd been glad to see both of them happy. He doubted Reggie would extend the same reasoning toward Aaron and Kacey.

Not like Aaron was planning to marry Kacey or anything. But he definitely wouldn't mind a repeat of their fiery night—if it wouldn't cost him the biggest business merger of his life.

"Hey, baby, you came in," a female voice came from behind Aaron.

He and Reggie turned to see a beautiful, pregnant Dominican woman Aaron immediately recognized at Camila. Camila's thick, dark shoulder-length hair was pulled into a ponytail at the base of her neck, and there was a blush beneath her light brown skin. She wore a pink V-neck *Momma's Kitchen* T-shirt that clung to her round baby belly and black leggings. Reggie stood to wrap his arms around her shoulders. Compared to Reggie, she looked like a munchkin.

Reggie placed a hand on her very round belly. "I decided to have dinner here tonight. How are you feeling? I wish you'd stop working in the kitchen."

"I'm no good a waiting tables, Reggie, you know that. I'd much rather help out in the kitchen." She turned to Aaron and held out a hand. "You must be Aaron. I'm glad to finally meet you." He took her hand, and she tugged on it until he stood. "We're practically family. Give me a hug."

Aaron laughed and returned her tight hug. "It's great to finally meet you, Camila."

"Same here. Reggie's told me all the crazy stories about you two in college. I can't believe that's the same man that I married. He's so straight and proper now." Love and affection for Reggie filled Camila's voice.

Reggie ran a hand over his head. "College was the time for that. Now I'm a man with responsibilities."

Camila pinched his cheeks. "Responsibilities doesn't mean you can't let go every once in a while. Or try to come in here and not scowl at every man in the building."

Aaron glanced around at the other waitresses. "I don't blame Reggie for being overprotective. He's got a family full of beautiful women."

Reggie's soft punch still tipped Aaron to the side. "Eyes in your head and off my family's assets." He grinned at Aaron, who held up his hands.

"You two sit down and enjoy the show while I put together something for you to eat." She kissed Reggie. "I'll come sit with you in a little bit."

Reggie kissed her again, an adoring look of love on his face. Camila whispered something to him in Spanish before winking and strolling back to the kitchen.

Aaron shook his head. "I never thought I'd see the day when you were smitten by a woman."

"I never thought I'd see that day either. Being on the road was my love for so long I didn't think I'd ever give her up. Plus, driving gave me an escape from my family."

"I get that." Aaron loved his family, but getting away and doing whatever he wanted without them poking their noses in his business was another perk of his job. "Your mom has a nice setup in here." He glanced around the restaurant.

"Yeah, she does. Building this place took a lot of hard work and sacrifice. When she first opened the place, so many people in town underestimated her, but she showed them. What sucks is that there are enough people who remember her rocky start and still try to bring it up every now and then."

"That's their problem, not yours."

"Easy for you to say. You don't have a mother with a reputation."

"That was years ago, Reggie."

Reggie shifted in his seat and looked uncomfortable. "She stopped having babies, but she didn't become a nun. I'll leave it at that."

Aaron decided to leave that alone.

The bartender from the night before headed their way—Monique, if he remembered what her name tag had said—Reggie's other sister.

She had two bottles of beer in her hand, and she placed one on the table in front of Reggie. "What's got you frowning now, big brother?"

"The usual. Monique, meet Aaron."

Monique's long lashes fluttered as she turned dark eyes his way. "Oh, I remember you. Decided to return and take the path of least resistance, huh?" She leaned over to place the beer on the table before Aaron, providing a generous view down the vee of her shirt. Aaron was proud of the way he pretended not to notice.

"Just came back for the food," Aaron said.

"What's that supposed to mean?" Reggie asked.

"Put up your shotgun, Reggie. I tried to take him home, but he turned me down and left alone." She rubbed Reggie's shoulders.

Reggie glared up at his sister. "Don't you have work to do?"

"Going back to the bar now." She smiled at Aaron. "I get off at eleven, in case you wanted to know."

"He doesn't," Reggie said.

Aaron chuckled as she walked away. "I think your sisters do this to you on purpose."

"I know they do it on purpose. They think I'm overprotective."

"Didn't you break one guy's arm for messing with a sister?"

Reggie shrugged. "That guy deserved it. He was older, and Kacey was still in high school."

Aaron leaned back in his chair and his brows drew together. "That's what happened?" Aaron remembered when Reggie hurried home from college to "handle" a guy messing around with Peanut. When Reggie came back, he glossed over most of what happened, only saying he broke the guy's arm during an *altercation*.

"Yeah, the jackass had her thinking he was in love. That he would marry her *after* she graduated. To say the family was pissed is an understatement."

"Okay, now I get the overprotective vibe." Especially when it came to Kacey.

"I'm not as bad as I was after that. And they flirt, a lot, but for the most part it's just for show. They tend to turn things up a notch when my friends are involved."

"Have any of them ever dated one of your friends?" Aaron tried to sound casual and sipped his beer.

Reggie scowled. "Hell no. That's much too close to home."

"I used to think the same, until Janiyah married my boy Fred."

"You were cool with that?"

Aaron chuckled and lifted his shoulder. "After watching them pretend not to like each other for years, it was kind of a relief."

That broke Reggie's scowl and he chuckled. "That sounds like an extreme case." Reggie's gaze shifted and his smile widened. "Aaron, this is my mom, Sabrina Holmes."

Aaron turned in his chair and met the warm golden eyes of a woman he would never have guessed to be Reggie's mother. Average height, but that was the only reason that word could be used. Her golden brown skin barely showed a hint at her age, a short and sassy haircut highlighted honey blonde, and a toned body that put women half her age to shame.

"This is your mother?"

"It is." Reggie stood again and gave her a hug when she reached the table. "Momma, this is my friend Aaron."

Aaron also stood and smiled. "It's nice to finally meet you, Ms. Holmes."

She waved a hand and shook her head. "Don't you dare call me Ms. Holmes. I'm Momma to Reggie, but you can call me Sabrina."

Aaron held out his hand for her to shake; instead she gave him a big hug. "Boy, we hug around here." When she pulled back, her amber eyes swept appreciatively over him and slim fingers clutched his upper arms. "So you're Aaron. I've heard so much about you."

Her hands squeezed his biceps. *Is she sizing me up?* Aaron cleared his throat and stepped back. "Likewise, Ms. Hol... Sabrina. Reggie is very proud of you."

"That's nice of you to say, Aaron. Let's have a seat."

Aaron gave Sabrina his chair and sat in the one on the other side of the table with Reggie.

"I am proud of you, Momma," Reggie said.

Sabrina patted Reggie's hand. "I know, baby." She looked between Reggie and Aaron. "You boys making plans for your merger?"

Aaron nodded. "We're going to spend the next few weeks discussing the possibility. And I'll get to see how Reggie runs the business."

"Sounds fun." Her voice was chipper, but somehow Aaron knew she didn't consider talks of merger fun at all. "In the meantime, you'll be on top of Kacey?"

Aaron was sipping his beer and nearly chocked at Sabrina's words. A devilish gleam lit up her eyes. "Pardon me?"

"I came by this afternoon. Kacey let me know you're in the apartment upstairs while you're in town."

He cleared his throat and shifted in the seat. "Yeah, I'm staying there."

Sabrina tilted her head to the side. "I'm surprised Reggie did that."

Reggie sat straighter. "Why? Aaron is a friend of mine. I can't let him sleep in a hotel when Camila and I have space right near us."

"I'm not doubting your hospitality, sweetheart." She patted Reggie's arm again. "Just, hearing the stories about you and Aaron and your wild times in college, I didn't think you'd trust to put such a handsome, sexy young man so close to your sister."

"Aaron is my friend, and he knows how I feel about my family. I trust him."

Aaron almost choked on another sip of beer. He'd thoroughly agreed with Kacey earlier when she brought up keeping what happened from her brother. Despite how alluring her eyes were, or how the sway of her hips momentarily hypnotized him, or, as if he'd ever forget, that she was the best sex he'd ever had, he wouldn't knowingly disrespect his friend like that.

Maybe he should come clean now. Surely starting their business merger on a lie was wrong morally, or spiritually, or something.

Are you crazy? he screamed internally. Reggie would call off the deal and possibly rearrange Aaron's face in the process. If he kept his hands to himself and they stuck to their agreement not to say a word to anyone, Reggie, and the rest of Kacey's family, would never know.

"Reggie has nothing to worry about," Aaron said. "I don't mix business and pleasure. Nor would I do my boy like that."

"That's good to hear." A definite note of steel lined Sabrina's silky voice, giving Aaron the distinct impression that Reggie wasn't the only one who didn't want him messing with Kacey.

"Speak of the devil, Kacey just walked in." Sabrina raised a hand and waved.

Aaron fought every instinct not to turn around and stare like a sprung-out kid. A few seconds later, she made her way to the table, dressed in the tight white button-up and fitted black pants all the waitresses wore. Her eyes jumped to his only briefly before she grinned at Reggie and Sabrina. That brief second sent a jolt of awareness down Aaron's spine.

"Didn't you get my call that we're fully staffed tonight?" Sabrina asked.

Kacey shrugged. "So I don't need to wait tables. But I do need to go over the deposits for the month and finish up the schedule."

"I could've handled that," Sabrina said. "You could have stayed home and taken a break."

Kacey raised a brow and smiled. "My break is over. My last semester started today, and I might as well get back into my normal routine. But don't worry, I'll let you close up."

"Oh, thanks for that," Sabrina said with sarcasm.

"Hey, you're the one who told me school comes first. I'm only a part-time manager." She leaned over to kiss her mother's cheek. "If you all need anything, I'll be in the back."

Her gaze swept the table again. Her eyes halted briefly on Aaron before she walked away. Sabrina and Reggie started talking. Aaron watched Kacey go. She didn't look back. She gave him no extra-long glances, no secret smile, no indication at all that she'd completely turned him out the night before. Her ability to act as if last night hadn't happened only made him want her more. He wasn't sure why, maybe because he was having a hard time not staring or grinning at her like a fool. Was pretending nothing had happened as hard for her as it was for him?

Aaron tore his gaze away from her swaying hips and sipped from his beer. He wasn't foolish enough to press and find out and end up ruining a friendship and potential business deal. Women were plenty, a fact that had kept him from acting foolish over one woman for most of his life. He'd remember his night with Kacey with absolute wonder but move on. That was the smart thing to do.

CHAPTER 10

Kacey *knew* he watched her walk away. She could feel his gaze on her back, pressing between her shoulder blades, daring her to turn around and look at him. She wanted to look. Was *dying* to look, but she wouldn't.

No distractions. She didn't have time for distractions. Not during her last, and most crucial, semester of school.

Then there was Reggie. Not that she really cared what Reggie thought about who she dated. If she really thought what had happened between her and Aaron would turn into something, she'd tell Reggie to shove his prehistoric ideas high up his rear end and get over it. But there was nothing serious between her and Aaron. He was a trucker. And even though the logical part of her brain knew that all truckers weren't scumbags just trying to take advantage of women, what had happened to her, the existence of her sister Ashlei, and the endless stories her brother used to tell about his life on the road before he met Camila kinda overrode any logical thoughts.

Kacey strolled over to the bar, where Monique was swiftly cutting up lemons. Monique looked at Kacey and shook her head.

Kacey looked around. "What?"

"Nothing, just you, here again. You were taken off the schedule for tonight."

"I make the schedule. I can come whenever I want." Kacey slid on to one of the bar stools at the end of the bar near Monique. There were a few customers sitting there. All had full or nearly full glasses before them. Three of the four had food in front of them. Kacey wondered if the fourth was waiting on food.

"You really need to learn to enjoy your days off."

"School's started, I'm out of days off. Besides, I'm not here to work the bar, or sing, I'm just going to go through the deposit slips and finish up this week's schedule."

"I'll be so glad when school is done and you can finally let loose that tight-as-hell ponytail of yours and have some fun." Monique scooped up the cut lemons and dropped them in a plastic bowl for later. She wiped her hands on a towel, then came over to lean a hip on the edge of the bar.

"Soooo," Monique said, sliding the words out through pursed lips. "Guess it's a good thing you didn't go home with choke me, spank me, pull my hair guy over there."

Kacey laughed and shook her head. Monique sure had a way with words. "His name is Aaron."

Monique shrugged as if that were insignificant. "Whatever. I didn't want to know his name last night, just the location of every birthmark on his body."

"You know Reggie is going to pop a vein if he hears you talking like that."

"And both you and Reggie know I don't care."

"Yes, we do." Kacey frowned. Would Monique tell Reggie to shove his opinions where the sun didn't shine and go for Aaron? Kacey definitely, from the bottom of her heart, did not want to see them together. Would Aaron be enough of a scumbag to actually sleep with her sister?

Umm, he's a guy and your sister is stacked.

Kacey straightened in her seat. "Hey, Monique—"

Monique's cell phone rang, and her sister pulled the bedazzled case out of her apron pocket. Her eyes lit up, and she pulled her lower lip between her teeth.

"I've got to take this call." Monique hurried around the bar. "Watch the bar for me."

"What... I'm not working the bar!"

Monique waved a hand and hurried to the kitchen door. Then she answered the call with a hushed "hello."

The doors to the kitchen swung back and forth for several seconds after Monique disappeared through them. Okay, maybe she didn't have to worry about Monique going after Aaron. The only time her sister got that excited was when she had a new guy in her life. Kacey slowly rose from the bar stool and went around the back. She checked on the customers, refilled drink orders, and verified that the fourth guy was not waiting on food. If he had been, she would have given Monique hell when she returned for abandoning her station with customers waiting.

She turned to where Reggie, Sabrina, and Aaron sat. Aaron's hair was a riot of curls and those bedroom eyes of his were wide and full of amusement. She found herself smiling, even though she had no idea what he was saying. He just looked like he could tell a good story, the way his hands were moving and the expressions that crossed his face. He wore carefree and happy as easily as she wore her Momma's Kitchen uniform.

His gaze flicked her way and stayed for a second. Her heart pumped wildly, and currents of awareness flowed down her arms. She was still smiling, she could feel it in her face, and his smile seemed to change, almost become some secret smile—a curve of the lips that said he remembered all the things they'd done the night before. A smile that was just for her.

The door to the kitchen opened. Kacey blinked and looked away from Aaron. *A smile that was just for her?* She was definitely going crazy. Caught up in a moment that didn't really mean anything.

Monique strolled back behind the bar. "Thanks for watching things for me."

Kacey nodded. "No problem."

Monique checked on the customers and then refilled a drink. She didn't look at Kacey, or start gushing about the latest hottie she'd snagged that had her so anxious to accept a call.

"Who was on the phone?" Kacey asked when Monique finished with the customers.

Monique waved a hand and started rinsing the dirty glasses at the sink behind the bar. "No one."

"You didn't act like it was no one."

"What are you talking about?"

"Come on, Monique. You were excited about taking that call. So tell me, who is he?"

"Why does it have to be a guy?"

Kacey chuckled. "Okay, is it a girl?"

Monique rolled her eyes so hard her fake lashes fluttered. "It's none of your business."

Kacey's smile fell away. "Really, you aren't going to tell me?"

"No, I'm not."

Kacey didn't like that answer. Monique never hid who she dated. She didn't care about people's opinions that way. The only way she would possibly care was if she was with someone she shouldn't be. Like the time she'd hooked up with one of Reggie's employees who also happened to be dating Camila's friend. That had been a difficult secret to keep, and Kacey had hated the entire situation. That was the first and only time, as far as Kacey knew, that Monique had dated a guy already in a relationship.

Kacey stepped over to Monique. "You aren't messing around with Julio again?" Julio was now married to Camila's friend.

Monique glared at Kacey. "Seriously?"

"I'm just asking. You don't usually keep secrets."

"Well, maybe I just don't want my family all up in my business this time." Monique snapped a towel off the counter and wiped her hands. "Jesus, Kacey, you always jump to the worst conclusions."

"Hey, I'm sorry. I just want to make sure you're okay."

"I'm fine," Monique snapped.

Kacey instantly felt guilty for assuming the worst. "I mean it. I shouldn't have said that."

"Aren't you supposed to be working on the books?" Monique said with a strong undertone of *chick, get out of my face*.

Kacey sighed and stepped back. She wouldn't get into it with Monique. When her sister was ready to tell her what was going on, she would. And in the meantime, she'd pray it wasn't Julio.

"Fine, I'm going to the office if you need me."

Monique spun back to check on a new guy who'd just sat at the bar. Kacey wished she could take back the entire conversation. She glanced quickly at Aaron, who was once again making her momma and brother laugh. She wanted to laugh, too, but the books needed to be done, the schedule made, and there were countless other things she'd find to do while she was here. She tore her gaze away from Aaron and went to the back, thinking of her one-night stand, Monique's affair with Julio, and wondering what was it about certain men that made the women in her family act so crazy.

CHAPTER 11

One week into her final semester, and Kacey wanted to bash her head into a wall. In fact, bashing her head into a wall was considerably more appealing than working on the thesis project her professor had ripped to shreds. After giving Kacey grief for using a personal goal for her project, the woman had thrown out nearly every source Kacey had spent the last semester gathering.

"Why so much research into fast-food chains? You're working on building a family restaurant. Start over," the woman had said, her red pen scratching out half of Kacey's literary review. Then she'd scoffed when Kacey defended her actions, using the rags-to-riches stories of how other famous chains had started with one location and the owner's dream.

Kacey tried to take some comfort that the woman hadn't recommended she find a new topic. But Kacey still felt as if she was starting from square one, and she begrudgingly admitted that even though her professor was a hard-ass, there were some nuggets of good advice beneath the pile of suggestions she'd dumped on Kacey. But now Kacey's plan to fill several sections of her thesis with research she'd done in previous semesters was out the window. Her final semester had just gone from hard to excruciating.

She reached into the bag of Twizzlers next to her laptop on the kitchen table and chewed one strawberry-flavored end. Twisting her head in a useless attempt to get the kinks out of her neck, Kacey sighed and stared at the blank space and blinking cursor on her computer screen after the words *"Literature Review."*

Sighing, she clicked on the Internet icon and navigated to the school's online sources for business journals. If she had to start looking for new information, she might as well start now.

Three sources in, a frantic knock on the door interrupted her. Swearing, she saved the journal article she'd been reading to her hard drive and went to the door. She swung it open, fully expecting her brother on the other side. Reggie tended to check in on her a few nights a week since she was a single woman living alone so close to him. She swore her brother would've fit perfectly in the Victorian age.

Her mind became as blank as her computer screen when she met Aaron's deep, soulful eyes. That sexy grin of his lit up his face, combined with slim-fitting jeans that molded to long, lean legs and a Spider-Man T-shirt clinging to his perfectly muscled upper body, made him more appealing than an A+ from Professor Hateful.

"Are you watching?" His voice rang with enthusiasm.

The words took at least two seconds to penetrate her brain. "Huh?"

"The match? The Coroner is beating King Rhames in a cage match for the title. It's crazy."

Another two seconds for comprehension. "You're talking about wrestling?"

"Yeah, I thought you were a fan. Tonight's match is great."

She *was* a fan. A huge fan, but she only watched on Sunday afternoon when she allocated three hours of the day to catch up on the shows she'd DVR-ed. There were too many to watch in that short time frame, but she watched based on importance. Wrestling usually sat up high on the priority list. Her biggest guilty pleasure: hot guys in skimpy outfits fighting in a ring. What wasn't there to love?

"I'm recording it."

"No, you've got to see this now." He stepped through the door and marched inside as if he belonged there.

Part of her considered telling him to get the hell out. The other part was too busy ogling his ass in those jeans.

As she'd suspected, she now knew that if she tried hard enough, she could easily ignore him...for the most part. Between work and class, she'd only seen him in passing over the past week. Those fleeting glances were enough to make her wish she was clutching something else at night instead of the teddy bear she'd owned since kindergarten. Particularly a certain guy who looked pretty darn good in a pair of jeans.

"If the Coroner wins, he'll be the new champion." Aaron plucked up the remote and turned on the television.

"I'm studying and can't get caught up in this right now." Kacey followed him into the living area.

The room filled with the sounds of fans screaming in the arena and the commentator's play-by-play of the action. Kacey marched over to snatch away the remote and kick Aaron out of her place. The Coroner took a metal chair and whammed King Rhames in the face. She gasped and scowled at the screen.

"No, he didn't!" Kacey said. Her eyes narrowed when one of the Coroner's flunkies distracted the referee so that the other could punch King Rhames in the corner of the ring. "They're cheating!"

Aaron's eyes were glued to the television screen. "When does the Coroner ever fight fair?"

"Never. That's why I can't stand him. He always wins his titles by cheating."

"He's cunning."

"He's sleazy."

Aaron sat on the couch, and Kacey plopped down next to him. "Come on, Rhames, get up and fight." She cheered for her current favorite wrestler.

"Rhames isn't out just yet. He always gets a second wind."

"I really should be studying," Kacey said, her attention riveted to the six-foot-five-inch wrestler with long black hair and bulging muscles beneath tan skin.

"Just watch till the end of this match," Aaron said.

"Just until this match is over."

An hour and a half later, Kacey and Aaron cheered during the final match when Jamie King, one of wrestling's biggest superstars, won the last match. A bag of chips along with her Twizzlers were between them, completely annihilated, and every bit of the tension that had plagued Kacey since Hateful Professor had kicked out all of her sources had disappeared.

"Wasn't that worth watching?" Aaron asked after the show ended.

"It was." She glanced at the clock and cringed. She'd be up late making up for this little indulgence. "But I still have a lot of work to do. I'm not going to get any sleep."

"Let it wait until tomorrow. One thing I know is that work done while exhausted always needs to be done over."

"Who says I'm exhausted?" Kacey's strong words were hampered by a yawn.

He cocked a brow and grinned. "How aren't you? School, study, work. School, study, work. Every day that I've been here, you've done the same thing. Working until all hours of the night after coming back from Momma's Kitchen."

"You don't know that."

"Yes, I do. Your light is on until late."

"How do you know how late my light is on? Are you keeping late hours yourself?"

She knew he did. She could hear his footsteps on the stairs going up to the apartment. Usually after she worked at the restaurant and was sitting at her laptop wishing her professor would win a trip to Abu Dhabi and never come back. And wondering if Aaron was spending his time with another woman since they'd agreed, like good adults were supposed to, to pretend as if their one-night stand had never happened.

"I'm used to being up late, and sitting still makes me antsy. There are no video games in the apartment, and only a few things on television are interesting to me. I get bored, and so I go out and walk until I'm tired."

"You walk? Late at night?" She didn't bother to mask her disbelief.

He nodded. "I have to move, otherwise I'd go crazy."

A fairly reasonable explanation. Or maybe she just *really* wanted to believe he wasn't out with another woman. "I have an Xbox if you need to play video games."

Crap! Why did she say that?

His sexy smile returned. "Are you offering?"

Saying no, never mind, or that the game system was broken was the best thing. Not offering up access to her apartment at any time. But withdrawing the offer now would make her appear foolish, or afraid. Certainly not eager for his company. Since, ya know, she wasn't.

Kacey shrugged and tried to appear flippant. "As long as you don't interrupt my studying." Who was she kidding? The man interrupted her ability to think clearly. No matter what she was doing, she'd just know he was in her space, breathing her air, looking delicious in a pair of jeans.

"I can connect the system upstairs."

He was giving her an out; maybe like a wolf hunting his prey, he could sense her fight-or-flight reflexes. His suggestion was a good one, except on the off chance she did take a break during the workweek, she wouldn't have access to the system.

"Can't. When I do take a break, it's with either Netflix or my DVR. I watch Netflix using the system."

"Are you sure?"

Not at all. "Yeah," she said with a relaxed laugh she wasn't sure how she managed. "I mean, we've both moved past that night. You'll just be playing a video game. I'll barely be here."

"Cool. Thanks." Gratitude filled his smooth voice, not a hint of innuendo or ulterior motive. Maybe he had easily gotten over the other night.

Maybe with the help of someone else.

She nodded. "Cool."

They sat on the couch, Aaron running his hands over his legs and Kacey studying the carpet. The awkward silence filled the space. Silence that gave her mind plenty of time to roam. And, boy, did her mind roam, wandering all up and through the memories of their night together. Normally she didn't let loose with a guy the way she had with him. Because she'd expected it to just be a one-night stand, she hadn't held back. And he'd loved it. Maybe she should have been upset that he'd let go before her;

instead, knowing she'd made him lose control, especially when he'd tried so hard not to, thrilled her.

He stopped rubbing his leg and placed his hand on the couch. Their pinky fingers brushed. Electric heat shot through her. They both jerked their hands back.

"I should go," Aaron said.

"That's a good idea," Kacey said, though she didn't want him to go. She jumped up before that thought could really sink in. He slowly rose. Their eyes met, he smiled, her heart thumped.

Kacey spun around and walked to the door. His footsteps followed. They reached for the doorknob at the same time, and the tips of their fingers brushed again. The touch was the spark to the electric tension that had built up over the past few minutes and ignited a line of flames up her arm.

Pull back.

Kacey's hand didn't move. Neither did Aaron's. He slowly traced his fingers over the back of her hand, the featherlight touch throwing more gasoline on the flames burning within her. His long fingers lightly gripped her wrist. Her pulse pounded against the soft pressure of his thumb, and he made slow, easy circles across the vibrating point. Pleasurable circles she felt all over her body and down to her dampening core.

This time her mind didn't wander over the memories of their night together. They ran directly there. Dashing back and forth over every sensual detail, so quickly that her brain went into overload with longing for more.

He pushed her hair aside and ran his finger across the birthmark on her neck. Her heart drummed, and her breath stuttered. She slowly lifted her gaze to his. His deep, dark eyes were hot with the same memories she couldn't suppress. She lost all thought of time, space, everything. Only the memory of their bodies pressed together, his lips on hers.

"Good night, Kacey." His voice was a soft whisper, full of the withheld desire coursing through her.

"Good night, Aaron," she whispered.

He stared at her lips. A little line formed between his brows. Did he want to kiss her as much as she wanted him to? She clenched her teeth to prevent licking them, prevent herself from being so obvious. Because if he followed up on that silent invitation and kissed her, there was a pretty good chance he wasn't walking out of that door.

He eased his hand away from her wrist. She had a feeling the imprint of his fingers on her wrist would be with her for the rest of the night. With one last, longing look, he opened the door, and went rigid. Reggie stood on the other side, his furious expression a dose of cold water on the moment.

• • •

Aaron would bet two years of his company profits that Reggie wanted to beat the crap out of him. If Reggie had access to Aaron's thoughts, and how hard it had been to convince himself to walk away from Kacey instead of taking those full, luscious lips of hers in what would definitely have been one hell of a kiss, he'd bet ten years profits.

"What are you doing here?" Reggie's sharp gaze jumped from Aaron to Kacey and back.

Aaron shrugged. "I just—"

"The water heater is acting up again," Kacey said. "He asked about hot water."

The scowl on Reggie's face lifted, but suspicion lingered in his gaze. "Why didn't you call me?"

Kacey leaned her head to the side and eyed Reggie as if he'd asked if she knew how to tie her shoes. "I can handle some tenant issues. There's no reason for me to call you."

Reggie stared at Aaron. "Cold showers may be good for you."

Aaron couldn't agree more. Though thoughts of Kacey while in the shower might still generate steam. "Don't worry, Reggie. I'm not overheated." *When I'm out of your sister's presence.*

Aaron gave Kacey a grateful smile. "Thanks for checking on the water."

She shrugged. "No problem. I'll call the plumber tomorrow to check on things."

Reggie watched both of them. Aaron didn't blame him for his suspicion. Though he and Kacey tried pretending there hadn't been that night between them, completely hiding his attraction was damn near impossible. She was sassy, always ready with a smart comeback to keep him on his toes. And even though their professional wrestling debates from earlier should have warned him, she was one hell of a fan. Watching the match on television with her had been more fun that he'd imagined. He'd remembered her saying that King Rhames was one of her favorites, and as soon as the match started, he hadn't cared about staying away from her and only wanted to spend more time connecting with her.

She'd wanted him to kiss her. Even though she didn't lean forward or lick her lips suggestively like some women, he'd seen what she wanted in the depths of her eyes. Now she wore a hurry-up-and-leave expression that proved she was more adept at pretending disinterest when others were around than he was.

Aaron's heart was still pounding and his body on hyper, Kacey-is-near alert.

"I'll just go back to my place." Aaron made a move to step around Reggie.

Reggie held up a hand. "Did you ever hook up with that woman again? The one you spent the night with when you first got into town?"

That was unexpected. Reggie hadn't brought that up since they'd first discussed Aaron's one-night stand in his office. It took everything in him not to glance at Kacey, a guilty gesture that would surely put Reggie on high alert. He hated lying to his friend. He didn't do drama, and he would prefer to have everything out in the open, but confessing the truth now was a little too late.

Really, what could he say? "Hey, by the way, Reggie, that woman that I had great, mind-blowing sex with is your baby sister Peanut. Small world, huh?"

Yeah, that would go over well. He'd rather keep his arms and legs intact. "Nah, I haven't seen her."

"Describe her to me, maybe I know her." Reggie looked at Kacey. "Or you might know her, Kacey."

"That's okay," Aaron said. "I'd rather not have your sister helping me hook up again."

"And I'd rather not help him hook up with someone else."

Had her voice sounded...possessive? He did look at her. Her thick lips were pressed into a thin line. She quickly glanced at Reggie.

"You know what I mean."

Aaron hoped she meant that she didn't want him with another woman because she hadn't forgotten about how good they were together.

Reggie grinned and playfully hit Aaron's shoulder. "Come on, I can't believe you're not interested in hooking up with her. The way you described the sex, I thought for sure you'd be spending most of your nights in town with her."

Aaron's face heated. Kacey crossed her arms and glared at him.

"Really, Reggie. Let's not talk about this in front of your sister."

Reggie shook his head and chuckled. "Don't be embarrassed. I've already told Kacey how much of a player you are. She can't be surprised to hear how easily you charmed the panties off a woman your first night in town."

Kacey grunted and turned away. "Actually, I'd prefer not hearing about it." She marched into the living area, her back stiff.

Aaron had earned his reputation honestly. He loved women. But he didn't want to go over his previous conquests in front of Kacey. Maybe because the sex with her had felt different, special, even if their relationship wasn't any different than the other no-commitment ones he'd had.

"I think we can stop talking about this now," Aaron said.

Reggie tapped him on the shoulder. "Excuse her attitude. She's been that way ever since Dewayne."

Aaron frowned. "Dewayne?"

Kacey spun around and nailed Reggie with a sharp stare. "Stop it, Reggie."

Reggie glanced back at Aaron. "The guy I told you about."

Oh, that asshole. Dewayne. Stupid name for a stupid man.

Kacey's angry gaze snapped between her and Reggie. "You told him about that?"

Reggie didn't appear the least bit fazed by the anger in his sister's voice. "Aaron remembered when I came home to handle that situation. He knows your history."

"My history has nothing to do with your friend." Kacey glanced at Aaron. The cool, confident stare she normally gave him was replaced with something else. Vulnerability, maybe a bit of fear. She hadn't wanted him to know about Dewayne. Maybe due to embarrassment, or because she didn't like her brother gossiping about her.

No, that drop of confidence went deeper than embarrassment. He'd had that same look whenever a woman accused him of being afraid of commitment. For a brief second, the truth that you'd once let yourself fall in love, and the relationship ended badly, showed in your eyes. He didn't want to hurt another woman the way he'd hurt Denise. Kacey didn't want her heart broken again.

Aaron eased toward the door. "I'll take that as my cue to leave. Thanks again, Kacey."

He opened the door and hurried out before Reggie or Kacey could say anything more. He was disappointed and frustrated. He didn't regret his night with Kacey. Hell, no man could regret a night that great. So the disappointment made sense. But the itchy frustration crawling up his spine? That would keep him up all night. He wanted her, but he could see any liaison they had ending in a devastating crash and burn that would be ten times worse than his young-love breakup with Denise.

Kacey's door opened. "Aaron, hold up." Reggie's voice stopped Aaron.

Aaron turned on the step to face his friend. "Yeah?"

"Kacey is going to be pissed that I mentioned Dewayne, but I thought you both needed the reminder."

"Why would you think that?"

"Because I know you. You seduce women without even trying. I don't need you to hurt my sister."

Damn, had Aaron's struggle and frustration been that obvious to his friend? Aaron gave his nonchalant smile and relaxed his body. "Reggie, man, I'm here for the business, that's all. I'm not going to lay a hand on any of your sisters."

Reggie's tense shoulders lost some of their cinderblock hardness. He uncrossed his arms and took a step closer. "Honestly, if it were Monique or even Ashlei I wouldn't care as much. They've got their wild sides, as much as I hate to admit that," he said with a quirk of the brow. "But Kacey's different. After that mess she hasn't been really serious with any guy. I know she's no nun, and she dates, but she's a lot more guarded. One day that guard is going to come down. Probably fast and without warning because she's kept it up for so damn long. That's great, because I want her to be happy." His brows drew together, and he stared at Aaron. "But I'd rather see her let it down for a guy who'd treasure her, not a guy just out for fun."

Reggie's speech was good, and heartfelt, and full of the type of love and protection any good older brother would give. But every word ramped up Aaron's frustration. A small part of him knew he could be that guy. But not here, not now. He didn't want to be the husband in a small town, eventually serving on the PTO and selling wrapping paper to coworkers at Christmas as part of his kid's school fund-raiser.

"Aaron, you're my boy and all, but—"

"I get it," Aaron broke in, the frustration edging his voice. "And, by the way, if I did go after your sister, if I was the guy she let her guard down for, I wouldn't hurt her. She's cool, smart, and hardworking. If I had her, I'd treasure her."

Reggie's brows drew together, and his lips formed a thin line. Aaron lifted his chin, still frustrated, but a little less so having spouted the words. Before Reggie could answer with more brotherly indignation, Aaron turned and jogged up the stairs.

CHAPTER 12

Kacey slammed the cordless phone on the bar in Momma's Kitchen. Just what she didn't need, a server calling out on Saturday night. She chewed on her lower lip to keep from swearing and stared at the schedule for the day. She didn't doubt her cousin Deborah's sick excuse. One phone call to her aunt would prove whether or not Deborah was lying. But rearranging the schedule to accommodate the night's crowd would only stop Kacey from getting out of there before they opened for lunch.

"Why are you frowning like someone just ripped out your weave?" Monique's voice came from Kacey's left.

"I don't wear a weave," Kacey said, staring at the schedule. *I could take one of the new servers out of training and give her Deborah's section.*

"Then why are you frowning as if someone ripped out *my* weave?"

"I'd laugh if someone ripped out your weave." A newbie set loose in the biggest section. That would spell Saturday night disaster. Kacey eyes scanned the list of employees off for the weekend.

A sharp tug at the back of Kacey's head pulled her backward. "Hey, crazy." She spun and slapped Monique's arm. "Why are you pulling my hair?"

"If you're going to frown, I might as well give you a reason." Monique's grin said she enjoyed the hair pulling regardless of the reason. She leaned against the side of the bar next to Kacey. Her long weave was flawless, and her curves were on excellent display with the top few buttons of her white *Momma's Kitchen* shirt open and her fitted black pants.

"Deborah called out sick. That's why I'm frowning." She turned back to the schedule.

"Damn, that's really going to screw up the rotation."

At least Monique understood Kacey's frustration. "I might have to come in and work."

"Weekend nights are off for you, remember? This is your last semester, I can't have you flunking out because you work weekends." Monique slid the schedule away from Kacey and looked over the spreadsheet.

Kacey frowned and slid the schedule back. "It's only one night."

"Moderation is not your strong suit. One night will turn into every night." Monique slid the paper back.

Her sister made a very valid statement. Kacey already felt guilty for taking weekends off when school was in. Her momma owned the place, but Kacey had been running the business for the past three years. Keeping the shifts fully staffed, handling the books, and being on top of the orders were all her responsibility. She felt like she was dropping the ball taking off nights when school was in session.

Kacey rubbed her eyes with the heels of her hands. "Ugh, between the short staff and the hateful professor I'm going to lose my mind."

"We're interviewing for waitresses today, so get over the short staff thing," Monique said. "Hateful Professor is stupid. Your thesis idea is great."

Kacey dropped her hands and placed a hand on her hip. "You're only saying that because it's to help this place grow."

Monique hugged Kacey from the side. "That doesn't make it less great." She dropped her arm and stared at the schedule. Before long her arched brows drew together in a frown.

Kacey leaned over and once again glanced over the names of the waitresses off tonight. "I guess I can call Jamelah and see if she can work. I think she can use the extra hours."

"Or we can just split the section between two others and give a few tables to the girl we hired last week."

Kacey frowned at the diagram of the restaurant with the location of the tables and the sections they were broken into. "That would work." She grinned at Monique. "Why am I the one getting the master's degree? You can run this place."

Monique laughed and tossed the schedule on the counter. "You overthink things when you're stressed and feeling guilty."

"I do not."

"Yeah. You do." Monique's eyes lit up. "You know what you should do?"

"I don't know if I want to hear you suggestion."

"You need to get laid."

Kacey rolled her eyes. "Why is that your solution to every problem?"

"Because sex is a proven cure for stress."

"Here's the problem: There's no one for me to have sex with."

"You've got two very good options," Monique said.

Kacey raised a brow, curious to know her so-called options, but just then Monique's phone rang. Her sister pulled the phone out of her pocket and glanced at the screen. "I've got to take this."

"Then take it." Kacey leaned against the counter and smiled at Monique.

Monique's eyes narrowed before she turned and answered her phone. "Hello?"

Kacey frowned at her sister's tone. She'd used her *I'm trying to impress the caller* tone. The one their momma used when she'd talk to bill collectors, teachers, and sometimes a new guy she'd met. Monique again disappeared behind the doors into the kitchen. Kacey straightened and started to follow, but she stopped herself. Instead of worrying about who her sister was talking to, she reworked the floor setup to cover for her cousin.

Several minutes later, Monique came back out from the kitchen. "Okay, so you've got one doable option and another good option."

Kacey looked around the empty dining room, then back to Monique. "Are you talking to me?"

"Umm, who else would I be talking to? I'm finishing our conversation from earlier."

Kacey pointed to the phone in Monique's hand. "You're not going to enlighten me?"

Monique ignored the question. "Your doable option is to call up Howard and get old but reliable sex."

Kacey was too through with Monique's words to even care that her sister had ignored the question. "Not happening." One fantastic night with Aaron and now Kacey doubted she'd ever be able to accept mediocre sex again.

Monique grinned and flipped her hair over her shoulder. "Or..." She dragged out the word. "You can waltz up the stairs to the apartment above your place and give Aaron a try."

As if she hadn't thought of that several times already. The only thing stopping her was the fact that he'd only be here for a few weeks. And that he'd bragged to her brother about getting laid his first night in town. And that he was a ladies' man who probably had a woman in every town he visited. Her life was good, and she had more important things to do than becoming another notch on a bedpost. Like figuring out how to make the professor from hades not hate her thesis project.

"Also not happening," Kacey said. "Look, I've got a vibrator, I'll be okay."

Monique grunted. "You're always so busy working and studying you probably won't even take the time to use that."

"Not all of us have secret callers to take care of our needs," Kacey said, again pointing to Monique's phone.

Monique slid the device, now in a purple case that matched her new nails, into her back pocket. "Are you really planning to keep your hands off of Aaron? You two had definite chemistry the other night."

Kacey decided to let the subject go. Monique would tell her who her secret caller was eventually. "Yes, I'm going to stay away from Aaron." Interest lit up Monique's eyes, and Kacey pointed at her sister. "We both are. Reggie is really excited about this partnership, and you know he'll stop the entire process if Aaron so much as touches one of us."

Monique shrugged and leaned her back against the bar. "Fine, we'll both stay away. Though I wasn't really that interested anyway. Do you think your professor will eventually get over her heartburn about your thesis project?"

Monique changed the subject so fast Kacey frowned. Normally her sister loved to find ways to get under Reggie's skin. For her to so readily agree that she would stay away from Aaron meant she had other things occupying her mind. Which only increased Kacey's concern about the secret calls. She really hoped

Monique wasn't going down the road to becoming a side chick. Her sister deserved so much more than that.

But she didn't want to get into another fight. "Don't get me started on my professor," Kacey said. "I did finally find some new references after she tossed out two-thirds of the ones I previously had."

Monique patted Kacey on the shoulder. "You'll do great."

"I'm not so sure this time."

"You always worry and freak out, but in the end you pull through with an awesome GPA. I know you can do it this time." Monique hugged Kacey. "We're all counting on you."

"Gee, thanks for not pressuring me," Kacey deadpanned.

Monique lifted a shoulder. "That's what I'm here for. If you don't mind, I'm going to use the office computer for a second before you go in."

"Yeah, sure."

"Okay, thanks. It'll just be a minute, so occupy yourself." She waved her hand around the bar.

"Does that mean I can't come in while you're on the computer?"

Monique strolled to the door. She waved her hand but didn't look back. "You can find something to keep you busy for ten minutes."

Kacey did, but keeping busy didn't keep her mind from wondering what her sister was up to. And her curiosity was only piqued more when Monique finally did let her into the office and Kacey realized the history on the computer had been deleted.

• • •

After Kacey and Monique interviewed three potential waitresses to help out during the busy weekend shifts, Kacey dashed out of the restaurant to make her way to the school's library. She'd wanted to stay and help out. The Saturday lunch crowd had been thicker than usual, and she always hated leaving the place when things were busy. Monique had hastily pushed Kacey out of the door with a sly "Don't you have more references to look up?"

Kacey hopped on her white Northwoods women's bicycle and started her trek across town to the school. Monique might recommend sex for stress relief, but riding her bicycle around town allowed Kacey to work out her frustrations with every turn of the pedal. By the time she reached downtown, her heart was pumping and much of her frustration had lessened.

She eased around a corner onto Main Street. She spotted Aaron strolling down the side of the street in her direction and tilted her head to the side. Common sense said to wave and keep going, but he'd grinned at her and raised his hand in a friendly wave, the afternoon sun bringing out a reddish tint to the edges of his curly Afro. Well, ignoring him would be rude. Kacey looked both ways before crossing to his side of the street.

"Where are you going?" she asked. Her voice was breathless, not just from the bike ride but from the effect of his dark gaze on her.

"To the library. You?"

"The same." His eyes lit up and she shook her head. "The school's library. I'm still looking for references for my project."

He turned and walked down the sidewalk in the direction she was heading, not fast enough to say he wanted the conversation to end, so Kacey slowly pedaled beside him in the bike lane.

"How's the hunt for references going?"

"Frustrating as hell. Let's talk about something else."

He nodded. "Fair enough."

"What are you going to do at the library?"

"Check out a book."

Kacey twisted her lip and glanced at him from the corner of her eye. "But you don't have a card."

He stopped and faced her. "Do you?"

She stopped as well. "Yeah."

"Then let me use yours."

"So you can go out of town with books due and I get hit with the fine? Uhh, no."

Aaron chuckled. "I wouldn't do that. Let me use your number to check out e-books instead."

"Can you do that?"

"Yeah, I do it all the time. Since I'm not in one place long enough to get a library card, my friends usually let me use their numbers."

Female friends? she wondered. "Why don't you just buy books?"

"Most of the time I do, but sometimes if I'm unsure about a book, I'll check it out at the library first."

"Ah, so selective." She started cycling again and he picked up his steps to follow her.

"So, can I use your number?"

"I don't think so. My library card number is only for serious commitments. One-night stands need not apply."

He chuckled. "Oh, really?"

"Really."

"How do I become a serious commitment?"

She snorted. "You? Never gonna happen. But in general, buy a house here, love my family, be ready to settle down and have a few kids."

He cringed. "You're one of those."

She stopped the bike again. "One of what?"

Aaron faced her. "All or nothing."

"I guess I am. Anything wrong with that?"

"Not at all," he said, shaking his head. He slid his hands into the back pocket of his navy blue shorts and gave her a *no big deal* kind of shrug. "All-or-nothing women are the best type, for an all-or-nothing guy. I'm just not there yet."

She grinned at him. "I pretty much know you're not."

He got a weird look, as if her words may have struck a nerve, before he turned his head to glance down the street. "What are you doing when you finish at the library?"

"If I find what I need, start working on my literature review."

Aaron met her eyes, his carefree, friendly look back. "Nope, wrong answer. After hours in the library, and I know it'll be hours because you drive yourself ragged, you'll need a break."

"I take breaks on Sunday afternoons."

"No reason why you can't take a break this afternoon with me."

His teasing smile and bedroom eyes were so very tempting. "I won't have time," she said in a weak voice.

"Just a few minutes with me at the county museum."

She stopped in the middle of getting ready to pedal again to give him a disbelieving look. "Museum?"

"It looks interesting, and it's between the college and the library. Meet me there in three hours."

"Why would I want to go to the museum? Why would *you* want to go?"

"Why not? It'll be fun."

"Aaron..."

He placed his hand over hers on the handlebars. "Just thirty minutes at the museum and that's all. Then you can go back to driving yourself crazy with school and work, solving the world's problems, or whatever else it is you stress about."

She put her hand on her hip, mostly because the feel of his on hers was sending crazy flutters through her midsection. "If you're going to be insulting, then I won't meet you."

He gave her a smile that would liquefy iron. "I think you will."

She shook her head and started pedaling down the street—but not fast enough for him to not keep up. "You're so cocky."

"And you're very sexy when you're trying to pretend like you don't like it."

She rolled her eyes, and her heart rolled in her chest. "Whatever. 'Bye, Aaron." She pushed ahead, leaving him behind.

"See you in three hours, Kacey," he called out.

She waved a hand but didn't turn back. She should leave him waiting. But deep down she knew she'd be watching the clock to count down the hours until she met him again.

CHAPTER 13

Two hours and fifteen minutes later, Aaron checked his watch and grinned. Forty-five minutes and he would meet Kacey. Maybe not the smartest decision given his last conversation with Reggie, but the moment he'd seen her on that bike smiling and glowing in a pair of short lavender shorts and an orange top, he'd known he wanted to see her again. Besides, he didn't have much to entertain him that day.

Reggie had plans for the day with Camila, plans Reggie didn't sound thrilled about. Aaron also could have unhooked Bertha from the trailer and driven over to Chattanooga for the day, but he wasn't in the mood to do that. So he'd chosen to do what he normally did when in a new city, play tourist and visit the sites listed on the town's Chamber of Commerce website. Hence the reason for asking Kacey to go with him to the county museum. It might not be exciting to most people, but he always enjoyed learning the little quirks about the history of the various places he visited. No better place to do that than the museum.

He strolled toward the college so he could catch Kacey when she left. He didn't doubt she would find an excuse to skip out on hanging with him. He passed a ball field with a group of boys playing baseball, and he stopped to watch. His cell rang about ten minutes after he'd leaned against the fence.

He pulled out the phone and raised a brow when he saw his sister's best friend Liz's number.

Aaron cringed. Normally he wouldn't mind chatting with Liz, but with Janiyah's grand expectations about Aaron and Liz's few hookups, he worried what this call was about.

"Hey, Liz," Aaron answered.

"I'm just giving you a heads-up about Janiyah." Liz's straightforward drawl came through the phone.

Aaron chuckled. "Too late, Kareem called a few days ago. Is this about her getting it into her head that you and I are a couple?"

"Yes. I think this pregnancy has gone to her brain and now she wants everyone married and happy."

Aaron leaned forward and watched the boys playing baseball. They appeared to range in age from ten to twelve, and they spent more time arguing and stumbling through plays than actually playing.

"Did you tell her we're just friends?" Aaron asked.

"I did, but she barely listened. I figured I'd call so you wouldn't think I put the idea in her head."

"I didn't think that. We both knew what was up when we hooked up."

"Yeah...but you know Janiyah. When she goes in, she goes hard."

"Tell me about it. Don't worry, I'll set her straight."

"That would be great. I've talked till I was blue in the face."

Liz sighed and Aaron pictured the redhead rolling her eyes behind her purple square-framed glasses. Aaron liked Liz, and not just because they'd hooked up several times. She'd been Janiyah's sensible anchor for years, and she kept his sister from making too many mistakes. But behind her dry sense of humor and straitlaced exterior, she had a fun side that she only let out on few occasions. It had been enough of a juxtaposition to pique Aaron's interest in her. And when things ran their course, she'd agreed to move on with no hysterics or drama. They'd remained friends, which made her even cooler in his book.

"How are things with you and that architect?"

Liz grunted. "Going. Where, I don't know, but for now we're kinda on again."

"You can do better, Liz."

"Now you sound like Janiyah. She thinks you're better, so watch you who say that around."

Aaron nodded, even though she couldn't see. The boys on the field started arguing again. Aaron frowned; there was enough talent on the team for them to be playing better. He wondered where the coach was. If they had direction, they could be decent.

"I'll do that. Hey, Liz, I've got to go."

"Sure, I'll talk with you later."

Aaron agreed, then hung up the phone to watch the kids. One boy hit a foul ball that flew to where Aaron stood. Aaron easily caught the ball. He jumped the chain-link fence and jogged over to the kid who'd hit the ball.

"Thanks, mister," the kid said. He was short and thick with dark skin and a head full of dark, curly hair.

Aaron tossed the ball over to him. "You guys aren't bad."

The kid snorted, and another boy who played umpire behind him snickered. "How long have you been watching us play?"

Aaron shrugged. "For about twenty minutes."

The umpire shook his head. "Then you definitely haven't watched long enough to know that we suck."

"You don't suck. Most of you hit pretty well, and you've got some speed on the team. You're just not utilizing your strengths." Aaron looked around for another adult. "Where's your coach?"

A few other boys ran over. The tallest, a lanky kid with sandy skin and green eyes, sized Aaron up. In the few minutes Aaron watched them play, he'd noticed the boy naturally took the lead on the field. "That's my dad."

"Is he here?"

"He got deployed. Two weeks ago. He did a good job coaching us."

Aaron held up his hand and took a step back. "Hey, I'm sure he's a great coach. He played ball?"

The kid kicked the dirt and glanced away. "Not really, but he watches it a lot."

"You can learn a lot from watching, and even more from playing."

The kid's head snapped up. "You played?"

"A little. All of high school and in college for a year. I tried out for the minors, but changed my mind before signing the contract."

The stocky kid's eyes widened. "Why in the world didn't you sign the contract? Are you crazy?"

Aaron laughed. The kid sounded a lot like David had back when he'd turned down the contract.

"I guess you can call me crazy. It just wasn't for me. I still play games here and there." Not as much as he'd like. Aaron did miss playing sometimes.

The unofficial leader of the group leaned his baseball bat over his shoulder and narrowed his eyes at Aaron. "So, what, you offering to coach us now?"

"Whoa, hold up, I'm not saying all that," Aaron said, holding up his hands. "You guys have talent. I've just got a few suggestions on how to utilize that."

"Like what?" the boy asked.

The rest of the team surrounded Aaron and stared at him with a mixture of interest and skepticism. There was no way he was going to coach the team, but spending a few minutes helping them out wouldn't hurt. Especially since their coach was away.

"Well, for one you've got the wrong guy playing shortstop. He'd do better as a first baseman. Then you can put your first baseman in that position." Aaron pointed to another tall kid who'd run the bases in no time earlier. "You're fast, and you'd do well there. Your shortstop should be fast and have mobility."

The tall kid frowned. "But I've never played shortstop."

"Trust me," Aaron said. "You'd make a great shortstop." The kids appeared skeptical. "Come on, let me show you."

Aaron ran the kids through a few defensive drills with the tall kid, named Lenny, at shortstop instead of first baseman. When Lenny easily accomplished a double out, where the previous shortstop had struggled, the team immediately perked up and asked Aaron for other suggestions. Aaron got caught up in helping the kids. Laughing, running, and listening to the good-natured rivalry between the kids brought back the happiness he'd once felt when he played. He'd liked to win when he played ball, but even more, he liked the camaraderie that he'd gotten from his team. The feeling that no matter what, win or lose, the team had his back.

"You're good on defense," Marcus, the green-eyed kid he'd identified as the leader, said. "But can you hit?"

Aaron waved a hand and blew air through his lips. "Can I hit? Of course I can hit."

Marcus tossed the ball from one hand to the other. "Bet you can't hit my fastball."

A few of the boys on the team snickered, and the others let out a few "oohs." Aaron never backed down from a challenge. "All right, kid, let me see your fastball."

The boys cheered and Aaron strolled over to home plate. Movement at the fence caught his attention. Kacey leaned against the fence, her bike on the ground beside her and a big grin on her face. Something primal stirred in his chest—a mixture of exhilaration and possessiveness—knowing she stood there waiting for him. Her orange top brought out the red undertones of her skin. His gaze slid over her slim curves. How in the world had he ever thought she was too skinny?

"Sorry, fellas," Aaron called to Marcus but didn't take his eyes off Kacey. "But I've got a date."

A round of catcalls rang through the team. Kacey shook her head, the ponytail she seemed to prefer wearing swishing back and forth behind her head.

"Don't use me as an excuse to avoid Marcus's fastball," she yelled from the fence. "I've seen it, and even I'm not sure you'll hit it."

Aaron's brows rose, and he gently swung the bat back and forth. "Oh, you're doubting my abilities?"

She shrugged. "You're the one trying to run away."

The boys laughed. Marcus pointed at Kacey. "That's what I think, too, Miss Kacey."

Aaron got into stance beside the plate and smirked at Marcus. "Throw the ball."

Marcus's fastball was good. Aaron would admit that, and to give the boy, and the team, the boost of confidence they needed, he missed the first two pitches on purpose.

Kacey leaned over the fence. "What's that about your abilities?"

Aaron shook his head and got into stance. This time when Marcus pitched, Aaron hit the ball with strength and precision. A resounding *crack* as the bat struck the ball silenced the boy's snickers, and they all watched, openmouthed, as the ball flew over the back fence.

Aaron propped the bat on his shoulder. "I could run the bases, but why waste the energy?"

The stocky kid, Jerry, jumped up and cheered. "That was awesome!"

The team ran over, including Marcus, and raved over Aaron's home run.

Marcus raised his hands. "Hey, guys, calm down." He turned to Aaron and crossed his arms. "You're an all-right player, so I'm going to make you an offer."

Aaron cocked his head to the side. "Oh, really?"

"Really." The boy rubbed his chin. "I'm going to let you coach us, seeing as how my dad's out of the country."

The boys quickly grew excited. Aaron shook his head. "Today was fun, but I'm only in town for another week."

"But you're going into business with Mr. Holmes, right?"

Aaron's brows drew together. He knew the town was small, and news traveled in small towns, but he hadn't expected the local kids to know his business. "Yeah."

Marcus shrugged as if things were settled. "Then you've gotta come back. We've got another ten days until the season starts with the recreation commission. We can meet here on Tuesdays and Saturdays and get prepared."

Lenny slapped his hands together. "That's a great idea!"

Aaron felt the tightening noose of responsibility around his neck. The kids were fun, and he had enjoyed playing ball with them, but he couldn't commit to coaching. He didn't live here. He was far from settling permanently in Resilient or anywhere. Hell, his apartment in Columbia basically served as a permanent hotel room, he was in and out of town so briefly.

"I really can't, boys."

The disappointment in their faces sucker-punched him. He could practically see the confidence they'd gained in one afternoon drift away.

Aaron sighed. "Look, I'll help out while I'm in town. I'll come back on Tuesday and next Saturday. Maybe we'll throw in Thursday afternoon, too."

The smiles returned, though not as bright as before. Marcus looked around at the team. The boys nodded. Marcus turned back to Aaron and held out his hand. "Deal."

Aaron smiled and shook the boy's hand. "Deal." He glanced at Kacey, still leaning against the fence watching him. "Now, I've really got to go. Here's another lesson: Never leave a pretty girl waiting."

The boys laughed and teased as Aaron jogged away from the group and over to Kacey. Her brown eyes sparkled like topaz in the sunlight. Admiration, or something close to it, shone in their depths. The urge to lean over the fence and kiss her senseless struck. He licked his lips in anticipation and leaned in. Her eyes widened and her lips parted. Aaron blinked and looked away. If the kids knew he was working with Reggie, then he was pretty sure word would get back to Reggie if Aaron kissed Kacey in the park.

"Nice hit," she said. He swore disappointment filled her voice.

"Hey, you doubted my skills."

"I never said that."

"You implied."

Her smile sent heat through his veins. "Maybe I did. Just a little." She held her thumb and pointer finger a few centimeters apart.

"Just a little, huh. Oh, okay," he teased.

They stood staring at each other, smiling like two kids who'd just learned Santa Claus was real. Something pulled him, and he placed his hands on the fence beside hers and leaned in closer. Just to be near and feel the heat from her body.

"So, you still want to go to the museum?" she asked, the bright smile still on her face.

"Not really."

"What do you want to do?"

"Take you home and make love to you."

Her eyes widened. Aaron leaned back. "Did I say that out loud?"

She nodded. "Yeah." She looked away, her breasts rising and falling with her rapid breaths. "We agreed we wouldn't."

"Yeah. I know. My bad, it just slipped out." He cleared his throat and ran a hand over his head. "How about some pizza?"

She frowned at him. "Pizza?"

"Sure, there was this pizza place downtown that looked interesting. We can order a pizza and kill some time."

"I can't do that."

"Why, are Momma's Kitchen employees not allowed to eat at other restaurants?" He asked with mock shock.

Her bright grin returned. "No, it's just the pizza there isn't that good."

Aaron waved a hand. "Excuses."

Her thick lips twisted in a cute way that had him leaning closer again. He imagined them against his...better yet, running along his body.

"Fine. But don't blame me if you get heartburn," she said.

"For another date with you, I'd take heartburn."

Her eyes sparkled again, and the corners of her smile softened in a secret way that caused a pull in his chest. Aaron hopped over the fence. Kacey took a step back and he picked up her bike. Otherwise, he'd say to hell with the field full of kids and kiss Kacey Randal absolutely senseless.

CHAPTER 14

Aaron eyed the half-eaten pizza on the table and Kacey chuckled. She'd tried to warn him they should have only ordered by the slice instead of an entire pizza. He'd insisted, and because she'd wanted to hang out longer, she'd let him.

Kacey gave Aaron's shoulder a playful push. "Aren't you going to eat any more?"

He shook his head and rubbed his stomach. "I'm pretty full."

"I'll ask for a box." She lifted her hand to catch the waiter's attention.

Aaron quickly lowered her hand. "That's okay."

"Don't tell me you're going to waste all of this pizza?" she asked with mock disbelief.

"Fine, I'll admit you were right. I should have just ordered a slice."

"A man who actually admits when he's wrong?"

"It happens so infrequently that I'm not fazed."

"Or maybe it happens so much that you've gotten used to it."

Aaron leaned back in the red leather booth and leaned his head to the side. Her fingers itched to dive in to the springy curls on his head. And when he ran a hand over his jaw, her body remembered what it felt like to have the hint of his beard rub against her neck, breasts, and shoulders.

"How does this place stay in business?" Aaron looked around at the fairly full seating area.

Kacey shrugged. "The only other pizza available is a chain delivery place on the outskirts of town or frozen from the grocery store. But the reality is that the owner, Luigi, is a local that everyone loves and he makes the best desserts. You may not order pizza from him, but you will order cakes for every event."

"Then why isn't it just a bakery?"

"Luigi loves pizza. Unfortunately, he hasn't realized that that his gift of cake-making doesn't translate to fantastic pizza."

"That explains the crowd." Aaron looked around the room. "And the lack of pizza in front of most people."

Kacey grinned and took a sip from her soda. "Yep, appetizers and desserts are what you order when you come to Luigi's Authentic Italian Pizza Parlor."

Aaron laughed, the rich sound infusing her senses and making her mouth water more than the rich smell of chocolate and fresh baked pastry of Luigi's famed cannolis.

Luigi strolled out from the back. He scanned the crowd, and when he spotted Kacey, he grinned and came over. A tall, thin man, with dark, wavy hair and a mustache that was perfectly curled, Luigi looked the part of some great Italian chef with his white chef's jacket and dark pants. But his look was the only thing authentically Italian about Luigi. He'd grown up in Resilient with Kacey, who'd known him as Larry in grade school, and his family had been there for at least three generations. Luigi was created when Larry returned from culinary school after college.

"How was everything, Kacey?" Luigi asked.

"Everything was good as usual," she said.

Luigi rubbed his hands together. "Glad to hear it. And what about you, sir?"

Aaron nodded. "It was definitely different from any other pizza I've tried. And I've tried a lot of pizza."

Kacey leaned an elbow on the table. "Luigi, meet Aaron Henderson. He owns his own trucking company and is in town working with Reggie."

Luigi's dark eyes widened. "Ahh, so you're the guy Reggie's bragged about. It's nice to meet you." He took Aaron's hand and briskly pumped it up and down. "Any friend of Reggie and Kacey's is a friend of mine. Here's what I'm going to do—I'm going to give you both a free cannoli tonight."

Aaron's head jerked back and forth. "That's okay, really."

Kacey placed her hand on his arm. "Don't listen to him. We'll take them."

Luigi slapped his hands together. "Great."

"And bring us a box with the check. Aaron wants to take the rest of our pizza home."

Luigi grinned on his way to the back. Aaron turned suspicious eyes on Kacey. "Are you trying to punish me?"

"Not this time. I promise you, you're going to want the cannoli."

Luigi came back with an empty pizza box, the check, and two wrapped-up cannolis. Aaron insisted on paying for the entire meal at the register, and after waving good-bye to Luigi, they were once again strolling down the sidewalk. Kacey pushed her bike while Aaron carried the leftovers.

"Hey, I meant to tell you earlier, but that was really nice of you to offer to help the boys with their baseball team," Kacey said as they turned off Main onto Maple Street toward the house.

"They really aren't that bad. What I show them in a few days should help."

"I think I remember Reggie saying something about you turning down a baseball contract."

He shrugged as if turning down the offer to play semi-pro sports was no big deal. "It just wasn't what I wanted."

"I thought most guys lived and breathed sports."

"I don't live and breathe anything. Baseball was fun, and I played for fun. When they put that contract in front of me, suddenly baseball became a job. I didn't want to lose the fun."

"How could you possibly lose the fun?"

"Responsibility kicks the fun out of most things."

Kacey frowned. "I'm not following you."

"Once you take the fun out of an activity, the things that made you enjoy that activity takes second place. If you turn a hobby into a career, then it's all about making that hobby more profitable. If you do the same with a sport, then it's more about statistics and being at the top of your game."

Kacey pulled her bottom lip between her teeth and thought about his words. Then she had to ask. "And relationships?"

He glanced at her. "Relationships are the same. When you go from being friends having fun to a relationship, there's the expectation that things have to become serious."

She stopped pushing the bike and turned to face him. "You're afraid of responsibility."

"I wouldn't say all that."

"I would."

Aaron shifted the pizza box in his hands. His carefree smile was one that easily labeled him as a guy who thoroughly enjoyed being free of all responsibilities. "I just don't want unnecessary expectations put on me."

"How did you end up running a business?" She started walking again and he followed.

"Things just worked out. I wanted to travel and get paid, so I figured, 'What the hell, I'll drive a big rig for a while,' thinking it would make an interesting story one day. Turns out I really liked seeing parts of the country that aren't in tour guides. Then one day this guy said I was just a driver. I was, and never had a problem with that, but the way he said it, he made it sound like being just a truck driver was derogatory. I'm slightly competitive." He held his thumb and pointer finger close together. "So I bought another truck and hired a guy to drive it for me. Before I knew it, I had a fleet."

He made his success sound so easy. And for a guy like him, success probably was. He breezed through life with the relaxed and carefree attitude of someone blessed with perpetual good luck. Though she didn't doubt he also worked hard, she had a feeling that Aaron didn't have to work hard for much of anything,

"Basically you became successful just to prove someone wrong?"

"You make that sound like a bad thing."

"What drives you? What are your hopes, your dreams, your ambitions? I get up and do what I do every day because of my drive to make my momma's legacy into something even bigger than what it is today."

Aaron placed a hand on the handlebars of the bike to stop her. "Why?"

"Because I'm proud of her and what she accomplished."

"Or is it because you get to ram it into the noses of the people who looked down on your mother for having four kids by four different men? And because despite all that your family has accomplished, some people still see her past and wonder if you'll go down the same path?"

Kacey sucked in a breath. "Why would you say that?"

He gave his usual no-big-deal shrug. "Because it's the truth. I'm not saying anything is wrong with your reasons, but your reasons are not because you have a hope, dream, or ambition tied to some noble cause. Just like I wanted to prove to that guy I'm not just a driver, you're proving to people that you're not your mother's reputation."

She spun away and marched down the street, too angry to wait to see if he'd stop. Her determination wasn't driven by revenge or some sense of proving something. She was proud of her momma. Proud of the business. She loved working there and didn't know what she'd do if she wasn't there.

You would have left Resilient. And you'd be spending your nights having fun instead of studying.

Kacey shook the thought out of her head. Yes, back in high school she'd wanted out of the small town, but who didn't want out of a small town when they were in high school? Her momma had needed help at the restaurant, and Kacey did love the place. She loved singing there, seeing the regular customers, the teasing of the staff.

But is that enough?

Of course it was. She was pissed at Aaron for putting stupid thoughts in her head. No one could just leave responsibilities behind and do whatever they wanted. No one but guys like Aaron, who were afraid of being a grown-up.

"Kacey." Aaron's voice, followed by his quick footsteps, came up behind her. "Kacey, I'm sorry. I shouldn't have said that."

She stopped and glared at him. "I love what I do. I'm happy to help my momma's business. That's what I do. I support my family. Whether it's getting a degree so that I can open a second restaurant or staying away from playboys like you so my brother can expand his business."

She snapped her mouth closed and clenched her teeth. Anger always made her say way too much.

Aaron slid his hand across hers on the bicycle seat. His long, warm fingers wrapped around her wrist, and he stepped forward until the bike pressed into his body.

"If it weren't just about supporting your family, what would you do, Kacey?" His voice dipped low. The question was more than just a few words, but an invitation to admit that she really hated their agreement to stay away from each other in the best interests of her brother.

I'd go home and make love to you. "But my motivation is about supporting my family. I don't live off of what-ifs. Just like I don't shirk responsibility."

His fingers on her wrist flexed, and his mouth tightened. For the first time, frustration replaced his constant look of relaxation and devil-may-care attitude.

They'd stopped in front of a boutique on Maple Street. The door to the store opened, filling the air with the cheerful sound of the wind chime at the door. Kacey glanced at the couple coming out of the store and tensed. Aaron released her wrist and turned.

The guy, tall and lanky, with the same rusty brown skin as hers, dressed in a pair of chino shorts and a white polo, grinned. "Kacey, how's it going?"

Kacey returned the smile. "Hey, Dad."

Cliff Randal strolled over and gave Kacey a hug. "What are you doing out here?"

"I'm walking home. I tricked Aaron into having dinner at Luigi's."

Cliff turned to Aaron and chuckled. "Luigi's, huh? I hope you ordered something other than pizza."

Aaron held up the pizza box. "To be fair, she did try to warn me away from ordering an entire pizza." Aaron held out his other hand. "Aaron Henderson."

Cliff shook Aaron's hand. "I know who you are. Good luck with the merger." He stepped to the side to indicate the woman who'd come out with him. "This is Brenda."

Brenda didn't stroll over, but she did smile and lift her hand. "Hello."

Kacey waved back. "Hi, Brenda."

"You are coming to your daddy's birthday cookout on Saturday?" Brenda asked.

"I may have to work," Kacey said. She could get off, but hanging out with her dad's family, overhearing the remarks from them about how grateful she should be that he'd taken care of his mistakes, was about as high on her priority list as getting her toenails removed.

Cliff's smile dimmed somewhat. "I'd love it if you came by for a few minutes."

Kacey started to come up with a reason why she couldn't, but Cliff gave her a hopeful look. Her dad's side of the family might like to rub it in her face, but she was grateful for her dad's willingness to try. She nodded. "I'll drop by for a few minutes."

"Good. Can't wait to see you." He looked at Aaron. "Come by, too, if you like. You two have a good night." Cliff strolled over to Brenda and wrapped an arm around her shoulders. Brenda snaked her arm around his waist so tight Kacey wondered if her dad could breathe. Cliff threw up his hand in a wave as they walked down the street to where his black Suburban was parked.

"Your dad and his girlfriend seem nice," Aaron said.

Kacey watched the Suburban disappear down the street. "That's his wife."

"Oh."

Kacey slowly continued down the street, and Aaron followed. "Have they been married long?"

"Why would you ask?"

"She stayed back. Almost like she was still unsure of how to relate to her new stepdaughter."

"Cliff and Brenda have been married for nearly thirty years."

"Oh." Aaron nodded. Then his brows drew together and he stared at her. "Oh."

"Yeah, oh. We're cool, but I'm a constant reminder of her husband's indiscretion."

"A little awkward, I'd guess."

"That's a nice way of putting things. I don't know why they stayed together."

"He must love her."

"Then why did he cheat with my momma?" The million-dollar question that had bugged her all her life. Why, if he loved Brenda? Why did her momma always have to be the "other woman" instead of ever finding the guy who loved her?

"People do stupid things," Aaron said.

Like ignore their dreams and work hard to make up for a parent's mistake. The thought didn't revive her anger. Instead a heaviness filled her chest and questions she'd never asked before swirled in her head. Along with thoughts of Dewayne, Harold, Julio, and Aaron. Why were she, her momma, and sisters always the women for fun, never the women for keeps? Why did her momma, sister, and yes, even she go for those fruitless relationships?

Kacey pushed the bike and walked faster. "Yes, people do."

CHAPTER 15

On Monday morning at six thirty, Aaron picked up his cell phone and called his best friend/brother-in-law, Fredrick Jenkins. Fred owned his own accounting firm and usually got up early in order to be the first one in the office. Aaron often called Fred early in the mornings or late in the afternoons when he knew his friend wasn't in the midst of a busy workday.

Fred answered on the fourth ring, right before Aaron was about to hang up. What sounded like a blender and loud talking came through the phone before his friend's voice.

"Hello?" Fred answered sounding exasperated.

Aaron frowned. "Is everything okay?"

Aaron went into the kitchen and checked the fridge. Not surprising, there was nothing of interest in there. The bare shelves were reminiscent of the shelves of the fridge in his apartment back home. That was where the similarities ended, though. Everything about this apartment was clean and comfortable. From the matching green living room furniture and sturdy oak tables, the queen-size bed with a mattress that had to have been constructed in heaven, and the simple kitchen with cushioned white chairs around a white dinette table. Not lavish by any means and all purely functional, but compared to the sparse furniture he rarely used in his own apartment, the place was five star. Made him consider actually taking the time to properly furnish his own place back home.

"Oh, Aaron, hey, I didn't look to see who was calling." The whirling sound increased in the background.

"What's that noise?"

"Janiyah is making breakfast smoothies. Apparently we're getting healthy before the baby arrives." The sound of his sister's voice rose over the noise of the blender in the background. "I'm not complaining about getting healthy, baby." Fred sounded like he'd pulled the phone away from his face. "I'm just saying nine months is a long time to only drink smoothies for breakfast."

"Is this a bad time?" Aaron asked.

"Nah, I'm good. I just have to choke down some strawberry kale concoction your sister is making. And don't you try to sneak in any bananas."

Aaron guessed that last part was for Janiyah. He could picture his friend, standing in his regular button-up shirt and tie, rubbing his nose beneath his glasses while Janiyah exasperated him yet again. It was one of the things Aaron was sure Fred loved about her. No one ruffled Fred's feathers better than Janiyah.

"She's lost her mind, hasn't she?" Aaron asked.

"Let's just go with overly concerned. About everything."

Aaron chuckled and shook his head. "I can't believe she's going to be a mother. That you're having a baby."

"Neither can I, man." Fred's voice filled with awe. "We waited twelve weeks before saying anything, but it still hasn't quite sunk in. Janiyah is driving David crazy. She's over there asking Sandra tons of questions and watching everything they do with Davina," he said, referring to David's daughter, the newest member of the Henderson family.

"Ha, I bet she is driving him crazy. What about you? Is she making you go crazy?"

"Not all day every day," Fred said with a laugh. "Your sister is already full of energy; so now imagine her pumped up on pregnancy hormones."

Aaron cringed. "Better you than me."

"Good thing I love the woman, or else I'd throw her out for making me drink kale every morning." Fred raised his voice, again probably for Janiyah's benefit.

"Shut up, Freddy!" Janiyah's words were clear, and the sound of the blender had ended. "Here's your breakfast. Hey, Aaron!" She yelled the last part.

"Tell her I said hey."

"I will," Fred said. "So what's up with you? How are things going with your college buddy?"

"Not too bad, actually. He's got a good setup, and combining our fleets will be profitable for both of us."

"That's great, Aaron. Glad to see things are still going well."

"They are. But that's not why I'm calling." Aaron went into the living room and sat on the cushy green sofa.

"What's up?"

Aaron thought about his last conversation with Kacey and the biggest thing that had bugged him since they'd parted. "Do you think I'm afraid of responsibility?"

"Say what?" came Fred's confused reply.

"You heard me. Am I afraid of responsibility?" Kacey's accusation had stuck to Aaron like hot asphalt. She had to be wrong. He wasn't afraid of responsibility. He ran his own company. That meant something.

"Well, in a way, yeah."

"Damn, you just gonna say it like that?"

"If you call me with a question, I'll give you a straight answer."

Exactly why he'd called Fred.

"I don't think you avoid responsibility because you can't handle it or anything," Fred said. "You and Janiyah are a lot alike. You don't want the typical ordinary life. For some reason you both like to do things your way and on your own terms, which means if there is a hint of traditional in something, you want no part. You're looking for the next new, shiny, non-traditional thing."

"You got Janiyah to be happy with the house in the suburbs, job, and kid thing. That's pretty traditional."

"That's because I'm not changing who she is. Believe me, she still lives and works on her own terms."

"I can't see myself doing that. Settling into the routine. Hell, it annoys me now that I can't go on the road as much because I have to handle the office stuff."

"Aaron, you're not looking at your success the right way. You've got staff to do the work, now you can really just travel for fun. No deadlines, no deliveries, no pressure. You can handle the office stuff, go on vacations, and still have a successful business. It's evolution. The only thing that remains the same is that change is constant."

"Where in the world did you hear that?"

"I don't know, somewhere." There was a pause. "Ugh, this smoothie is as bad as it looks."

"Toss it out."

"Nah, she made it, I'll drink it. Then I'll stop and grab something on the way in to the office. Just don't let her know," Fred said with a laugh. "Hey, are you really okay? What made you ask that question?"

"Nothing really, just a conversation I had with this woman."

"She shot you down?" Fred asked, surprise in his voice.

"Not really. We'd already hooked up, but we can't anymore."

"Damn, Aaron, please don't let Janiyah know you hooked up with someone else. She thinks you and Liz are really hitting it off."

Aaron rolled his eyes heavenward. Again with this Liz thing. "Liz and I slept together a few times then agreed to see other people. Now we're just friends. She's seeing that architect."

"Janiyah says he's just a rebound thing and that you two will be back together again."

Aaron groaned and realized this thing with Liz was going to be a bigger headache than he'd expected. Exactly why he never should have slept with his sister's best friend. Janiyah had seen happily-ever-after in every relationship since she and Fred got married.

"Look, I'll handle the situation with Liz and make it very clear to Janiyah that I'm not getting serious with her best friend. I'm not trying to get serious with anyone."

"Hmm, it sounds like that fear of responsibility is rising up again," Fred said with mock surprise.

Aaron wished his friend were there so he could punch him in the shoulder. "You know what, I'm gonna let you go. Thanks, Fred."

"Hey, anytime. I'm always happy to rain the truth on you."

• • •

Reggie stomped back into his office and slammed his cell phone on the desk. "That woman drives me crazy sometimes."

Aaron slowly sat back in his chair, where he'd been reviewing the latest profit-and-loss statements for their businesses, and eyed Reggie. His friend paced back and forth, his mammoth muscles bunching with frustration beneath his blue uniform shirt as he ran a hand over his face.

"There are a lot of women in your life," Aaron said slowly. "Which one is driving you crazy?"

Reggie took a deep breath and dropped his hands. "Camila. I love her, I swear, but...damn."

"What happened?"

"She wants to go to a party."

Aaron raised his brows and waited for more. Reggie stared at Aaron, then held out his hands as if waiting for Aaron to get upset.

"Is the party at the gates of hell? Because I don't see a problem."

"She's pregnant," Reggie said, again with an expectant expression.

Aaron frowned and tried to understand his friend's frustration. "Okay, so she can't drink. Which means you can't. Is that why you're upset?"

"Our days of partying are over. She's pregnant. We're about to become parents. We shouldn't be hanging out, acting foolish with a bunch of people with no kids."

"Reggie, what's the big deal? You're having a kid, but that doesn't mean you suddenly lose your ability to have fun."

Reggie shook his head. "You don't understand. We have to set the example now. Start living the lives we want our kids to emulate. But the closer we get to her due date, the more she wants to go out, party, travel. Why can't she just be happy?" The confusion in Reggie's voice went way beyond the simple question of why Camila wanted to go to a party.

Back in college, Reggie had partied with Aaron, but he'd also always been the more responsible of the two. His friend's transition from wild playboy to role model of the year didn't surprise Aaron. Yet Aaron didn't see the link between going to a party and setting a bad example for his kid. Unborn or not. Another reason why he wasn't ready for marriage. What if Kacey felt the same as Reggie?

Aaron shook his head and almost slapped his face. *No thoughts of Kacey and marriage.*

He jumped up from the chair and clapped his hands. "What do you want for lunch?" He didn't want to get into Reggie's issues with Camila and he damn sure needed another topic to discuss.

Reggie stopped staring in the distance and turned to Aaron. "What?"

Aaron rubbed the back of his neck, which was as stiff as his truck bed after spending the entire morning going over spreadsheets. "I'm starving and will eat pretty much anything." He thought about the leftover pizza sitting in his fridge. "Except pizza from Luigi's."

Reggie smirked. "Yeah, I heard about your date there with my sister."

Aaron froze in the middle of stretching his arms above his head. He'd been sure the kids had reported he'd left the park with Kacey, but when Reggie hadn't brought it up this morning, he'd hoped maybe they hadn't. Reggie seemed way too chill about Aaron and Kacey's "date." Surprising. Aaron had expected his friend to come out with more brotherly indignation.

Aaron lowered his arms. "It wasn't a date. We ran into each other and both wanted something to eat."

Reggie crossed his thick arms. "Honestly, Aaron, if I thought you could be serious about her, I'd say okay. I want her to get married, be happy, all of that."

Aaron stood and held up his hands. "Hold up, I'm not dating your sister. I like her. She's cool and easy to talk to, but you and I both know I'm not ready to settle down the way you have. I like partying too much."

"I don't know, the other night you said you'd treasure her. Got me thinking you're ready to give up the single life."

Though Reggie teased, Aaron was eager to get off this topic of conversation as well. "I was tired. It was late. Now, can we figure out lunch?"

"Are you sure? Because with us going into business, if you two were serious I'd deal. Keep things in the family, so to speak." The smirk left Reggie's face and he got the serious expression Aaron knew all too well.

"Where is this coming from, Reggie?" Aaron asked. He couldn't mask his surprise at Reggie's one-eighty.

Reggie shrugged. "The 'treasure her' comment, I guess. You seemed sincere. And again, I like things staying in the family. Figured you two together wouldn't be so bad if you meant what you'd said. So tell me, *is* there anything going on?"

Aaron's shoulders tensed. Now was the time to come clean. He didn't. Couldn't. His outburst and the trip to Luigi's were giving Reggie dangerous ideas. He already had Janiyah practically planning his wedding. He didn't need Reggie doing the same.

Aaron waved his arms back and forth in front of him and shook his head. "There's nothing going on. Seriously."

Reggie studied him, then finally exhaled heavily. "All right. I'll take your word and won't bring it up again." Reggie snapped his finger and pointed at Aaron. "Oh, by the way, I heard you agreed to coach Marcus Kestner's team. You sticking around for a while?"

"Hold up, I didn't agree to coach them. I just offered to help out while I'm in town."

Reggie chuckled. "Kids hear what they want to hear. He's already bragging to half the town that he's got a former professional baseball player coaching their team."

"What? I'm not professional. I turned down the contract."

Reggie gave Aaron a *what can I say?* look. "Again, kids tend to only hear parts of the story. His grandmother is happy someone stepped in to help. Marcus's mother passed away a few years ago, and with his dad in the military now, she's the one who's raising the kid. Baseball is his life, and his dad supports him. But with his constant tours overseas there's only so much he can do, ya know?"

"I get it, but I'm not here permanently. I'm happy to help the kids, but coaching them..."

"Don't look so panicked." Reggie's smile returned. "The kids like you and they're proud of your help. Don't worry, they won't get too attached." Reggie glanced at his watch. "Let's go to Momma's Kitchen for lunch."

Aaron perked up at the thought of going there. Not just because he'd see Kacey, the food was good too. "You don't get tired of eating there?"

"Nah, I don't mind during the lunch hour. It's the dinner crowd that annoys me. The girls aren't singing during lunch, so there are less guys hanging around trying to hit on every female relative I have."

Aaron hadn't heard Kacey sing since that night, and he wondered if she missed being onstage. He'd figured out that she didn't work nights when school was in session. Maybe he'd ask her, if she was still speaking to him after the other day. "Let's go."

CHAPTER 16

Kacey wiped down the bar, then asked the two guys in business suits sitting on the end if they needed anything else. After refilling their drinks, she went back to rolling butter knives and forks in napkins for the evening shift. Her fingers flew in a quick, efficient rhythm, and she tossed the tightly rolled utensils into the basket next to her.

She glanced around the place, at her momma making her rounds in the seating area, greeting diners at the tables, making sure to smile and rub the backs of the men. Flirting never hurt your tips—a favorite phrase of Sabrina's. Kacey's gaze went back to the vacant stage. There was no music during lunch, only dinner, when she didn't work. Singing onstage was part of her outlet when she was stressed about the long hours working at the restaurant. Even that was unavailable to her because she didn't work nights while in school. She worked hard all of the time and barely had time to enjoy herself.

Kacey threw another rolled set of silverware toward the basket. It missed and landed on the floor. Mumbling a curse, she bent and snatched up the fork and knife, now unwrapped and dirty after sliding across the floor. She'd never been this irritated at work before. She always looked around and found comfort, pride, a sense that this was where she belonged even though she gave up so much of her free time to make the place grow.

There was only one place to land her irritation: squarely at Aaron Henderson's doorstep. She loved her job here. Loved the fact that she'd be able to confidently handle opening a second restaurant and maybe even one day a third. She was not here out of some crazy need to pay for her momma's mistakes. And who was he to say they were mistakes anyway? Neither she nor her siblings would be around if her momma had been some old-school virgin. Working here was a way to thank her momma for all of her hard work and her sacrifice. For doing whatever was necessary to make this place successful.

But is it your dream?

Kacey gripped the utensils in her hand, wishing she could sink the fork directly into Aaron's wonderfully muscled thigh. Forget Aaron Henderson and his insistence on putting his nose where it didn't belong. She didn't want to be rich or famous. Didn't want to go to Hollywood and become a singing star. So what if the only dream she had was to help at the family restaurant? Was it wrong to have stayed in Resilient instead of moving somewhere else? Wrong to dedicate her life to her momma's business? Wrong to be committed to her family?

Hands slapped the bar. "Hey, can I get some service?"

Kacey rolled her eyes and sighed. "No, Reggie, you can't." She turned to grin at her brother, but her gaze glued to Aaron beside him and her smile withered away.

He looked good. Relaxed and happy with that sexy *I don't have a care in the world* smile that seemed to always stick to his perfect lips. He leaned on the bar, his light blue T-shirt draping his slim form perfectly. Dark eyes sparked with enough mischief to make her want to ditch work and run off into whatever adventure he'd cooked up for the day.

Her eyes narrowed. The man shouldn't look so sexy when she was still pissed at him.

"What brings you two in here?"

Aaron grinned. "I would say the stellar service, but I'm thinking you're not feeling the customer service today."

"Just depends on the customer." She looked at Reggie and gave him a smile. "What can I do for you, Reggie?"

Reggie glanced from her to Aaron. "What did I miss? Are you mad at Aaron?"

"Why in the world would I be mad at Aaron?" Kacey asked, eyes wide and a hand to her chest. "It's not as if he's swept into town, knew me for one day, and then decided to make broad assumptions about my life."

The smirk on Aaron's face diminished. "I made no assumptions. I just pointed out how hard you work."

Kacey stalked over to the bar and gripped the edge. "I work hard because I want to work hard. Maybe you should try it sometime."

Reggie shook his head. "Hold up, Kacey. Aaron does work hard. I can vouch for that."

Her customers at the end of the bar waved a hand for the check. "I've got to get back to work. Reggie, just tell the guys in back what you want." She went to check on the two customers.

She didn't look at Aaron or Reggie as she closed out their tab. Reggie got up and walked into the kitchen. She knew Aaron was watching her, and pretending as if his intense stare wasn't making her want to squirm took everything she had. Lashing out at him in front of Reggie had given her only a second of satisfaction.

Spinning away before she felt the least bit guilty for taking out her own frustration on him, Kacey took the dirty dishes into the back. Reggie came over to her immediately.

"What was that about?" He pointed to the door in the direction of the bar.

"What was what?"

He crossed his huge arms and drew his brows together. "Don't play dumb with me, Kacey. You're mad at Aaron and I want to know why."

She carefully placed the dishes in the pile near the dishwasher and smiled at the guy working the machine. "He's just annoying sometimes," she said, turning back to Reggie.

"I know you—when someone is annoying, you usually find a way to avoid them. You don't lash out at people unless..." Reggie's arms fell to his side and his frown became murderous. "Did you two hook up? He said there was nothing going on—"

Kacey held up her hands and shook her head. "Whoa, wait a second. No, we didn't hook up. And don't you think I'd be happy if I'd had sex with him?"

Reggie scowled and stepped back. "Dang, Kacey, really. You'd be happy if Aaron was serious about a relationship, but you'd be angry if he acted like Dewayne and just got his kicks with you and then tossed you aside."

Not flinching was a monumental task. They'd be a hundred years old and Reggie would still think Kacey was the same foolish girl who'd fallen for the okey-doke from some player. Seeing the pulse in his temple explode by telling him things were the other way around, that she'd used Aaron for her own pleasure then tried to walk away without a second glance, would almost be worth him getting the poor stupid "Peanut" image of her out of his head.

"It's nothing like that," she said. "He just said something that struck a nerve. He wasn't even trying to be mean, not really."

"You're just taking out your bruised feelings on him."

She shrugged. "Something like that."

Reggie sighed and crossed his arms again. "And it has nothing to do with him hitting on you or stepping over the line."

"No. He's really a decent guy...when he's not making commentary on how hard I work."

"You do work hard. Honestly, I think a guy like Aaron would be good for you." When Kacey raised a brow, Reggie chuckled. "Okay, not *exactly* like him. But you do need someone who'll help you relax and enjoy yourself every once in a while."

"Really, you want me to relax and have fun. Is that before or after you rip the arms off of any guy who looks my way?"

"That's because most guys who look the way of this family expect every woman in it to be loose. You know, for a second I thought Aaron was really feeling you. If I knew he would stick around and do right by you, I'd be okay with you two together."

She shouldn't ask, shouldn't want to know. "What made you think that?"

"The last time I warned him off, he said if he had you he'd treasure you. Silly me, I thought it meant he could get serious, but he's still talking about leaving. And when I'm not around, he does his own thing, so I'm thinking he's hooking up with that woman he first met when he came into town."

Her mind spun. First with the "treasure" comment, then with Reggie's thought that Aaron was hooking up with someone. "He's sleeping with someone?"

"I don't know for sure, but knowing Aaron, he's got some woman he's interested in."

The cook called over to tell Reggie his food was ready. Reggie nodded. "Just be nice to Aaron for a few more days. He's not that bad."

Kacey grunted a kind of agreement. Aaron wasn't bad; she just wasn't in the mood to be friendly to him. Her momma came into the kitchen.

"Hey, Momma, can you watch the bar for a few minutes?"

Sabrina shrugged. "Sure. Is everything okay?"

"Yeah, I'm just going to take a quick break."

Kacey slipped off her apron and then went out the back door. A pile of crates was stacked against the building, and she sat on one of those. She pulled a handful of Laffy Taffy out of her pocket. After opening one and shoving the sour apple–flavored candy into her mouth, she flipped over the wrapper to read the joke.

"What did one casket say to the other?" she read aloud. "Is that you coffin?" Kacey chuckled and shook her head.

The back door opened, and Aaron came out. He glanced to the right then to the left, where she sat. When he saw her, his eyes lit up. He grinned and Kacey's heart flipped.

"What's got you smiling?" He strolled over and stood next to her.

Kacey stopped smiling and shifted anxiously on the crate. "Why are you back here?"

"Reggie said I needed to apologize for upsetting you, so I came to do that."

"Is that the only reason you'll apologize, if my brother demands it?"

He ran his hands over the thick curls on his head. "Actually, I figured I'd come and demand an apology from you."

"Excuse me? Why would I owe you an apology?"

"Because you've put me in an awkward situation. Normally, if I state my opinion and someone doesn't like it, I move on. People not liking what I have to say isn't that big of a deal. But see, you're different. I didn't say what I said to hurt your feelings. But apparently I did, and because of that I kind of care."

Kacey smirked, but only to keep from grinning at his declaration. "Kind of care?"

"Yeah, can you believe it?" He shook his head, but humor filled his eyes. "Which means, since I *kind of* care, I should do something to make up for upsetting you."

Kacey leaned her elbow on her knee then rested her chin in her hand. "I'm still not getting why I owe you an apology?"

"How can you not get it? You've caused me emotional strife. People get sued for much less than this."

Kacey sat up. "Are you planning on suing me?"

"That depends."

He leaned his arms on either side of her on the crate. The breeze brought over the scent of the Dove soap she'd put in his apartment and his underlying scent. Spicy, enticing, masculine. His chocolate brown eyes, dancing with his constant sense of humor, stared into hers. Kacey wanted nothing more than to kiss him.

"On what?" she whispered.

"On you allowing me to throw a party in your honor."

Kacey raised a brow. "A party?"

"Well, more like a cookout. I know you really don't want to go to your dad's birthday party on Saturday even though you promised. I'm not saying you should ditch, but maybe if your brother is hosting a cookout on the same day, you'll have a reason to skip out early."

"Reggie isn't having a cookout."

"Reggie isn't having one yet. I'll put the idea into his head, he'll fire up the grill, and you'll have a reason to leave your dad's place early. But I'll leave out the part about it being for you."

She leaned back, needing space, distance, between her and his warm body. "Why is that?"

"Because I don't want to give him any ideas about us." Aaron leaned in closer. "He thinks there's something going on. He even gave me the okay to date you."

Kacey drew in a shaky breath. "No, he didn't."

"He did." Time froze as his dark gaze glided over her face, pausing at her lips. She didn't lick them, but man, if she didn't want to kiss him. Aaron suddenly straightened. "Until he realized that I'm not looking to settle down anytime soon. We both know that you're the kind of woman a guy settles down with."

She hid her disappointment with a blasé look. She hoped that was how she looked, anyway. "Too much of a commitment for you?"

"It is," he said with no preamble. "As you pointed out, responsibility isn't my strongest trait."

"I shouldn't have said that. Your business proves you're responsible."

"And I shouldn't have questioned your hard work for your momma's business."

"No. You shouldn't have." He flinched and she lifted a shoulder. "But I can see how it might look like I've forsaken my own dreams for my mother's. Maybe I did let her dream become my own, but I don't regret that. I want nothing more than to open a second restaurant, start a franchise. And, yeah, maybe a tiny bit is to prove that what my momma started turned out better than expected."

"There's nothing wrong with wanting to prove the people who doubted you wrong. That need to do better drives all competition. Recognize that, embrace it, and before you know it you'll have four restaurants open. I think you can do it, Kacey."

His words of praise filled her with warmth. She knew she could, but sometimes when she was in the middle of a semester and had to stay up all night on a paper after working all day in the restaurant, she wasn't sure. More so this semester with the rocky start with her professor. Those times made her wonder if she really wanted to keep at it. He'd seen the inner struggle she tried to hide and called her on it. That was what had really pissed her off before.

"You think so?"

"I know so. You're kind of a hard-ass."

Kacey chuckled and shook her head. "And I guess you can be responsible enough to give good advice every once in a while."

"Responsible in business, but very irresponsible when it comes to relationships."

"I'm too busy to get involved in a long-term relationship. I can appreciate it when a man is honest about what he wants."

Aaron's eyes narrowed. He backed up and waved a finger. "I'm not falling for that."

"Falling for what?"

He shook his head. "Never mind. I'm being crazy." He slapped his hands together. "So, are we cool with the cookout idea?"

"Yeah, I guess so."

"Great. I'll get on Reggie." He picked up her Laffy Taffy wrapper. "I love the jokes on these."

She grinned. "Me too."

He read the joke silently and chuckled. "That's pretty funny."

"I thought so."

He met her eyes, and his good-natured smile heated her from the inside out. She could fall for a guy like Aaron, if she was ready to fall. He'd make it easy with his smile, personality, and optimism. But she didn't need to fall in love. Not with a guy in town for a few weeks who even admitted he was irresponsible when it came to relationships.

"I'd better get inside."

She wanted just a few more minutes. "You didn't apologize."

His brows drew together as if he were in deep thought. "I did, remember? I'm throwing you a party."

Kacey chuckled and rolled her eyes. "There is something seriously wrong with you."

"Yeah and you like it." He winked and her insides trembled.

She laughed to herself as she watched him go. A woman could definitely fall in love with a guy like that.

CHAPTER 17

Aaron accepted a beer from Tara, one of several attractive, single women Reggie and Camila had invited to the cookout. Aaron knew Reggie had invited them to try to find out whom Aaron had sex with his first night in town. Aaron didn't mind the obvious attempts at hooking him up because he was determined to get Kacey out of his mind. Hopefully before she left her dad's party and showed up here to distract him further.

"Thank you," he said to Tara and slid over on the cushioned bench set off from the patio in Reggie's well-landscaped yard.

Tara sat next to him. She flashed a smile that invited him to move closer. Her dimpled cheeks, dark skin, and a bright yellow sundress that perfectly clung to her curvy figure were exactly what he'd normally go for. His lukewarm reaction, on the other hand, was proof his growing interest in Kacey was getting way out of hand.

"You're very welcome," Tara said. "So, tell me, how long are you in town?"

Aaron shrugged and sipped the beer. "For at least another week, maybe two."

"Not enough time to have any fun." Tara licked her full lips and cocked her head to the side.

His lukewarm interest remained the same; still, he had to try. *Why did trying have to feel so hard?* Flirting was never hard for him.

"I can squeeze in a little fun."

"Hmm, I bet you can. Tell me, Aaron, what do you like to do for fun?"

She took a slow sip from her beer bottle, letting her tongue linger on the rim before pulling it away.

"Baseball, gaming, meeting new people, and seeing new things."

"Has anyone shown you around town?" Tara leaned her head to the side and played with the end of her long ponytail, which dangled over her shoulder right above her breasts. The motion drew his eye to that location, but didn't stoke his fire.

"No."

Her dark eyes brightened. "Then I can show you around. What are you doing tomorrow evening?"

Aaron thought about the wrestling pay-per-view event coming on the following night. He'd considered asking Kacey if she wanted to watch it with him, but spending more time with Kacey would only have him falling further into her trap. Not one she'd purposely set. She didn't have to, because women like Kacey *were* the traps. Good-looking, easy to talk to, fun to hang around. He could get comfortable with a woman like her, and if he got comfortable he'd think he was falling in love. Which was no good because he knew what a mess he'd made the last time he'd thought he was in love.

Aaron shook his head. "I'm not doing anything tomorrow night."

Tara's grin widened. "Great. Take my number and give me a call. I'll show you a good time."

He shook the discomfort that tried to settle in as he put Tara's number into his cell phone. He and Kacey weren't together. They wouldn't be together. They'd shared one night and agreed to move on. Plus, she came with more drama than he needed in a relationship. Being with her meant staying in

Resilient. Watching her drive herself into the ground from the responsibility of running the restaurant. Days working with Reggie in an office and nights sitting on the couch with Kacey, watching wrestling before going to bed and making love.

Which on the surface seemed cool. Except one day he'd realize he was just like his dad. Stagnant, boring, and stuck.

Marcus ran over to Aaron and Tara. "Hey, Aaron, will you throw some balls for me?" The kid bounced on his feet.

Aaron chuckled. "Sure, kid." He looked to Tara. "Excuse me."

"I'll watch," Tara said.

They stood and Tara slipped her arm through his. Aaron led her over to where Marcus and a few other kids were tossing a baseball back and forth. He threw a few balls and gave the kids a few pointers before agreeing to join Reggie in a game of corn hole. Marcus flanked his left and Tara glued herself to his right. Tara asked to be his partner and turned out to be pretty good at aiming the beanbags toward the hole.

Monique kept score, and even though she clearly cheered for her brother and his partner, Julio, she had to concede when Aaron scored the winning shot. Tara jumped up and pumped her fist. "Yes!" Aaron chuckled at her competitive streak. "We did it, Aaron." She raised her hands for a double high five.

Aaron slapped her palms, then automatically pulled her in for a hug. She pressed her soft curves hard against his body. She slipped her arm around his waist, and they turned to face Reggie. Aaron didn't pull away.

Aaron lifted a shoulder. "How about a rematch?"

Reggie shook his head. "You're feeling cocky, I see."

Tara's arm around his waist tightened. "Of course we are."

Kacey walked over and Aaron's laughter died away. He forgot all about Tara's soft body the second his gaze landed on Kacey. The light blue dress she wore had a halter top and fell in loose folds to her feet. The thin material clung just enough to her shapely legs to make him imagine them without the material covering them. Her long hair was twisted at the back of her head, accenting the graceful lines of her high cheekbones, her slim chin, her plump lips. He smiled at her, until he met her eyes, which narrowed in on him and Tara. His smile drooped.

Aaron took his arm from around Tara's shoulders and stepped to the side. Tara gave him a confused look, then glanced at Kacey.

Kacey turned away from Aaron and smiled at her brother. "Sorry I'm late. Things took a little longer than I expected at Cliff's."

Reggie shrugged. "No big deal. How was the party?"

Kacey lifted a shoulder. "It was all right." Her lips tightened and Aaron frowned. She didn't sound like things had gone *all right*. "How did the game go?" Kacey pointed to the corn hole sets decorated with University of Tennessee orange and white.

"We lost," Reggie said. "Those two beat the crap out of us."

Kacey's cool stare returned to Aaron and Tara. "Really."

Tara leaned into Aaron's side. "Yep. We make a pretty good team."

"Looks that way. Sounds like you need a rematch."

Tara nodded. "That's what I said."

Reggie picked up the beanbags and separated the orange from the white. "Then let's do this."

Aaron wasn't in the mood for a rematch. He wanted to talk to Kacey and find out what had happened at the party to cause the tightness around her eyes.

"You guys have fun," Kacey said and turned to leave.

"Hey," Aaron called. She glanced at him. "You okay?"

Her lips spread in an overly bright smile. "I'm perfect." She turned and walked away.

Perfect, hell. Something had happened. He had an urge to follow her, but he let Tara turn his attention back to the game. Following Kacey would pull him further into her trap. He needed to avoid the trap. But his eyes and brain didn't want to cooperate, and both strayed to her too much during the course of the next game.

He didn't even care when Reggie and Julio won. He tried to pretend as if he wasn't watching Kacey as she sat with her mom and sister Ashlei on the deck. Or when she went to the grill and only ate half of the hamburger on her plate. Or when she sat with one of Reggie's friends and spent twenty minutes talking and laughing with him. Aaron ignored the need to interrupt, pull her to the side, and get her attention on him.

Kacey meant long term. Kacey meant a relationship. He wasn't good with relationships, but he damn sure didn't like the way that guy put his hand on Kacey's knee.

"You know, we can get out of here," Tara said from where she sat next to him on the bench.

He looked into Tara's big, hopeful eyes. "You know I'm only in town for a short time," he said.

She smirked. "I know, and all I'm interested in is a good time while you're here."

All the invitation he needed. The perfect way to ensure Kacey never looked his way again. "That's good to know."

Tara cocked her head to the side and toyed with the end of her ponytail again. This time his gaze didn't follow the movement. Aaron glanced to where Kacey stood getting a canned drink from one of the coolers on the deck. She looked up and their eyes met. For the briefest second, he swore he saw hurt in her expression before she quickly looked away. She slammed the top of the cooler down and rushed into the house.

"So, what do you say? Want to get out of here?" Tara asked.

Aaron frowned and turned back to the woman who could rescue him from the trap. Suddenly leaving with her didn't feel like a rescue. *I'm not ready to settle down. I'm not the guy Kacey needs.* But he couldn't walk away without knowing what had her so upset.

"Give me a second, okay?"

"Sure."

Aaron stood and followed Kacey into the house. The music and conversation from outdoors became a hum in the background of the cool, quiet interior. Camila and some other ladies sat around the kitchen table, and another group of ladies and kids sat in the attached living area. For a moment Aaron second-guessed following Kacey inside. He had no idea what he wanted to say to her, and he definitely couldn't say much in front of everyone in here.

Camila glanced at him. "You need anything, Aaron?"

Aaron glanced at the gathered people. Kacey wasn't with any of them. "Yeah, the bathroom."

Camila pointed toward the hall. "It's right down the hall."

He nodded. "Thanks."

One of the ladies stopped him. "I think someone is in that one. Try the one upstairs."

Aaron glanced at the closed bathroom door in the hall. Kacey could be there, but asking for her specifically would only have them wondering why he was so interested in Reggie's sister.

"I will, thanks," he said. The ladies went back to talking and Aaron went down the hall, hesitating before the bathroom door, but then he kept going. He'd go upstairs for a second then come back down. Take off with Tara and forget about getting further involved with Kacey.

Upstairs he easily found the other bathroom, but since he didn't have to use it, he decided to check out the upstairs. Not because he wondered if she was up there, but because he hadn't seen that part of the house yet.

Yeah, tell yourself that.

He peeked into the master bedroom, and the two other bedrooms upstairs, one of which was being converted into a nursery. Aaron grinned at the light blue walls and the crib in the corner. Reggie, married with kids. He still couldn't believe it. Seemed like all the guys he knew were settling down, leaving him as the only bachelor left. He wished them all well, and he knew that one day, way in the future, he wouldn't rule out the same. Just not right now. He was too restless right now to settle down with one woman. Which was why he should just go down and leave with Tara, no matter how much a relationship with Kacey intrigued him.

Aaron grunted and quickly backed out of the nursery. He ran a hand across his face. "Don't even go there," he said softly. They lived in two different states. He still had to straighten out the confusion over Liz. Hell, he still talked to half of his off-again, on-again hookups frequently. Not the behavior of a guy ready for a relationship. He would be crazy to give up a single man's dream. Not to mention it had the potential to ruin this merger if things went bad.

Yet he still checked the last closed door on the second floor. He opened the door to find a washer and dryer and Kacey, sitting on the dryer, sipping from a canned strawberry margarita.

Aaron froze, forgetting all about his off-again, on-again relationships as memories of his night with Kacey heated his blood.

She glared at him. "What are you doing in here?"

She was angry. It couldn't be because of Tara. She'd spent more time talking to that dude downstairs than paying attention to him and Tara. He came into the laundry room and leaned against the inside of the door frame. "I'm snooping. What are you doing up here?"

"Getting away from the noise." Her plump lips twisted into a smirk. "Why are you wasting time snooping? I thought you and Tara would have taken off by now."

Aha...so she had paid attention. "I didn't want to leave with her just yet."

Kacey cocked a brow and harrumphed. "Why is that?" She lifted the can to her lips for a sip.

"I wanted to check on you."

The can jerked in her hands and drops of the red margarita spilled on the front of her dress. She swore and wiped them briskly. "You don't have to check on me."

"I know I don't have to, but that doesn't change that I want to. How did things go at your dad's party?"

Her hand gripped the small can, causing a slight bend in the aluminum. "The same as always. He was glad I was there. His family was cordial. Brenda's family wasn't."

Aaron's body tensed. "Were they rude to you?"

Kacey put the can down and tried to wave it off, but her lips were tight. "Not exactly. Just a little cool with their reception. It's normal. Not many of them are happy to have Cliff's bastard around."

Anger shot through his body. His hands balled into fists. "Did they call you that?"

"No. No one's called me that since I was four and the entire situation first came out."

Aaron cursed and ran a hand over his face. "How could someone say that to a child?"

"It wasn't exactly to me, just about me. In the middle of a grocery store as Cliff tried to keep my momma and Brenda from fighting."

Aaron frowned and his mouth dropped. "You're kidding."

She took a sip from the margarita. "I wish I were. The entire situation with them started out so volatile. Now they all act as if everything is cool and they didn't once fight over Cliff in the middle of the grocery store."

"Maybe they matured."

"Or maybe they're just crazy," she said with disgust. "I don't get it."

"There's nothing to get. Your mom and Cliff got together and you were born, which to me is a great thing no matter the circumstances. Things were bound to be bad when the situation got out, but then cooler heads prevailed and they all learned to deal with the situation because regardless of how the adults behaved, the sweet, beautiful girl who came from that had nothing to do with it."

Kacey's wide, dark eyes turned to him, and something tightened in Aaron's chest. "You don't have to feel bad for their mistakes. They found a way to make things work and you had the love of your mom and your dad. A lot of people don't get that."

"I know, but is it wrong that a small part of me wanted what you had? Two parents, married, in love."

"Boring," Aaron said, waving his hand. "When you look up 'perfectly boring married couple,' you see my parents. They worked, took care of me and my siblings, and worry about us in between family meetings and Sunday dinners. No excitement at all."

She rolled her eyes, but smiled. "If you had my family, you'd appreciate boring."

Maybe he would. He did appreciate his parents and the stability they provided. But even with all that, he didn't envy their life. The weight of responsibility that he and his siblings put on them.

"Always trying to one-up me," Aaron said. "It's why I like you."

Her dark eyes met his. Something sparked and her sad expression turned into a sweet smile.

"I like you too, Aaron," she said, her voice a low, melodic sound that sent another type of heat through his body. Kacey smirked. "Sometimes."

Aaron chuckled and her sexy laugh joined his. "Only sometimes, huh?"

He also liked her sense of humor, and her teasing jabs. They made him want to kiss her. Made him think about how much he'd liked kissing her and how great her slim legs felt when they were wrapped around his waist. How easily he'd lost himself when they'd slept together.

Kacey shifted on the top of the dryer. She picked up the can and ran a finger across the rim. "Well, you've checked on me. You can go back to Tara now."

To hell with Tara. "I don't want to."

She sipped from the can and licked those wonderful full lips of hers. "What do you want?"

No hesitation. "To kiss you."

CHAPTER 18

Kacey's already speeding heartbeat jumped another level. She should insist he go back to Tara, finish her drink, and go home. But the second she'd seen her family friend pressed up on Aaron, her brain screamed "mine" and she'd wanted to grab Tara by her long ponytail and jerk her away from Aaron's side. Especially since Aaron didn't appear to mind the attention. She was already emotional from Cliff's party, which she could blame for the extra shot of jealousy coursing through her. Besides, *she* had walked away, and he followed.

"Then kiss me," she said in a soft but confident voice. Though he could still walk away and go back to Tara.

Aaron closed the door and strolled across the small space to stand before her. A thrill of victory swelled within her. He'd made his choice, and she had no intention to squander her triumph.

Pulling on her skirt, she slowly lifted the material to gather around her thighs and spread her legs. She motioned with her head for him to come closer.

"If I kiss you I can promise you, I won't stop at that."

Kacey grabbed the waistband of his dark blue shorts and jerked him forward. "I'm familiar with your lack of self-control."

She licked her lips, thinking about how he'd lost the cool façade he carried around right before he climaxed.

"So you think I have little control?"

"I'm not complaining."

His large hand slid up her thighs and gripped the soft flesh. "Let's test your self-control."

"Mine isn't the one in question."

"Remind me of that when we leave this room."

Aaron cupped the back of her head with one hand and kissed her. Kacey clutched his red cotton T-shirt and pulled him in. She didn't care about anything thanks to the magic of his kiss. The sweet glide of his tongue against hers and the firm pressure of his body had her slanting her head to the side to get closer.

She breathed deep, and fast, getting drunk off the smell of soap, sweat, and the spicy masculine fragrance that heated her blood. She knew all the reasons why they shouldn't be here, how easily they could get caught, and she didn't care. All she wanted was Aaron, who'd called her beautiful and said the situation with her parents wasn't her fault. Something she knew, but she liked hearing from another person.

Now she needed him. Wanted him. And based on the urgent grip of the hands on her head and thigh, he felt the same. The kiss was full of the same thoroughness that he'd shown that first night, but edged with the pent-up desire they'd tried to ignore.

Aaron's hand on her thigh slid up to the throbbing pulse between her legs. Kacey spread farther, and pushed her hips forward. A deep moan rumbled through his chest, and his long fingers massaged her through the damp material of her panties. Pleasure pulsed through her body. She gasped, her head falling back, and she bit her lower lip to hold back her shout. Aaron pressed hot kisses along her neck, alternating between fast brushes of his lips and light nips with his teeth. His body was rigid, tight with desire that she wanted unleashed.

Had only two weeks passed since they'd had sex? She felt as if she hadn't been touched in over a year.

Pushing her panties aside, Aaron's fingers slowed their quick movements to gently knead her wet folds. Kacey's mouth fell open. Her nails dug into his shoulders.

"Oooh, yes." The words were a loud moan.

Aaron sucked the sensitive spot at the base of her neck. "Control, Kacey, you don't want anyone to hear you."

The hand on her head dropped to her breast. He squeezed before lifting the flesh and lowering his head to pull at the tip through her dress. She clamped her lower lip between her teeth and stifled a moan. Thoughts of control were irrelevant when he touched her like that. Kacey reached for his erection, but he pulled his hips back.

"Not yet," he said in a deep, rumbling voice.

Aaron straightened. His lids were low over his hypnotic, dark eyes and he stared into hers. He gathered the ends of her dress around her waist and pushed the material further up and around. Kacey's short, fast breaths sounded ten times louder in the small space. The sound was anxious and urgent, giving away how much she wanted this. He slipped his fingers into the waistband of her panties and pulled. Kacey lifted her hips, and he eased them down her legs. The slow scrape of the material against her legs made her breath come faster, harder.

He stuffed the wet material into the pocket of his shorts. Again she reached for his waistband, her fingers trembling with the need to get to the growing hard bulge clearly visible behind his zipper.

"Not yet." His teasing, sexy smile split his lips.

"I don't have all day," she said in a rush.

"This won't take all day." Sure hands gripped her hips and pulled her forward. Cool air and his scorching stare covered her exposed sex. "Control," he said before licking his lips and lowering his head. Then his tongue was there, slowing running from bottom to top in long, sure strokes.

Kacey cried out. Then bit her lip. How could she possibly keep up a façade of control when this man had a tongue that should be in the sexual hall of fame? His full lips covered her swollen nub followed by steady pulls. Make that *his entire mouth* needed hall of fame recognition. Aaron raised a hand to palm her breast, his fingers making delightful circles around her nipple while his mouth created magic between her legs.

Voices came from the other side of the laundry room door. Kacey stiffened; her eyes popped open. Oh, God, she couldn't be caught like this. She tried to push Aaron away, but damn the man and his hall of fame tongue because he made quick, lazy flicks across her clit. Blood rushed through her ears. Her lids fluttered closed, and the hand at his shoulder gripped and pulled forward instead of pushing away. His soft curls brushed her fingers and who was she to not succumb to the temptation and dig her fingers into the thick mass?

"The nursery is over here," Camila's voice came from the other side. Followed by another female's.

They needed to stop. He'd made his point, and she had definitely lost control. Aaron slid his finger into her, and she clenched around the thick digit.

"Mmm, damn, Kacey, I love it when you squeeze me," he said, his lips brushing against her.

Kacey bit her lips, but the movement barely stifled her moans. Aaron's lips covered her clit again. The voices continued. Kacey lost herself in the pleasure. One hand balled into a fist on the cold surface of the washing machine, the other held Aaron's head in place. Aaron started the quick flicks and her hand jerked, knocking over the can of strawberry margarita. The can tumbled between the washer and dryer. The sweet smell of the drink filled the room.

She was sure someone had to have heard and would burst through the door. Aaron added another finger and then slid his fingers in and out in long, deep strokes. The president could walk in right now, there was no way she'd be able to stop. Her teeth pressed into her lower lip, and the sound of Aaron's efforts combined with her muffled moans and heavy breaths echoed in the tiny area.

She gripped his hair and twisted her hips. "Oh God, oh God, oh God," she cried out. Control snapped. Her orgasm exploded through every cell within her. Strong spasms rocked and pulled at her midsection, and she slapped her hand against the washing machine then pulled her lips between her teeth to keep from yelling again.

Aaron's fingers slowed and he moaned against her still trembling flesh. After one final intimate kiss, he stood and stared at her in the eye. His lips lifted in a cocky grin. "Good job maintaining control."

Kacey's head fell back and she panted. A lazy grin spread across her face. She was too sated to care that he'd won this round.

"But I'm not done."

Kacey lifted her head. He was a blur as she looked at him through slitted lids. He reached into his back pocket and pulled something out. Kacey's eyes widened.

"You carry condoms in your pocket?"

He opened the small foil pack and slid the protection over his long, curved cock. "I'm always prepared."

He griped her hips, pulled her forward, and then slid, fast and hard, into her. Kacey's head fell back again. "Oh my God, yes!" she said in a long, slow moan.

He pulled her forward, one hand at the back of her head, the other clenched to her hip. He kissed her neck and pounded into her with sure, steady strokes.

The pleasure was intensified, her body still sensitive and on high alert from her orgasm. She lifted her legs to wrap them around his waist. Her hand gripped his butt and added her own push to his strokes.

"Squeeze me, Kacey." Aaron's low, desire-filled voice rumbled against her neck.

She did, feeling every thick ridge and the unique fit of him within her body. Her legs shook. She focused on the pleasure, lost everything, and opened herself up to accept the exquisite ecstasy created by their union. The trembles started low in her midsection, then steadily spread out until they burst into another orgasm. She clenched him; her shoulder muffled his cry as his own orgasm tore through his body.

Kacey didn't care who heard. Not at this moment. This moment was too perfect to care about anything else.

• • •

Kacey left the laundry room first, after cleaning up as much of the spilled strawberry margarita as she could with one of the towels in the laundry room. She went out the back door. Aaron was to come out a few minutes later and make his way to the backyard. To her surprise, when she walked through the kitchen no one stopped her or asked where she'd come from. Camila just smiled and kept on talking. Kacey's face flamed. She could only hope her sister-in-law and whomever she'd shown the nursery to hadn't overheard Kacey's lack of control in the laundry room.

The cookout was going on in the backyard as it had before she'd gone upstairs. People laughing, talking, the grill still smoking and covered with enough food to feed the entire neighborhood. Which, knowing Reggie and Camila, they'd invited.

She glanced at Tara, sitting on the bench near the house looking at her phone then looking at the house. Probably checking the time and wondering where Aaron had gone. Kacey grinned, thoroughly pleased that Aaron would not be going anywhere with Tara.

"Where have you been?" Monique's voice broke through the noise in the background.

Kacey turned to her sister, sitting in one of the patio chairs on the deck. Her younger sister, Ashlei, and her momma flanked her. Very rarely did a weekend come when at least one of them wasn't working the restaurant; a family function was usually the only excuse when this happened. The staff knew how to handle things and would call if something came up. Still, Kacey mentally reviewed the schedule to try and remember who was managing the place in the family's absence.

She was about to ask, when another tremble vibrated her midsection. She grinned and let thoughts of work drift away for once.

"Around," Kacey said. She slid over a chair and joined her family.

"You haven't been around. I would have seen you if you were around."

"Quit worrying about me and where I've been," Kacey said. She looked over at her momma. "Cliff said hi."

Sabrina waved her hand as if she didn't care. Her smile was a bit triumphant, though. "Cliff always says hi. They didn't give you any trouble?"

Kacey glanced away and shook her head. "No trouble. Just the same old, same old. Who's watching the restaurant today?" Work would at least get the subject changed.

Sabrina crossed her legs and leaned back in the chair. "I left Jamelah in charge. She can handle things for a few hours, and I'm going back to oversee the night crew."

Kacey nodded, but frowned. Jamelah was being groomed for manager, but she'd never worked a weekend shift alone. "Are you sure she can handle the place? Saturday afternoons can get busy."

Sabrina shrugged. "We're only ten minutes away. If anything drastic happens, she'll call. Besides, things get busy when the live singing starts later."

"You sure you don't want me to—"

"You get weekends off to study, Kacey. It's the last semester, so get over it," Sabrina said, shutting down the conversation.

"Fine," Kacey said, raising her hands in surrender. "So what are you all yakking about?"

Ashlei giggled behind a can of strawberry margarita. Kacey thought about the can she'd just knocked over and her own triumphant smile broke out.

"We're talking about men," Ashlei said.

Monique shifted in her chair. "Get it right, we're talking about one man." She glanced over at the back of the house. "One man in particular."

Kacey followed her sister's gaze to Aaron coming around the back of the house. He waved at the four of them, his easy grin brightening his handsome face. His glance stayed on her a second longer than the rest of the ladies, and he licked his lower lip before drawing it into his mouth and slipping his hand into the pocket that held her panties.

Tingling started between Kacey's thighs and heat flushed her face. She shifted in her chair and grinned. She checked out her momma and sisters to see if they'd noticed, but their eyes were still glued to Aaron.

"You're talking about Aaron?" Kacey asked.

Ashlei nodded. "Yeah, wondering who he's hooking up with. Reggie is determined to find out who he spent the night with when he first came to town."

"Why?" Kacey asked.

"To prove it isn't one of us," Monique said with a snort. "That's why he invited nearly all the single women he knew to this cookout."

Sabrina pointed to Tara, whom Aaron made his way to. "I think we know who the mystery woman is."

"Why would you think it's Tara?" Kacey asked with a laugh, enjoying their speculation and the fact that she herself might be the mystery woman no longer crossed their minds. She normally didn't like keeping secrets from her family, but she wasn't burdened by guilt for not spilling this one. She gave everything to her family, the business. Aaron was her fun fling, and she would enjoy what moments they could sneak in, without angry looks from Reggie or warnings to guard her heart that were sure to come from her sisters and momma. She could handle this; she wasn't seventeen and starry-eyed anymore.

"Figuring out who was easy," Monique said. "She quickly superglued herself to his side. She didn't waste any time putting her marks on Aaron."

"She wouldn't have a chance if we were in the running," Ashlei said with a groan. She glared at Kacey. "Why did you have to make us promise to stay away from him?"

Sabrina swatted at Ashlei. "It's for your brother, so get over it. You all know Reggie would go crazy if one of his sisters slept with his business partner. Let Tara have him and keep your brother from having an early heart attack. He's already having palpitations because his wife is showing signs of being stifled under his holier-than-thou attitude."

Ashlei huffed and Monique grunted. Kacey only slightly felt bad for going against her promise with her sister to stay away from Aaron.

Aaron sat down next to Tara. They talked for a few minutes, then got up and strolled to the front of the house.

Monique smirked. "Looks like Tara is ready for a private conversation with Aaron."

Kacey clenched her teeth, her triumph deflating. She reached into the cooler before her family noticed her annoyance, but they just switched the conversation to the other men at the cookout. Kacey sipped on another strawberry margarita. The taste and smell of the drink reminded her of a few minutes earlier. Aaron's soft lips against her most private parts, the slide of his fingers, and her body's explosion in passion.

"What's wrong with you?" Monique's voice broke through Kacey's memory.

Kacey stopped twisting in her seat. She sucked in a deep breath and tried to stop panting as if she'd just run a marathon.

"Nothing's wrong."

"You're squirming and you've got this weird look on your face."

Ashlei watched her with narrowed eyes. "Yeah, you do look kinda flushed."

Kacey checked her phone. Aaron and Tara had been gone for close to ten minutes. She hated to admit it, but jealousy and suspicion crept into her. Crazy, juvenile emotions. Aaron might be a playboy, but he didn't seem like the kind of guy who'd do that to her and go off on a date with another woman right after.

As if you really know him.

Kacey put down the drink. "I've gotta pee, that's all." She hurried into the house and rushed through the kitchen to the living area, where she slid back the blinds to look out of the front window.

Tara leaned against the side of her gray SUV parked on the side of the road, and Aaron stood in front of her. His arms were crossed and the easy smile he always wore lifted his lips. Kacey's lips pressed together, and pain twisted her chest. She watched as they talked and then Tara leaned in to give Aaron a hug. She got into her vehicle and drove off. Aaron stood watching.

Kacey left the window to hurry out the front door and march over to Aaron. Aaron slowly turned away from the road back toward the house. His easy smile was still on his face. Kacey waited for the guilty look to come; instead he continued to grin.

"What was that?" She pointed down the road.

"That was me telling Tara that we wouldn't be going out tomorrow night."

Kacey crossed her arms. "Oh, really?"

"Really. Unless I don't have a reason to cancel. I've got her number." He pulled his phone out of his back pocket. "I can give her a call and reschedule."

"Don't be a jerk."

His teasing grin never left. "Don't be jealous for no reason." He strolled over until he stood over her, then slid his arm around her waist and pulled her against his body. "I'm more interested in finishing what I started upstairs than going out with Tara again."

Kacey rubbed his hard chest, and heat swelled within her. "I'm not acting jealous."

"Yes, you are. Admit it, you like me." He leaned down and kissed the side of her mouth. A thrill went through Kacey's body.

"I like you, but I know this isn't turning into anything permanent."

That hall of fame mouth of his worked against her neck. "I'm glad we're on the same page with that."

She was about to lose control again. She pushed against his chest and met his eye. "And we still can't tell Reggie."

He stopped smiling and his brows drew together. "Are you sure? I think he'll understand."

She shook her head. "He wouldn't like it. Not after we both claimed nothing was going on. Besides, if we're only going to screw around for a few days while you're in town and then move on, there's no need to upset him."

He sighed and continued to frown. Kacey hoped he understood this was for the best. After a few seconds he nodded.

"Fine." He released her and stepped back. "Then I guess kissing you on his front lawn isn't a good way to keep this thing a secret."

"Probably not."

"We can go back to the laundry room."

She wanted to jump up and down and scream, "*Yes, please!*"
"No, but I am leaving in a few minutes to study. You can leave later and slip in around the back."

"I think I can do that."

Kacey bit her bottom lip to suppress her eager grin. "Cool."

"Cool." He winked, then leaned over and kissed her cheek. "I'll be leaving sooner rather than later."

She watched him walk away. Well, she watched his perfect behind as he walked away. Everyone told her to loosen up and have some fun. Fine, Aaron would be her fun. He was a fling, and she was older and much wiser and knew this was a friends-with-benefits type of relationship. Plus, he was only in town for another week, maybe two. No one fell in love over a few days anyway, so her heart was safe.

She made her way to the front door, determined to prevent any hint that she and Aaron had come from the same place. She reached for the knob and the door flew open. Monique came out and shut the door behind her, a smirk on her face.

"You want to tell me what that was about?"

Kacey glanced away, her heart hammering in her chest. "What are you talking about?"

"The little kissing thing between you and Aaron. I thought we were keeping away from him."

"We were, but this just kind of happened."

"Were you planning to tell any of us?" Monique raised a brow.

"There's no need to tell anyone. We're just having a little fun while he's in town."

"Your 'little fun' will make Reggie go ballistic if he finds out."

"Then he won't find out." She grabbed Monique's hands. "Don't tell him."

"Kacey, I don't like lying to Reggie."

"It's not a lie, and don't be so high and mighty with me. You didn't tell him about Julio before, and you're not saying a thing to me or him about your secret phone calls."

Monique jerked her hands away. "Fine, keep your secrets. But we both know you can't handle sneaking around behind people's backs. Reggie will find out and you'll end up heartbroken because his friend ran game all over you."

Kacey's hand balled into fists. "Guess I should ask you for pointers on secret affairs. I saw how cozy you were with Julio earlier."

"You think I'm still screwing with Julio?"

"Who's calling you?"

Monique scoffed and raised a hand. "Kacey, I love you, but if I look at you any longer I'm going to cuss your ass out." Monique turned and went back into the house.

Kacey spun away from the door, her arms crossed tightly over her chest. She pushed aside any guilt. If her sister could keep secrets, then so could she. Movement at the side of the house caught her eye. Sabrina was on her cell phone, talking with a big smile on her face. One guess who that was. Sabrina always called Cliff after Kacey told her he said hi. Every female in her family kept secrets. Out of the three of them, her thing with Aaron was the least of their problems. She only hoped her decision didn't blow up in her face.

CHAPTER 19

Kacey checked the schedule for the day and prepared the deposit from the previous night's earnings. She quickly stuffed the money and credit card receipts into the thick green deposit bag and zipped the bag closed. Popping out of her seat in the back office of Momma's Kitchen, she checked the time and grinned. She was right on time. A quick trip to the bank and she'd be off to meet Aaron.

Over the last week they'd found every moment they could to sneak off together. Reggie was convinced Aaron was sneaking of with Tara, so he hadn't said anything to her. Everyone assumed he was with Tara, except for Monique, who only rolled her eyes whenever Kacey said she was going to be busy "studying" all day. Honestly Kacey hadn't gotten much of any work done since giving in to her desire for Aaron.

She hurried out of the office and found Monique filling the ketchup containers at the bar.

"Hey, I'm going to take the deposit and then I'm gone for the day."

Monique stopped tapping one ketchup bottle onto another. "Gone for the day? I thought you were at least staying through the lunch shift." Monique's tone of voice had lost its frigid nature in the week since the party.

Kacey strolled over to her sister. "I'll work the night shift to make up for it."

"Don't you need to work on your thesis tonight?"

She did. She was so far behind from where she needed to be that on any other day she'd be pulling her hair out. But she still had time to finish and get the next section turned in to her professor. Aaron left to go home the next day and she could pull an all-nighter and work all day Sunday and get her work done.

If she wasn't too torn up about him leaving.

"Don't worry about it. I've got plenty of time to get things done." Kacey looked over her shoulder toward the door leading to the kitchen, where Sabrina's voice could be heard giving directions to the cooks before they opened for lunch. "Just tell Momma I'll be back later."

"You're going to see him, aren't you?"

Kacey stopped in the middle of turning away to stare at her sister with a raised brow. Monique hadn't called Kacey on her sneaking around, and Kacey hadn't brought up her sister's secret phone calls and sudden need to delete all of her browsing history on the computer. She hated fighting with her sister, but if Monique had her secrets then Kacey could have hers.

"I'm sorry, is that judgment I hear in your voice?"

Monique grunted. "Believe it or not, it's concern. You sneaking around with Aaron isn't right."

"I'm not sneaking around with Aaron, I'm going to Chattanooga. I need to interview someone at the tourism office and the department of commerce for my thesis."

All true, but Aaron had agreed to make the trip with her.

Monique scoffed and tossed her hair over her shoulder. "I still don't think it's right. If you just told Reggie—"

"Who's calling you, Monique?"

Monique eyes narrowed, and her glossed lips pressed into a line. "I'm worried about *you*."

"And I worry about you. But we're both adults and we can make our own decisions."

"Just because I'm not telling you what's happening with me right now doesn't make what you're doing right. Reggie is going into business with him and you two are hiding things from him. That's wrong."

Kacey ignored her guilt. Reggie's business and Kacey's love life were completely different things. Once Aaron left, the fact that she'd slept with him a few, okay, several times wouldn't matter.

"I'll be back later." Kacey grabbed her purse from beneath the bar and stalked toward the door.

"Last time you said you knew what you were doing and you ended up looking foolish and heartbroken," Monique said. Kacey froze but didn't turn around.

"Face it, Kacey, the reason you're the good sister is because you're the one looking for the same thing Reggie has. Someone to fall in love with and make a happily-ever-after. Aaron isn't that guy. And by the time you realize that, you'll be crying in your bedroom just like you did last time."

Kacey's hand balled into a fist. She turned to glare at Monique, who only watched with a sympathetic look in her eyes. If there'd been malice in her sister's face, she could have handled that better. She could fight that. Not the sympathy.

Kacey gritted her teeth and shoved through door into the heat and the sun. She blocked out Monique's warnings. She wasn't in love with Aaron and she wouldn't fall in love with him. But she wouldn't let her sister's doubt ruin her last day with Aaron.

• • •

Reggie's lawyer slid two copies of the new contract across the conference table in his office to Aaron and Reggie. "Well, gentlemen," he said. "Once you two look these over and agree on the terms, we can finalize the merger."

Aaron grinned and skimmed over the first page of the contract. He couldn't believe how far he'd come. The business he'd started on a whim years ago would be an actual player in the freight industry, and he'd laugh at everyone who'd scoffed at him being *just a truck driver*—all the way to the bank.

Aaron nodded. The first few pages looked good to him. "I'll take a copy home for my lawyer to review. Though I doubt she'll find any issues."

Reggie slapped Aaron on the back, pushing Aaron forward. "We're really doing it."

"Yes, we are."

"I'll admit, when you first brought this up I wasn't sure, but the projections of the profits we'll make, plus the broader reach we'll have, will instantly put us at the top of many businesses' lists."

"I told you it would, Reggie. This merger is good for both of us." Aaron rolled up the contract and tapped the paper on the desk. "I should have the signed copy back to you by the end of next week."

"Hand-delivered or scanned?"

"Probably scanned. I know Marcus really wants me to make it back next week for his baseball game, but I've got to make sure things are good back home."

Disappointment clouded Reggie's eyes. "I understand. But if you stuck around and coached them, they could make the playoffs."

Aaron nodded. "They can make it without me. They're good." He glanced at Reggie's lawyer. "Thanks for helping us with this."

"My pleasure." The middle-aged guy stood with Aaron and Reggie, and they shook hands.

After the lawyer left, Reggie turned to Aaron. "Want to celebrate with lunch at Momma's Kitchen?"

Aaron smiled but shook his head. "No, I'm going in to Chattanooga this afternoon. I ordered some team shirts for Marcus and the guys. I want to surprise them with them tonight."

"Guilty conscience, huh?" Reggie smirked.

Aaron grinned and rubbed his jaw. "Hey, even though I won't be there, I want them to look like a team."

"I hear you. Have fun in town. I'll see you in the morning before you roll out."

"Most definitely."

"You taking Bertha to Chattanooga?"

Aaron shook his head. "Nah."

"Then how are you getting there? You need a ride?"

Saying that Kacey was taking him sat on the tip of Aaron's tongue. He hated keeping the secret from his friend, but revealing things today would only ruin the potential deal. Especially after he and Kacey had spent the last week sneaking around to keep Reggie in the dark.

"I've got a ride. I'm trying that new app where people pick you up."

"Are you sure? That's crazy."

"If the person looks crazy, I'll call Tara or someone to take me." Aaron grinned.

Reggie laughed. "Tara would love to take you. I know that's who you've been sneaking off with." Reggie's big hand slapped Aaron's shoulder. "You thought I didn't know you were sneaking off to see someone? Come on, Aaron, I watched you sneak it in with women while we were in college. Not that I blame you. She's fine and you're single."

"Yeah..." Aaron hedged. Yet another lie to his friend and business partner. "I'll check you later, all right?"

They shook hands and gave a one-armed hug before Aaron left and made his way to the park, where he helped Marcus and the rest of the team practice. That's where Kacey said they'd be least likely to be spotted when she picked him up. He strolled through the park to the front entrance. Not soon after, Kacey's green Honda Accord pulled up. Kacey's bright smile, visible through the windshield, had his own lips curving upward.

Damn, he was falling into the trap. He felt the downward spiral just as sure as he felt the sun on his face. Even more surprising, what freaked him out was not that he was falling, but that he wasn't freaked out about knowing he was falling. If he were in town a few more days, he would come up with reasons to settle here. Spend the days working in the office letting other drivers pull the loads so that he could go home and cuddle with Kacey on the couch after coaching the baseball team. All would be great—until the itch to do something different settled in. The itch always came. A few months with Kacey would be great, but it wasn't worth hurting her like he'd done to Denise.

Aaron leaned his hands in the open passenger window and bent over. Kacey turned to face him with a sexy twist to her lips.

"Need a ride, handsome?"

"I'm waiting on a friend of mine," he said.

"Girlfriend?"

"More like *special friend.*"

"Well, since your *special friend* is coming, I'll just leave." She eased the car forward.

Aaron jumped back. "Hey, hey!"

The car stopped, and Aaron leaned into the door again. She watched him with a teasing glint in her eye.

"Yes?" She drew out the word. Aaron loved this silly side of her, when she wasn't stressed out from work or school.

"Forget my special friend. I'd much prefer to ride off with you."

"I bet you say that to all the ladies." She unlocked the car door. "Get in."

"Now, hold up a second. Before I ride off with some sexy lady, I need to check out the ride."

She raised a brow. "Oh, really?"

"Yeah. I've watched you get around town on a bicycle the entire time I've been here. This is the first time I've seen you behind the wheel of a vehicle. I'm a trucker and the safety of the ride is the most important thing."

Kacey rolled her eyes, and Aaron laughed. He was only giving her a hard time as he pretended to check out the vehicle. He was pretty sure that as meticulous as Kacey was about everything else, her car would be in excellent condition. He gave a cursory glance at the tires and frowned. The tread was way too low.

"Kacey, get out of the car."

"Are you seriously checking out the car?"

"Just get out of the car for a second."

Her huff of frustration was audible even over the hum of the engine. She got out and dragged her feet around to where he stood. "Yes?"

"When was the last time you changed the tires?"

She shrugged. A sure sign that he wasn't going to like whatever she said next. "I don't know. I bought it pre-owned two years ago. The previous owner mentioned something about tires, but I never got around to it."

"Why not?" He couldn't believe someone would actually neglect their tires that long.

"I don't drive often. Most of the time I'm riding my bike around town."

He pointed to the tires. "These are not safe. You need to change them."

"Okay, okay, I'll change them." She sounded about as convincing as a kid saying they wouldn't peek at their birthday presents.

"I'm serious, Kacey. I've seen what can happen during bad weather when cars on the road have old tires. They hydroplane in the rain. The driver loses control and can cause a major pileup. It's nothing to play around with."

"I hear you. I'll do something." Again with the voice that didn't convince him.

"Kacey, promise me you'll change them. I would go crazy if you were hurt because of a preventable accident. I can't even begin to think about that happening to you. Please, for me."

Her mouth fell open, and her eyes grew wide as silver dollars. Aaron snapped his mouth shut. Those words weren't supposed to sound so...caring. Granted, he did care about her, but he sounded like Reggie worrying over Camila. When had he started feeling that way about Kacey?

"Okay, I'll change the tires." Her low concession finally convinced him she was telling the truth.

A weird tension pulsed between them. He could see the question in her eyes. What was going on with them? They'd agreed to have a little fun, not get serious and protective. *Get it together, Aaron. You are not that guy.*

He gave her his carefree grin and a half shrug. "Good. I can't have my only special friend in Resilient, Tennessee, hurting herself."

The mood was broken as Kacey smirked and rolled her eyes. "Of course not. Come on, enough with the three-point inspection. Let's go already. Unless you're too afraid to ride in my car."

"I'll ride, but no speeding, tailgating, or texting while driving."

"I don't do any of that anyway. But thank you for the driving lesson, Mr. Henderson." She said the last part in a silly, childlike voice. "I never would have thought of that."

Aaron wrapped his arm around her waist and swung her around. Kacey yelped then giggled. "Stop it, Aaron."

"You want to play, I'll show you how to play." He slowly set her feet back on the ground. She sighed and rested her hands on his shoulders. A bone-deep feeling that Kacey in his arms was right on all levels swept through his body.

He let her go and stepped away before he got lost in that feeling. Fell further into the trap. Kacey either didn't notice his retreat or didn't care because she just laughed and started toward the front of the car. "Let's go."

CHAPTER 20

"I can't remember the last time I came down here," Kacey said to Aaron.

They were sitting along the riverfront in Chattanooga. Nearby, seven fountains sprayed water at the base of the city's public art exhibit that paid homage to the Trail of Tears, the time when the Native American tribe of Cherokees were forced out of the south. Aaron had been to Chattanooga several times and always liked coming to the Riverfront. He turned away from staring at the fading sunlight reflecting off the river to look at Kacey. She leaned forward with her arms on her thighs. Hair escaped from her ponytail and clung to the side of her face with every breeze.

While she'd interviewed people for her thesis, Aaron had hung out in the waiting areas. At the tourism office, the receptionist had openly flirted with him, until he mentioned being a truck driver. After that, her interest in her computer had increased tenfold. Aaron didn't care, he wasn't interested in hooking up with her, but it reminded him of the way people scoffed at his hard work. Even more reason to make his business a success. He hated lying to Reggie, but Kacey was right—if they'd told him the truth knowing they wouldn't become anything serious, the deal would have been ruined. He'd worked too hard to let that happen.

Aaron used his finger to slide a few tendrils of hair out of Kacey's face. "That long?"

"Yeah. We came once in high school to see the Passage Memorial and visit the aquarium. I remember thinking this entire place was beautiful. But now, if I ever come to Chattanooga, I go straight to whatever appointment I have and then go back home. I don't stop to enjoy the scenery."

"Whenever I visit a new town I always take the time to visit the local sights."

"Really?" The pitch of her voice rose.

"Really. It's why I drive. I like seeing new places and meeting new people. I've been to every state in America."

She sat up and gave him a disbelieving look. "You can't drive to Hawaii."

"I know that. I took a cruise to Alaska and a friend of mine has a place in Maui and invited me there for a week a few years ago."

"That's a nice friend."

Aaron shrugged. "She's big on house parties, so there were about a half a dozen of us there for the week. But we had a good time."

"Was it a couples' party?"

"Why would you think that?"

"Half a dozen is six people. Just wondering if it was couples." She broke eye contact and glanced down at the long blue and green skirt she wore.

There'd been three guys and three ladies that weekend, but they weren't really couples. He'd only known Carla, whom he'd met in California the year before during a job. They'd had a quick bit of fun before he'd left the state and hooked up again when he'd come back. That week was a blur of parties, drinking, and acting like a spring breaker on the beach. He still kept in touch with the guys from that weekend.

"I guess you could say that."

A line appeared between her brows, and she stared at the fountains. Aaron used to tell the story of his weekend in Hawaii to all of his male friends. Reggie would usually ask if Aaron still kept in touch with Carla or if he planned to go back to see her again. He'd always been proud of his history with women. The frown on Kacey's face made him wish she'd never seen that side of him.

He tugged on her elbow, but she resisted. Aaron tugged harder. "Come on over here."

She tried to glare at him, but he gave her the smile that usually got him what he wanted. She rolled her eyes and shook her head but let him tug her over against his side. Aaron kissed her forehead and wrapped his arm around her shoulders. He was going to miss her. A lot more than he'd missed any other woman. The thought was petrifying and not because he'd never felt that way before, but because he didn't know if she'd miss him just as much as he'd miss her.

"How are things going with your thesis?" he asked.

Kacey stiffened against him. "Coming along."

"Are you sure?"

"I'm just a little behind, but I'll get caught up this weekend."

When he was out of town. He knew he'd pulled her away from her studies and sometimes her work at Momma's Kitchen. Selfish of him, yes, but honestly he wanted to spend as much time with her as he could before this thing ended.

"Are you ready to go home?" she asked.

"I always look forward to being back home, but this time I'm not too anxious."

"Why?"

Getting Janiyah straight about Liz topped the list. That wasn't going to be fun, but Kacey didn't need to hear that. "Baby fever is running rampant in my family. My youngest sister texted me today to say I had to be in town for the gender reveal party she's having in two weeks."

Kacey chuckled. "That'll be fun."

"I am very happy for my sister, but going to a gender reveal party is only going to serve as a platform for my family to ask when I'll settle down and start to make babies. My mom hoped all four of her kids would fall in love and settle down. Now that three of the four have, and two of the four are providing the next generation, I'm the only one left to pressure."

"What's so bad about finding someone and having a family?"

"Nothing, in theory. I'm just not ready for that much. My dad loves us, but he never seemed to relax. Even on vacation. He was always worried about the welfare of his family. Food, clothing, and providing things we needed. And if it wasn't us, then there were the pressures to keep his business successful. Marriage and family comes with an automatic increase in a man's stress. I haven't found a reason to add more stress to my life. I'll love my wife and kids. They'll be all that I can think about. Right now, I'd like to only think of myself and Bertha."

Kacey sat up. She clasped her hands in her lap and looked at the water. "I can't fault you for that."

Aaron's eyes widened, and his head tilted to the side. "Really? I thought you'd use that in your *you're afraid of responsibility* arsenal."

"Being honest about what you really want in a relationship is responsible," she said. "It's easier to lie and act like getting married one day is your ultimate goal. It's harder to say that you don't want that. Don't believe in that."

"You don't?"

She leaned back against him, and Aaron wrapped his arm around her waist and breathed in the clean scent of her hair, feeling more content that he could ever remember.

"I know some people are happily married. But marriage is a lot of hard work and a lot of compromise for things that shouldn't be compromised on. I keep saying that when I'm finished with school, and get the second restaurant open, I'll be ready to settle down. But if I achieve that, then I'll have to work harder to manage two places instead of one. The Chattanooga restaurant will become my number-one priority...even more than the home restaurant is now. Throw in a husband and kids that will require me to put them first, and it seems like that's even more stress in my life."

"You can find a balance. Lots of people do. And having a guy compromise some of his time with you to build a successful franchise isn't too much to ask."

"But me compromising when he finds someone else to give him that attention, I can't do."

This wasn't about her, but her mom, Cliff, and Brenda. "Not every guy is like that."

"I know," she said. "I just don't want to possibly pick the one who is like that and find myself in that situation."

"No matter who you pick, I don't think you'll have a problem with that."

She tilted her head back to look up at him. "How could you possibly know that?"

"Because you're fiercely loyal and dedicated. You stick beside your parents regardless of the awkward situation they put you in. I know you're not comfortable keeping us from Reggie, but you don't want him to hurt his business because of his protectiveness over you. You're busting your ass in school, but you still feel guilty if you can't relieve Monique or Ashlei at the restaurant. If you had a husband, you'd be just as dedicated and loyal to him. Any man who earned that from you would be crazy to throw it all away."

If she picked someone who appreciated those qualities in her. She'd make the perfect spouse for someone equally as ambitious as she was. The quiet backbone of support any man would need. The kind of support he never considered would make handling the pressure of being a provider easier for a man.

They were quiet for several minutes. Aaron wrestled with the feeling of sinking further into the trap. He was a guy who could appreciate all those qualities in her. Would even be able to handle her close-knit family. But how long before he got bored? Sure, he loved Resilient, coaching Marcus's baseball team, going to Momma's Kitchen for lunch in the middle of a workday to see Kacey and her family, and spending time with her after a long day. But did he love that more than he loved his current lifestyle? He couldn't answer that with a strong yes, so that question was best left alone.

He nudged her side with his elbow and pulled a handful of Laffy Taffy out of his side pocket. "Want one?"

Her eyes lit up and she grinned. "Where did you get this?"

"Don't worry about that." He pulled back the wrapper on the candy to read the joke. "What did the egg say to the frying pan?"

She frowned as if considering the answer while stuffing a piece of candy in her mouth. "What?"

"You crack me up."

They both chuckled, and Aaron pulled her against him again. He kissed her forehead and when he pulled back, her eyes sparkled in the waning sunlight. He lowered his head and kissed her, reveling in the way her body completely went soft against him. She tasted like the strawberry candy, and he could eat strawberries until the end of eternity. He probed and deepened the kiss, pulling her closer against him until she twisted and wrapped her arms around his neck. He lifted a hand to take one of her small breasts in the palm of his hand. Her hardened nipple was prominent beneath the material of her blouse.

He didn't want to leave her tomorrow, but he had to get home. And he didn't want to go back to Resilient and spend the night separate from her or trying to sneak into her place late at night when there was little chance of Reggie or someone else seeing.

He leaned back. "Let's get a room."

Her desire-filled eyes cleared and focused on him. "Seriously?"

"Yes. I don't want to spend the night without you by my side. Please, spend the night with me."

CHAPTER 21

The next morning Kacey suppressed a heavy sigh and trudged up the steps to her front door. Staying the night in in Chattanooga with Aaron hadn't been a smart idea. She'd talked a good game about not being sure if she could marry or compromise, but at the end of the night that's all it was, talk.

Maybe if they'd joked around, or talked about seeing who could lose control first, she could have walked away without her feelings becoming so jumbled and tangled. Instead he'd made love to her, slowly and sweetly, as if he too wanted to savor their last night together. By the time the sun rose, she'd been wishing Aaron could be the guy worth marrying. She'd even whispered that question to his sleeping face. Like an idiotic fool in love.

She would not get mopey and sad just because Aaron was leaving today. She would not acknowledge that her heart wanted to shatter into bite-sized pieces because their fling was coming to an end. She would not succumb to the urge to text him and see how he was doing later today or ask how his ride home had been. Doing any of that would only prove that Monique was right and she couldn't handle the quick fling that was their relationship.

She took a deep breath and shook off the melancholy that hovered over her, waiting to latch on and turn her into some sad, brokenhearted ninny. Last night was the end. They'd both known that was the end, and when she'd dropped him off about two blocks away so they wouldn't arrive home at the same time, he'd kissed her cheek and jumped out of the car without a backward glance. No way was she going to let that bother her. She knew the deal when she'd gotten into this.

She slid the key into the lock, but when she turned it to the left there was no telltale *clunk* of the dead bolt opening. Frowning, Kacey tested the knob and pushed. The door opened easily. Her heart thundered in her chest, and she sucked in a shallow breath. She slowly pushed the door forward and leaned to the side to peek through the door. Tension vibrated through her body, and she was ready to bolt down the stairs screaming at the top of her lungs if someone was still there.

"You can come in, Kacey," Reggie's voice boomed.

Kacey let out a heavy breath and pressed a hand against her pounding heart. She stalked through the door and glared around the room until her gaze landed on her brother sitting on the couch.

"What are you doing in here? I thought someone had broken in." Kacey slammed the door behind her.

He slowly rose from the couch and crossed his thick arms over his chest. "I was worried about you."

"Why?"

"Because you didn't come home last night. Everyone in the family was worried."

Kacey waved a hand and pushed aside the guilt for not letting anyone know that she planned to spend the night in Chattanooga. "There's no reason to worry. I'm a grown woman and can take care of myself."

"No one is doubting your abilities, Kacey. But when you text to tell Monique and Momma that you can't work because you have to get things done for your thesis, and then we can't find you here, at the library, or at school, we start to worry."

Kacey blew out a breath and pressed her hand against her forehead. She should have known they would come looking for her. "Can I just have one night to myself without it being a state of emergency?"

"Yes, but you still should check in," he said with all the authority of a father.

She dropped her hand and glared. "I don't have to check in with you or anyone else. How I spend my time is my business."

She marched past him into the kitchen.

"Are you spending your time sleeping with Aaron?"

Kacey froze. She gritted her teeth and mentally cursed Monique, the only person who could have put that thought into her brother's head. She slowly spun to face Reggie.

"Why would you even think that? It took longer than I expected to get all the interviews done, and since I was there I decided to check out some other restaurants downtown." Not quite a lie; she and Aaron had eaten downtown. "It got late and I decided to stay in town instead of drive back."

Reggie narrowed his eyes. "You see, I'd believe you. Because I know you typically never lie to me. Out of everyone you're the one I could always trust to tell me the truth."

"Why don't you trust me now?"

"Because when I texted Aaron last night to see where he was, he texted back that he was with Tara—but I saw Tara at Luigi's right before." Reggie took a step forward. "Just tell me the truth, Kacey." He stared into her eyes. "Are you sleeping with Aaron?"

She wanted to lie. To tell her brother to mind his own business, but she couldn't. Not when his gaze burned into hers. "Fine. Yes, I was with Aaron last night."

Reggie rose to his full height. "Are you sleeping together?"

Kacey sighed. "Yes."

"For how long?"

Might as well go all-in. "Since before I knew he was your partner. I met him on his first night in town, when he came into Momma's Kitchen. We hooked up that night."

Reggie clenched his hands into fists at his side. "You're telling me he's lied to me this entire time?"

"We didn't want to upset you."

"So lying makes the situation better. I even gave him my blessing when I suspected and he still lied."

Kacey slapped her chest. "That's my fault. I told him to keep it from you because I knew you'd overreact."

"You're my sister."

"Yes, but you look at me as if I'm some kind of virgin saint. I'm not, Reggie. Aaron came in, I wanted to get laid, and he was willing."

"Stop it, you sound like—"

"Like who, Reggie? Like Momma or Monique? Guess what. We're all from the same family."

"But you're not a whore!" he shouted.

Kacey sucked in a breath. Her eyes widened, and anger flashed up her spine. "Neither are they, Reggie."

"I didn't mean it like that."

"Then how did you mean it? I know Momma made mistakes when she was younger. I don't like having my dad's wife smile in my face when I know seeing me causes her pain every moment I'm around. Just like you don't like hearing that Momma can't even remember what your dad's name is. Or that Monique's dad was a traveling preacher, and that Ashlei's dad was some trucker who came through town. But that's the way things are. I don't hate or begrudge her for her mistakes, because she's done everything in her power to make a better life for us."

"I know that."

"Do you, really? Because you spent a lot of time trying to protect and defend our honor while simultaneously sleeping around with every woman you met on the road. Just like the only-wants-one-thing guys you warn us about."

He wiped his brow, looking flustered. "That's why I care, Kacey. I know what men think about easy women. You all are special."

"So were the women you left behind before you met Camila."

Reggie's shoulders went rigid. "Those women aren't my family. I don't want men to think that they can just take advantage of you," he said through clenched teeth. "Look what happened when you were still in high school."

"I knew exactly what I was doing, and the entire time I knew it was wrong. A mistake I learned from."

"You don't hear what the guys in this town say about the women in my family," he said with rage in his voice.

"Yes, I do. You can't protect us from the few people who can't see beyond the past to what our family has accomplished."

"You sleeping with Aaron behind my back doesn't help things either," he said. "Instead of telling me the truth, you've been sneaking around with him."

Kacey flinched. "I knew that if you found out you wouldn't want to partner with him."

"Damn right, I don't. I can't trust him."

A shadow passed by the window. Kacey had watched for that shadow enough to know it was Aaron coming in. Reggie spun to see what she was looking at.

"He's back. What did you do? Drop him off a few blocks down the street so he could walk home? Pretend as if you hadn't spent the night laid up with him?"

"Quit trying to make it sound dirty. It's not like that."

"If you can't tell your family who you're with, then it is dirty." He stomped to the door and wrenched it open. Reggie turned to jog up the stairs to the second-floor apartment.

Kacey chased him. "Reggie, stop. There's no need to ruin this deal. Your business is more important."

"Family is more important, Kacey," he said over his shoulder. "He disrespected my family by not telling me."

Reggie got to the top of the stairs and banged on the door. The door flew open. Kacey couldn't see Aaron, Reggie's body blocked the view, but she heard his wary chuckle.

"Reggie, what's up?"

"Are you screwing with my sister?"

"What... Come on, Reggie."

"Don't lie to me," Reggie said in a low, angry voice.

Kacey pushed past Reggie to stand between him and Aaron. Aaron stepped back and brought her with him. "Reggie, stop. He wanted to tell you but I asked him not to."

"Really," Reggie said with a bitter laugh. "How hard was it to convince him to lie? Not too hard, I suspect. That's his game. I've known him for years, and he only pretended to want to tell me in order to show you he cared."

Kacey glanced at Aaron, who frowned and rubbed his eyes. "Reggie, man, I wouldn't do that to your sister."

"Why am I supposed to believe that?"

"Remember what I told you?"

"I remember you lied to my face when I asked you straight-up if there was something going on between you and Kacey. I even gave you permission."

Kacey jumped forward. "I'm not a kid, you don't give anyone permission."

Aaron placed a hand on her waist and pulled her to his side. "I get what he's saying, Kacey." He looked at Reggie. "I wasn't sure what was going on with me and Kacey then. I knew I liked her and that something could grow between us, but I didn't want to say anything until I was sure."

"How in the world can I trust you?" Reggie asked. "Is that going to be your excuse if you make a deal without telling me? Or if you hire or fire an employee, or sign a new contract without telling me? *Oh, Reggie, I meant to tell you but I wasn't sure of your reaction.*"

"Come on, Reggie, you know I wouldn't do that in business."

"How the hell am I supposed to *know* that, Aaron?" Reggie said, tossing out his hand. "I can't trust you, and I can't go into business with you. I'm tearing up the contract."

"No!" Aaron said. "We worked hard on this, we both saw the numbers and this merger is the best thing for both of our businesses. We can't grow any other way."

"I'll find another way."

Kacey tried to stop Reggie from turning to leave. "Reggie, don't do this. Not over this."

"Reggie, I care about Kacey," Aaron called out. Both Kacey and Reggie turned to him. "I care about her a lot, and walking away from her this morning knowing it was the end of our relationship was the hardest thing I've ever had to do."

Kacey's mouth fell open. Aaron looked at her and Reggie with so much sincerity she wanted to believe him. A spark flared in her chest. Hope maybe, but something she hadn't allowed herself to feel in years.

"It was?" she asked.

He nodded and swallowed hard. "Yes. Kacey, I don't know what it is, but I haven't felt this way about another woman. The thought of settling down scares the shit out of me, but I don't want to leave you. I don't want to lose you."

Her heart swelled, and the feeling she'd tried to suppress gave way to a happiness she never thought she could feel. "I don't want to lose you either."

Aaron's relieved smile only made her want to jump into his arms. He looked to Reggie. "I know the way Kacey and I started was screwed up, but I want to be honest moving forward. I can't take back what happened, but I can make things right. I promised I'd treasure her. Let me show you I'm honest."

Aaron walked forward and held out his hand. Reggie looked at her happy grin, then glared back at Aaron.

"Are you serious?" Reggie asked.

Aaron nodded. "It's like you said about Camila. I don't want to go out with any other woman, and I damn sure don't want to see Kacey on the arm of another guy."

Reggie lifted and lowered his chin. He reached out and clasped Aaron's hand, and they shook. "Fine. If you mean it, and are done sneaking around, then I'm okay."

"I never wanted to do that, and I'm ready to be a one-woman guy," Aaron said. He grinned at Kacey. "If she'll have me."

He opened his arms and she accepted his hug. His body was rigid—surprising, compared to the easy grin on his face. She leaned back to stare into his face, but his was filled with a look of happiness and contentment. He wrapped his arm around her shoulder and looked at Reggie.

"And the merger?" Aaron asked in an urgent voice.

Reggie looked at the two of them and smiled. "Back on."

The tension left Aaron's body, and he held out his hand to shake Reggie's again. Kacey frowned. Too much knowledge of the games men played started doubts in her brain. Had she just been played?

Aaron turned to her with a look of joy and adoration in his eyes. "Kacey, I've never felt this way before, but tell me if it was just as hard for you to leave me this morning as it was for me to leave you."

Anxiousness filled his eyes, and his easy grin was gone. She pushed the doubts away. He couldn't fake that look in his eyes. "It was."

Relief swept across his features, and he kissed her quickly. "I'm going to make you happy."

CHAPTER 22

Aaron sat on his parents' back porch with his brother, David. Music played from the Bluetooth speakers around the patio, and sunlight glittered off the surface of the pool. The smell of the grill filled the air, and he expected their dad to be out there soon with burgers if he didn't get sidetracked by their mom. David sat next to him, feeding his ten-month-old daughter with an ease that scared the crap out of Aaron. David usually came dressed like a runway model even for family events. This Sunday afternoon, David wore a plain gray T-shirt and khaki shorts that Aaron wasn't sure had been ironed. A pink polka-dot blanket draped his brother's shoulder and he looked as if he needed a haircut.

Aaron's heart went from zero to sixty in his chest. Was that what kids did to you? Turn you into a shadow of your former self? Was he next in line?

"I messed up," Aaron blurted out.

David looked up from his daughter. He bounced his knee to gently rock her as if he'd been handling babies all of his life. "How?"

Aaron sat forward in the chair and ran his hands through his hair. He wanted to pull the curly strands out. "It happened during the merger. I met this woman..."

David chuckled. "Let me guess. You met her, she fell in love, you promised to come back and see her, but now she's acting all *Fatal Attraction* on you."

Aaron cringed and shook his head. "I haven't had that situation happen since Keisha two years ago."

"Okay, then how did you mess up?"

He cleared his throat and told David how Reggie had found out about him and Kacey the previous weekend.

"You lied?" David asked.

"No, nah, not really. I mean, I do care about Kacey. A lot. I wasn't ready to leave her and I had moments when I thought I could be with her long-term. But when Reggie confronted me, all I could think of was saving the deal."

Aaron's leg bounced, and he ran a hand over his head. "Now, when I'm on the phone with her, the conversation is still good. She still makes me laugh and we talk about everything, but she sounds different. Happier. And all I can think about is whether or not I rushed into things."

"Are you going back to see her soon?"

"I don't know, I mean, I've got to go back to Resilient, but before her I figured it would only be a few times a year. She hasn't asked when I'm coming back, but she said she missed me."

And he missed her. A hell of a lot more than he expected. But the feeling that he hadn't really thought through making them "official" bothered him. That entire afternoon seemed like a blur.

David looked down at Davina and checked the amount of milk left in the bottle. "You should talk to her and tell her what happened."

Aaron glared at his brother, whom he'd happily hit if he wasn't holding Davina. "Yeah, then I'll really be considered an asshole. I can't tell her or Reggie. Not until everything is done."

David looked up and shrugged. "Then what, you break up with her after the paperwork is signed?"

The million-dollar question. His lawyer had looked over the contract and everything was good. All he needed to do was sign the papers. But he hadn't signed yet. He didn't know what to do after he signed.

"I don't like feeling rushed into things."

"Then let things play out and see what happens. You said yourself you've got feelings for her. For once, just see where the feelings take you."

"I know where the feelings take me, and I'm not ready for that."

"For what?"

His niece gurgled and spit out the bottle. David grinned as if seeing a baby finish eating was the most adorable thing in the universe. David patted her on the back, again looking as if burping a baby and wearing a wrinkled T-shirt was normal for him.

Aaron pointed to his brother. "That. Marriage, kids, all of that."

"Marriage and kids aren't bad."

"They change you."

"Not really."

Aaron raised a brow. "When was the last time you got a haircut? And I'm not trying to call you out, but is your iron broken? You used to dress as if you were about to walk down a runway."

David shrugged as if it was no big deal, but he did run a hand over his head. "Some things just don't take as high a priority. Kareem's cutting my hair later, and I'd much rather have Davina spit up on this T-shirt than one of my other shirts. Besides, being with her doesn't mean this."

"Really? You reunite with Sandra and six months later she's pregnant. Fred and Janiyah get married and already she's pregnant. I wouldn't be surprised to hear Kareem say that Neecie's pregnant."

"Neecie's what?" Kareem's loud voice broke the peace of the afternoon.

Aaron turned to his brother, who'd just walked out from the sunroom, a glass dish filled with hamburger patties in his hands. Kareem's eyes were wide with something very close to panic. Aaron still hadn't gotten used to seeing his brother without his signature dreads, which he'd cut last year. Or in a color other than black, though the dark brown shirt and dark jeans didn't stray too far into the bright color realm.

"I was making a point to Aaron. Everyone is hooking up and having babies. I was telling Aaron that you'll be making the announcement next."

Kareem nostrils flared with a heavy breath, and he shook his head. "Hell, no. Not anytime soon over here. I love Neecie, and one day I want kids, but today ain't that day." He strolled over to the grill and lifted the lid.

"Kids aren't so bad," David said.

"I never said they were, but I need to figure out this relationship stuff before I go throwing a screaming, hungry kid in the middle of it."

Aaron nodded in agreement. After Kareem got out of prison, Aaron never thought he'd see his wear-all-black, growl-at-a-pit-bull angry brother as in love and relaxed as he'd been since getting together with his fiancée, Neecie. Getting Kareem out of all black had seemed like a miracle, but Aaron still couldn't imagine Kareem cradling a baby with a pink polka-dot towel on his shoulder.

Kareem glanced back at David and shrugged. "Not that your girl screams that much."

David chuckled. "I know she's a screamer."

Kareem turned back to the grill to drop a few patties on the hot surface. "Why ya'll talking 'bout babies anyway? Did Aaron knock up some chick?"

"No, I didn't," Aaron said. "But I did walk right into a shotgun relationship." He explained to Kareem what had happened with Kacey.

Kareem didn't interrupt or say anything right away. He finished with the burgers and wiped his hands on a towel hanging on the grill. When he turned, he looked at Aaron with a serious expression.

"You think she told her brother on purpose."

Right to the thought Aaron had tried to suppress. Aaron couldn't get over how Reggie just happened to find out about Aaron and Kacey the day he was supposed to leave. How he came barging at Aaron's door with Kacey right after him. He didn't want to think Kacey would do that. She wasn't that type.

"I don't think she would."

"You don't know that," Kareem said. "She was a one-night stand and you hooked up with her a few times while you were there. Women get hooked and try to find ways to make a man stay."

"But she wouldn't."

"What if she would?" Kareem countered.

David glanced from Kareem to Aaron. "How did she look when her brother broke the deal?"

"Shocked, and she told him he didn't have to do it." He frowned and thought about that day. "But then when I said I wanted to make things work, she looked...happy."

Kareem grunted. "Maybe because that's what she wanted."

The baby burped and David cradled her in the crook of his arm. "Don't listen to Kareem, Aaron. He's still hovering on the side of the neurotic."

"Shut the hell up, David," Kareem said without malice.

"Don't get mad because I'm speaking the truth. We all know your trust issues run deep. Especially before you got together with Neecie. Let's not assume the same with—" He looked to Aaron. "What's her name?"

"Kacey."

"I don't know. It sounds a little too convenient to me," Kareem said. "And it gives Reggie more of an interest in the company. If you're with his sister, he gets his say and then can use her to convince you to listen to his ideas more."

Aaron shifted. "How?"

Kareem shrugged. "Women get whatever they want in the bedroom."

David nodded. "That's true."

"I don't know." Aaron ran his hands over his face. "You all are making me think about stuff I hadn't even considered."

"Well, maybe you should," Kareem said.

David stood. "Look, don't let Kareem put doubts in your head. You're nervous because you had to 'fess up to your feelings for the first time. But if you're really unsure, then I'll do for you what you did for me."

Aaron lifted his head. "What's that?"

"Bring her to the family. Let us check her out."

Kareem nodded. "Yeah, do that. We usually can figure out what's up."

Aaron considered, then nodded. "Fine, I'll see if she wants to come to the gender reveal, but don't tell your wives. No way am I letting them know more about this situation."

• • •

After leaving his parents', Aaron went back to his apartment. Normally the sparsely furnished place made him feel at home. But today not so much. He missed the comforts of the apartment he'd had over Kacey's house. Or the warmth of Kacey's place. His one bedroom didn't have any family pictures or personal touches to make it feel like his space. Just a couch, some gaming chairs, and his monster flat-screen television and video game console. The only thing in his fridge was an empty pizza box, half of a soda of indeterminate age, and a box of baking soda Janiyah had insisted he needed the last time she visited. After partaking of Kacey's full fridge, he could fully appreciate stocking up on necessities.

He ordered a pizza and sat on the couch to play an online game. As he waited for the pizza, he wondered what Kacey was doing. Probably up working on her thesis. Trying to get caught up after he had hogged so much of her time before he left. If he called, he could imagine the exasperation in her voice that he'd interrupted her, but it wouldn't hide the pleasure that seemed to creep in whenever he did. She enjoyed spending time with him. Just as much as he enjoyed time with her. Maybe David was right and he should just let things play out and see what happened.

He stopped logging in to the online game and pulled out his cell phone to call. He scrolled through his recent calls until he got to her number. A knock on the door came right before he could press the button to call. Aaron tossed the phone on the couch and got up to answer the door. He pulled out his wallet to pay the pizza delivery person, but when he opened the door, he was greeted with Liz's smiling face.

"Hi," she said in a high, singsong voice. Her purple-framed glasses were crooked on her nose, and the normally neat knot that held up her strawberry-blond hair had lost its firm hold on her shoulder-length hair.

"Hey, Liz, what are you doing here?" He glanced around as if someone else would be able to explain her appearance.

"Janiyah called and told me you were in town," Liz said. She took a step forward and ran her hand up his arm. "She also said you were going home where you'd be all alone and needed some company."

Aaron gritted his teeth. He was going to kill his sister. "She did, huh?"

"Yes, she did." Liz wrapped her arms around his neck and pressed against him.

"What happened to you and the architect?" He could guess. Aaron knew he was the fun in between her off-again, on-again relationship with the guy. That hadn't bothered him because he had no claims on Liz.

He wondered whether there was a guy in Kacey's life who'd like to fill in the void while Aaron was away. Aaron hadn't done long-distance since Denise. That was before he had his business and he could stay in Texas almost full-time. He and Kacey hadn't talked about how often they'd see each other. Another side effect of their spur-of-the-moment relationship act. Aaron remembered the guy who'd drooled over Kacey at the bar that first night. Was that guy filling Aaron's place while he was out of town? The idea made Aaron's stomach boil.

"I'm done with him. Totally done this time."

"You said that last time."

He took a step back, but Liz remained wrapped around him. Her step forward was unsteady and she stumbled. Aaron placed a hand on her waist to keep her from falling.

"I mean it this time, Aaron. He won't commit, and I'm tired of waiting around."

"I told you that the last time."

Liz grinned and twirled a finger in his hair. "You did, and you also helped me forget about him the last time." She wrapped her leg around his and slid her body up and down, pressing her full breasts against his chest.

Aaron suppressed a groan. He had enjoyed Liz's enthusiasm. "Liz, you can't keep running over here whenever you get mad at him."

"I didn't run. I took a cab," she said with a very uncharacteristic giggle.

Aaron narrowed his eyes. "Are you drunk?"

"Tipsy."

He scowled. "At least you didn't drive?"

She shook her head; the knot gave way and waves of hair fell around her face. "I figured I'd be spending the night." She rubbed her body up and down his again. "Help me forget, Aaron."

Liz grabbed his head and pulled him down for a kiss. She simultaneously slipped her tongue past his lips and palmed his cock. Aaron's eyes rolled back, and he nearly succumbed to the pleasure—but he didn't want to sleep with Liz. He wouldn't do that to Kacey. Whether or not he had doubts about their relationship, he'd never been one to cheat.

"Uh-hum, I got your pizza," a male voice said from behind.

Aaron pushed Liz off and wiped his lips. Her face was flushed and her hazel eyes sparkled with wicked desire. He knew what came with that sparkle. Aaron suppressed a groan and moved her to the side.

"Yeah, thanks, man," Aaron said. Liz went into his apartment while he pulled the money out of his wallet and paid the delivery guy.

Aaron closed the door and turned. Liz had plopped down on his couch, and only her feet were visible on the armrest. Aaron sighed and dropped the pizza and soda onto the coffee table.

Liz grinned up at him. "Ready for some fun?"

Aaron rubbed the back of his head. "Liz, how is this going to help convince Janiyah there's nothing between us?"

"She suggested that I come, but she doesn't know I took her up on the suggestion." Liz stood unsteadily and unbuttoned the top two buttons of her gray sleeveless blouse. "No one has to know."

"Liz, we aren't doing this."

She scowled at him. "Come on, Aaron, it's what we do. And right now, I need a distraction. A big one." She eyed his crotch. "You're just the right size."

She stepped forward and stumbled. Aaron caught her around the waist. "You're drunk, and we both know you're going to hate yourself tomorrow."

"But I won't be horny," she said, then broke out into a fit of giggles.

Aaron shook his head and took her into the bedroom. This was definitely not characteristic of Liz. He'd had a hunch that architect wasn't going to be what she wanted him to be. Now Liz realized the same, and she was crashing from that relationship pretty hard. A few swift steps got him into the bedroom, where he laid her on the bed. Liz rolled onto her back and pulled up her skirt, revealing bright pink panties. Aaron groaned. This was going from bad to worse.

"Come on, Aaron, one last time." She started pulling the underwear down. At the first glimpse of curly red hair, Aaron turned his head.

"I'm going to eat a slice of pizza and give you time to calm down. I'll take you home later." He hurried to the bedroom door and slammed it shut behind him.

Through the door he heard Liz curse, then the squeak of his bed, which meant she'd probably flipped over. A second later soft sobs replaced her cursing. Aaron grunted and rubbed his eyes. He'd give her a few minutes to get herself together and then take her back to her place.

Aaron trudged back to the living room. He felt like a jerk and he hadn't even done anything wrong. But there was a willing woman in his bed, and despite how much he hated his body for reacting, he was now rock-hard. He closed his eyes and took a deep breath. *Take Liz home. Come back, call Kacey, and get some very hot phone sex going on.*

Tonight was beyond messed up. Liz coming over unannounced, drunk no less, was not typical for her. Love made people do foolish things. How many women had he brushed off over the years? Had they done something similar? Would Kacey do the same if she found out a big part of his declaration had been to save the merger? He thought of her and that guy from the bar. Hugging, kissing, making love, all so that she could get over what Aaron had done.

"Damn," he muttered to himself and picked up the phone to call Kacey. He needed her to know he was thinking about her, and not because of the damn merger.

CHAPTER 23

"Today is my last day," Camila said with a heavy sigh and dropped the profits from the bar onto the desk next to Kacey.

Kacey looked up from balancing the books for the night to grin at her sister-in-law. "I know, your maternity leave starts tomorrow."

Camila rubbed her lower back and moaned. Kacey eyed Camila's rounded belly and wondered how she'd possibly managed to work tonight with all of that going on.

"I appreciate you helping out this long."

Camila continued to massage her lower back and lifted one shoulder. "I would have gone crazy if I'd sat at home for a moment longer than necessary. I could work at least two or three more weeks, but Reggie insists that I take my last month off. You know, so I can prepare to be the perfect stay-at-home mom," Camila said with an exaggerated eye roll.

"He's a worrier." Kacey picked up the money from the bar and added it to the rest of the money she was counting. "Don't worry, the baby will come and he'll get back to normal."

Camila looked doubtful, but waved a hand. "Well, he needs to be more worried about people tearing up our house than me working."

Kacey swung around. "What are you talking about? Did someone vandalize the house or something?"

"Not the outside. It had to have been during the cookout the other weekend."

"What happened?"

"Nothing really, just that someone was in the laundry room and spilled something red all between the washer and dryer."

Kacey's face burned, and she worked hard to keep her features neutral. "Say what?" Her voice rose with mock surprise.

"Yes!" Camila continued, not even noticing Kacey's embarrassment. "They tried to clean it up, but there is a red stain all down the side that won't go away. Who in the world would be in the laundry room anyway?"

Kacey shrugged and spun back to the stacks on money on the desk. She straightened the already organized piles. "That's crazy."

"I know. Anyway, Reggie doesn't seem to care."

Camila went on with her rant about people's lack of manners and Reggie's ability to care about her going out with friends more than someone spilling crap in the laundry room. Kacey's embarrassment slowly slipped away after realizing Camila didn't suspect either her or Aaron as the culprit for the red washer incident. Soon she tuned out Camila and Reggie's drama of the moment and got lost in memories of the way Aaron had made her spill the drink. She squirmed in her seat and smiled, then immediately her smile drifted away. How could they possibly make this work with him living in another state?

Does he really want us to work out?

It was the thought she'd tried to avoid pondering too long since he'd left the other day. On the one hand she didn't want to be the person who believed that a one-night stand could actually turn into a long-term relationship. But the long-neglected romantic Kacey, the one who'd dehydrated into nothing after having her heart broken so young by an older man, really wanted to believe.

Camila finally left and Monique came in. "The tables are clear and the floors are mopped. Are you done with putting together the deposit yet?"

Kacey zipped closed the bag of cash and receipts, then placed it in the safe. "Yep." She pushed the safe door closed and locked it. Jamelah had called in sick, so Kacey had jumped at the chance to fill in. Otherwise she'd be at home trying to study but really missing Aaron.

"Look, if you have a problem with me, then just tell me," Monique said.

Kacey stood and faced her sister. "What are you talking about?"

"You haven't spoken a word to me all night. Are you still pissed about the cookout thing?"

"No."

Monique crossed her arms and her long lashes fluttered. "Then what's the deal?"

"Did you tell Reggie about me and Aaron?"

Monique scowled. "No, Reggie came and asked me, point-blank, if you and Aaron were together."

"So you told him?"

"I told him that I didn't know what, if anything, was going on with you two. He suspected, and *you* gave it away when he came to your house."

"That sounds too easy."

"It wasn't hard for him to figure out. You two disappearing around the same time. Aaron saying he was with Tara but then we see her all by herself. You not answering your phone and just taking off for the night. It's almost like you wanted to get caught."

"I didn't want to get caught," Kacey said. She just hadn't thought spending the night with him in Chattanooga through. She'd hated the thought of him leaving so much that, when he'd asked, she'd just turned off her phone and gone with her feelings. No thought of her family or how they'd see things.

She ran a hand across her head and tugged on her ponytail. "I'm sorry for accusing you."

Monique propped her hip on the desk. "Why are you mad anyway? It worked out."

"No, it didn't."

Monique nodded. "Yes, it did. You were all giddy and falling in love over the guy. He admitted he felt the same, and now you two are together."

Obviously Reggie had decided to fill Monique in on the particulars. "I wasn't giddy and falling in love."

"Yes, you were. Yes, you are. Don't be embarrassed, he's feeling the same."

"I don't know if he really feels that way," Kacey blurted out. Monique raised a brow and Kacey slumped back into the chair behind the desk. "Everything was so rushed. I'll admit I didn't want to see him go. That a part of me hoped he was feeling something a little bit more and that he'd try to keep in touch."

"Like he does with all those other women he hooks up with," Monique said.

Kacey leaned back in the chair and stared at the ceiling. "Stupid, I know. I don't want to be one of the women he hooks up with when he rolls through a town. But I also didn't want that day to be the end. When he said all that stuff, I let myself believe him."

"Now?"

"Now I'm wondering if...if he only said it to save the deal with Reggie."

"If he did, he's a dick and doesn't deserve you or to go into business with Reggie."

Kacey chuckled. "I agree. But how do I know?"

"Ask him."

"As if he'd tell the truth."

"Then ask in a roundabout way. Keep your eyes open and rein in your heart. I know he's fine and obviously knows how to please you, but if you don't think you can trust him, you need to know sooner rather than later."

"You think I don't know that?" Kacey snapped then sucked in a breath. She already knew everything Monique said. Had gone through the same arguments with herself after Aaron left. The only problem was if she found out that were true, she'd once again have been played for a fool. Something she'd long thought she was smart enough to avoid.

Kacey shook her head and stood. "I've got studying to do tonight. I'm meeting with my professor tomorrow to go over my progress on my thesis."

"Are things getting better with her?"

"Yes. I got what I needed last weekend, but I was able to get a lot more done this week." Further proof that she met her goals much easier when there wasn't a guy around to distract her. Another reason to find out whether or not Aaron was only using her. If her last semester of school suffered because of a farce of a relationship, she'd never forgive herself.

"I'll open up tomorrow if you're going to be up late tonight," Monique said.

"Thanks." Kacey's cell phone rang. Frowning, she picked the phone up from the desk. "It's Aaron."

Monique checked her watch. "Nearly midnight and he's thinking about you. That's a good sign."

Kacey couldn't keep the smile from her face. "It could be." She answered the call and Monique slipped out.

"You do realize how late it is?" Kacey said.

"Yes, but I knew you'd be up. Are you studying?"

"No, closing up the restaurant."

"I thought you got nights off."

"I do, but I'm filling in for a sick employee."

"Well, that puts a damper on this call."

"Really, why?"

"I'd hoped for some hot and heavy phone sex to help me sleep."

Kacey's body heated. "You called for phone sex?"

"And to see how you were doing."

"Yeah, sure." Her smile was so big it hurt her cheeks.

"And to ask you out on a date."

"I think we've already been out on a date."

"This is an important date."

"What is it?"

"I'm coming up for Marcus's ball game next Thursday. I want you to ride back with me on Friday."

"You want me to come to South Carolina?"

"Yes, I'm inviting you to my sister's gender reveal party."

Kacey couldn't speak for a second. An invitation to meet the family wouldn't come from a guy who'd only blurted out he cared to save a deal. Would it?

"Why do you want me to meet your family?"

"Actually, my brothers are interested in meeting you. The woman who convinced me to tame my wild ways. They're dying to get a look at you."

"You told your brothers about me?"

"Yeah, why wouldn't I?"

He asked the question so easily, with a dash of confusion about why she wouldn't think he'd discuss her with his brothers. The dehydrated romantic Kacey plumped up with joy. Maybe he did mean what he'd said.

"Sure, I'd love to meet your family."

"Awesome," Aaron said with enthusiasm. "Now, how about that phone sex?"

"I'm at work, Aaron."

"The place is closed. Shut the office door and let's have some fun."

Kacey bit her lip and glanced around the office as if someone could overhear the conversation. She pushed the door closed and slid the lock.

"You've got five minutes."

His excited groan revved her up as she sat in the chair and slid her hand down her pants.

CHAPTER 24

Aaron leaned over with his hands on his knees. His heart bumped against his rib cage and he held his breath. Scanning the baseball field, he gave a signal to one of his boys on third base. He was glad he'd decided to come back. Not only because he got to see Kacey, but because he was back in time to coach the team. Just his presence alone gave the boys the extra bit of confidence they'd needed. At the top of the ninth, the game was tied at two and if they kept their opponent from scoring, he knew his boys would score and win.

The kid at bat for the opposing team, whom Aaron swore should be playing in a higher age group, shook out his shoulders and glowered at Marcus pitching. The kid had more strength than skill. But with a runner on first and second and with one out, if the tall kid hit a homerun, the game was over.

Marcus threw the ball. Tall Kid swung and hit the ball straight down the middle. One of Aaron's boys caught the ball and immediately pitched to Lonnie, whom Aaron had moved to the shortstop position. Lonnie easily outed the kid running from second to third before throwing to first. The first baseman caught the ball and outed the hitter. Aaron pumped his fist and clapped with the rest of the parents at the field. He waved to huddle his boys together.

"Great job, boys. Now all we've got to do is score to win this game." Aaron looked to Marcus. "Marcus, it's your turn. Their pitcher likes to throw high fastballs. Don't try to be a hero and knock one out of the park. If we're deliberate about what we're swinging at, we can win this."

"I got you, Coach," Marcus said.

Pride swelled in Aaron's chest as the rest of the boys looked to him for direction. He could blame his pride on being an avid baseball fan who had missed the game, but it was a lot more than that. He was proud of his team, his boys, and the progress they'd made.

The boys went back into the dugout, and Aaron gave Marcus another pat on the back. "You've got this, Marcus."

Marcus gave him a nod, then grinned and ran out to bat. Aaron once again held his breath and watched. Marcus did watch the first two pitches, both high fastballs that thankfully he didn't rush to hit. The third pitch was a beauty, Aaron sucked in a breath and hoped Marcus saw the sweet spot. When Marcus's bat hit the ball, Aaron couldn't hold back his yelp of pride. The ball flew over the heads of the opposing team and out of the park.

The smile on the kid's face as he ran the bases was priceless. The team rushed to Marcus as he came around home plate. It was all "great jobs" and "way to go" statements after the game. Aaron accepted the pats on the back and well wishes from the parents of the team members. He glanced over the heads in the crowd to where Kacey leaned against the fence. Her grin struck him straight in the chest.

I could love her.

The thought made the noise of the field fade away. His palms sweated and his heart pumped crazily. He wasn't good at love, and he damn sure couldn't *fall* in love. Loving her didn't mean he'd want to stay in Resilient; it only meant he'd see her cry when he realized he ultimately loved his life more than being the guy she wanted.

One of the boys bumped him and Aaron cleared his thoughts. He lifted his chin, motioning for her to come over.

"All right, boys," Aaron said, pushing thoughts of love aside and raising his hands and voice to talk over their excited voices. "Who wants some pizza?"

A round of "yeahs" was his reply. Kacey strolled up to his side, and he slipped his arm around her waist and pulled her against his side.

"Then let's head over to Luigi's for pizza and cannolis."

Kacey looked up at him. "Luigi's?"

"He's Marcus's uncle and he helped me with another surprise." She pursed her lips, and Aaron couldn't resist brushing his lips across hers. Kacey's arm around his waist tightened, and a spark flared in her eye. He did feel more at home than he'd ever felt in his life. But love?

She wore a cute green and blue maxi dress that he really wanted to get his hands beneath on the ride from the field to the restaurant. But several of the boys begged to ride with them. He, Kacey, Marcus, and Lonnie loaded up in her car.

He noticed she still hadn't changed her tires, but he decided not to get into that right now. They arrived a few minutes later at Luigi's, where a long table was set up for the boys.

"How did you know they would win?" Kacey asked.

"I'd love to say it was intuition, but I wasn't sure. I planned this pizza dinner for them win or lose."

Luigi came over and grinned. "Aaron, the boys tell me you all won. Great job! I hope you'll be in town for the rest of the season."

"I'll try to make as many games as I can," he said.

Aaron ordered enough pizza and cannolis for the boys and their parents. After everyone had eaten, Aaron stood and silenced the group.

"And now for the surprise." He looked at Luigi, who grinned. Luigi moved a piece of paper blocking a projector connected to a laptop.

Marcus jumped up and pointed at the screen. "Dad!"

Marcus's dad, dressed in army fatigues in a tent, waved. "Hey, Marcus! Hey, guys!"

Marcus looked at Aaron with a huge grin, then turned back to the screen. "We won!"

"That's great. I knew you guys would turn things around."

The team huddled around the webcam and started spouting off questions. Kacey grabbed Aaron's hand and squeezed. "How did you set that up?"

"I asked Marcus's grandmother for his dad's e-mail address and started chatting with him. I've been telling him what I've done with the boys coaching-wise, and then we worked it out for the webcam after the first game."

Her eyes went soft and loving. "You are wonderful."

He shrugged and tugged on the front of his shirt. "I know."

Kacey laughed and playfully hit his shoulder. He pulled her against him and kissed her, enjoying the pert fullness of her small breasts against him, and the fact that he could pull her into his arms without hesitation.

Someone cleared their throat. "Hold up, you two, there are kids around."

Aaron and Kacey broke apart to grin at Sabrina.

"Good to see you again, Aaron," Sabrina said.

Aaron nodded at Sabrina. "I'll be around."

"I know, now that things are all in the family."

Aaron glanced between Kacey and her mom. "What do you mean?"

"You and Kacey being together while you and Reggie are in business together. At first I didn't like the idea, but as long as you two are happy, it's fine with me. Plus, it keeps all the business in the family. That's the way I like things. Why do you think I only want my girls or my nieces handling the money at Momma's Kitchen?"

Kacey shook her head. "That's because no one else runs the place better than us. Not because we're family."

"You run it well *because* you're family," Sabrina said, then grinned at Kacey. "I'm guessing you'll be in late tomorrow."

"I'll be in at the normal time."

Sabrina hugged Aaron. He lifted the corner of his mouth in a half smile that he really didn't feel like giving. Sabrina's *keep it all in the family* speech was too damn close to what Kareem suspected.

Sabrina winked at Kacey before going over to speak with Luigi. The boys on the team were still telling Marcus's dad all of the details of the baseball game.

"Are you okay?" Kacey asked.

He stared into her eyes. No malice or sinister gleams reflected from her brown-eyed stare. He couldn't fall in love with her. Not completely. He hadn't started their "relationship" with the best of intentions. And though he knew his feelings went deeper than just a lingering desire to sleep with her again, what he didn't know was whether or not hers were just to keep things in the family.

"Just thinking," he said.

"About what?"

Marcus waved him over. Aaron lifted a hand in acknowledgment. "I'll tell you later."

● ● ●

After the party, Aaron followed Kacey back to her place. The place smelled like lemon cleaner and the living room lights reflected brightly off of the furniture. Kacey walked in front of him, and Aaron slipped his arm around her waist to pull her back against his front.

"Someone's been busy cleaning."

"And?"

"You didn't have to spruce up for me."

"I didn't. It was just time to clean."

He pushed her hair aside to kiss what he thought of as his spot, her cute birthmark, and brought up a hand to cup her breast. "Time to clean, huh?"

She spun in his arms, and Aaron lifted her by the waist. Long legs wrapped around him, and Aaron strode straight for the bedroom. He'd been hard and wanting her from the moment he left. Kacey tightened her legs around him, pressing his growing arousal directly on to the heat between her thighs. Who needed a bed? Aaron stopped midstride and pressed her against the wall.

Their mouths came together instantly, and he slipped into the sweet oblivion that came whenever they kissed. The oblivion that said *move ahead and take her to the bedroom and bury yourself deep. Forget everything except for the way you feel when you are in her arms.*

Plus, it keeps all the business in the family. Sabrina's voice rang through his mind.

Aaron lifted his head. "This 'all in the family' thing... That didn't have anything to do with us getting together, did it?"

Kacey's smile withered away, and a line formed between her brows. "You're thinking about this now?"

"I just want to know whether the idea of keeping things in the family ever came into play."

"Came into play how?"

"I don't know, maybe that had a slight influence in your feelings for me."

"What are you accusing me off, Aaron?" She pushed back and tried to squirm out of his arms, but he pressed his body forward.

"Look, you know I just say what I'm thinking instead of holding things back."

"Yes."

"And what your mom said made me think. Did you tell Reggie about us so that it could..."

He was surprised the heat in her glare didn't singe the hair off his head. "Are you accusing me of forcing us to be together?"

"I just want to know."

"I can't believe this." She squirmed and he finally let her go. "I don't want to force anything on you. I can't believe you'd think I try to coerce you into a relationship."

Aaron scrubbed his hands over his face. "I'm sorry." He dropped his hands. "I shouldn't have even brought it up. It's just that after your mom mentioned keeping things in the family, it made me think that you and me together does give your family an advantage on the running of the trucking business."

Her hands crossed straitjacket-tight over her chest. "How so?"

"Because I could love you, Kacey," he said in a rush. "And everyone knows that when a man falls in love, he does anything to make his woman happy."

He sucked in a breath. That was not supposed to come out yet. But hell, the words were true. He met her eyes and shrugged.

The anger melted from her face. "You could love me?"

"Yeah... I mean...we're easy."

"Easy?"

"I don't know how to explain it, but when I'm with you things feel easy. Like this could work."

"I didn't think you really wanted this." She pointed to his chest then hers. "I thought you only agreed because—"

"Because of what?"

"So you could keep the business. So you wouldn't ruin the deal."

He bit the inside of his cheek to keep from flinching. He'd be wrong to tell her that was part of the truth, wouldn't he?

"What kind of ass would I be to do that?"

The happiness in her face warmed his insides. Yes, he'd definitely be wrong to admit that he had felt that way. Why he'd agreed to their relationship didn't matter anyway. She was really feeling him and he was feeling her. There was no need to *not* see where things could eventually go with Kacey. They were great in bed together, he liked her more than any other woman, and he enjoyed being around her. He could at least try to make this work.

She wrapped her arms around his shoulders and pressed her body against his. "You would be the world's biggest ass if you had done that."

"The only thing that happened that day was your brother's accusations forced me to admit my feelings. I'm falling for you, Kacey, and I want to see where things lead."

She slid her hand into the front of his pants and wrapped her slim fingers around his growing arousal. "I know exactly where things are leading, Mr. Henderson."

Her hand squeezed him, and Aaron let the reasons for them getting together fade away. The only thing that mattered was going with what life threw his way, and right now life was throwing him a relationship that he wanted to try out.

CHAPTER 25

Normally when Kacey met a guy's family she would be so nervous she could barely breathe. Aaron didn't give her time for that. He wrapped his arm around her shoulder, gave her his relaxed grin, and strolled up to the front door of a beautiful two-story brick colonial where his sister and brother-in-law lived.

"I should be more nervous," Kacey said.

"They're going to love you," he said. "If my family is anything it's welcoming. My mother is going to gush over you as if you were one of her kids, my sister is going to drill you for every detail of our relationship, and my brothers will tease you. Except for Kareem; he still hasn't gotten the hang of teasing."

"He sounds like Reggie."

Aaron's brows drew together. "Maybe Reggie on steroids."

The front door swung open. A young woman with sparkling brown eyes and a yellow sleeveless blouse and white skirt answered. The bright smile on her face widened when she looked at Aaron, but a beat later she registered Kacey at his side and her happiness flickered to confusion.

"Aaron, hey," she said.

"Janiyah, hey," he said, mimicking her confused tone of voice. "You didn't think I'd skip the party, did you?"

She shook her head and the silky curtain of her hair swayed around her face. "No, never that." She met Kacey's eye with a tight smile. "I didn't know you were bringing a date. You never bring dates."

Kacey wasn't sure if his sister was happy or annoyed that he'd brought a date. The nervousness that hadn't popped up before slowly began to bubble in her stomach. "Sorry, I didn't mean to crash the party," Kacey said.

The slight frown on Janiyah's face instantly cleared, and she beamed at Kacey with the same carefree smile Aaron always wore. "I'm sorry, that was rude, wasn't it? Blame it on the pregnancy hormones. That's what Freddy does whenever I say things that sound kinda crazy."

Aaron chuckled. "What was the excuse before you were pregnant?"

Janiyah glared at him, but the humor still danced in her eyes. "You shut up, and come on in."

They entered the cool interior of the tastefully decorated house. The inside looked like it could have been in a home design magazine, except for randomly placed bright-colored paintings that didn't quite fit the décor.

"The house is beautiful."

Janiyah glanced over her shoulder and grinned at Kacey. "Thanks. The paintings are mine. I do them during wine and art night with my best friend, Liz." Janiyah raised her brow and looked to Aaron. "She's here today."

Aaron's steps stuttered. Kacey glanced his way, and he just gave her a quick smile that didn't quite reach his eyes.

"My bad," he said and tightened the arm around her shoulder.

They went through the entryway to a large living area filled with people. Janiyah clapped her hands. "Hey, everyone, Aaron is here."

There was a round of hellos before most went back to their various conversations. Kacey glanced around to try and see if she could tell who was family and who wasn't. Janiyah immediately crossed the room to a cute redhead wearing a soft pink sleeveless dress. Janiyah whispered something to the woman, and a slow blush crept up the woman's face. She turned wide eyes first on Kacey then to Aaron.

Aaron's gaze had followed Janiyah. He cleared his throat and scratched his jaw. "Hey, let me introduce you to my mom and dad."

Using his arm around her shoulder, Aaron ushered her to the other side of the room. Kacey fought the urge to turn back to Janiyah and the woman. Liz, she'd assume. And Liz and Aaron obviously had a history. Kacey didn't care as long as that history was dead and gone.

They approached a couple sitting at the bar overlooking the kitchen, the woman dressed in an emerald-green blouse and tan slacks and the man in a garnet golf shirt and black trousers.

"Mom, Dad, this is Kacey Randal," Aaron said, pride filling his voice. "Kacey, these are my parents, Loretta and Roger Henderson."

Kacey forgot about the redhead. His mother's heart-shaped face broke into a glorious grin, and she pulled Kacey into a big hug.

"Well, it's certainly nice to meet you," Loretta said. She pulled back and eyed Kacey from head to toe, her smile growing with each passing second.

"Nice meeting you, as well." Kacey's voice filled with her own delight at his mom's happy greeting.

Roger Henderson wasn't as enthusiastic with his greeting, but there was definite interest in his dark eyes. He shook her hand and gave it a quick squeeze before letting go. "Aaron didn't tell us he was bringing a friend."

"I don't have to tell you all everything," Aaron said, placing his hand at the small of her back.

"It's a very pleasant surprise," Roger said with a nod to Kacey. "Where are you from, Kacey?"

"Resilient, Tennessee. Aaron and I met while he was in town working on merging his business with my brother's."

Roger raised his brows, which also slightly drew together. "You're Reggie's sister? And he's okay with his sister dating his business partner?"

Aaron let out a heavy breath. "Dad, let's not have the 'don't mix business with pleasure' talk right now."

Roger nodded. "I just asked a relevant question."

Loretta placed her hand on Roger's chest. "All of our kids have found love in their own ways. I think we can let Aaron do the same."

Kacey swallowed hard and looked at Aaron. "They're going there."

He nodded. "I know." He pointed to the kitchen. "Hey, there's Fred. Let's go meet him."

He pulled her quickly away from his parents. "Sorry about that. I should have warned you, Dad is old-school and is probably itching to lecture me about the dangers of dating a business partner's sister. And my mom is champing at the bit to get me paired off like the rest of her kids. You'll get either a lecture on decision-making or questions about your dress size for a wedding if you talk to either of them."

Kacey chuckled and slipped her arm around his waist. She loved his sense of humor. Loved that he could quickly turn an awkward situation around. And this guy whom she loved so many things about had said he could fall in love with her. Which made admitting she was falling in love with him, too, so much easier.

She met his best friend, Janiyah's husband, Fred, who practically beamed with his happiness over the occasion. He hugged Aaron and also Kacey. She didn't miss the raised brow Fred threw Aaron's way when he thought she wasn't looking, but Aaron waved him off. She then met his two brothers. David was pleasant and filled Aaron in on stories of being a new dad. His wife, Sandra, joined them with a beautiful baby girl dressed in lavender. Aaron's brother Kareem watched her as if waiting for her to say or do something wrong. She didn't think the guy capable of relaxing or smiling until his girlfriend, Neecie, came over. Then he was all smiles and affection for her.

Janiyah rang a bell, and Fred joined her in front of the large stone fireplace. "Okay, everyone. Now's the moment we've all been waiting for." She pulled a white envelope out of her pocket and handed it to her husband. "Freddy, you tell them."

Fred kissed Janiyah's cheek, and she bounced on her feet like a schoolgirl. Kacey grinned at their happiness. She didn't know their story, how they'd gotten to be the ecstatic couple before her, but they appeared to be the epitome of happily-ever-after.

Aaron squeezed her hand. He grinned at his sister and friend, eagerly waiting for the announcement like everyone else. Kacey's heart trembled. Forget falling; she had already fallen.

"It's a boy." Fred's proud voice rang out over the hush of the room.

Aaron shouted "Whoo!" and clapped his hands with the rest of the people in the house. Janiyah and Fred were overrun by family and friends all kissing and wishing them well.

Kacey held back, letting the family and friends congratulate the couple. Aaron and Fred embraced and patted each other on the back. The redhead wrapped Janiyah in a hug, then they broke apart, squealed, and hugged again. Liz then moved on to hug Fred. When she faced Aaron, they had an awkward hesitation before they embraced. Aaron pulled back, but she leaned up and whispered something into his ear. Aaron's head lifted, and Kacey quickly looked away, pretending as if she wasn't watching. He lowered his head and then nodded at Liz.

"How about some music?" Aaron said. "I'll hook up my phone to the speakers and get this party really started."

He hurried over to Kacey and gave her a quick kiss on the cheek. "Fred has speakers wired through a port in the kitchen. I'll hook it up and be right over."

He went into the kitchen and pulled out his phone. Liz followed him. Kacey watched them from where she stood. Okay, so they needed to talk. Maybe to have closure or something like that. She wouldn't be upset, but when Aaron pulled Liz farther into the kitchen and out of Kacey's line of sight she frowned.

The music came on, a new pop song that had a loud bass beat. Kacey maneuvered through the people toward the kitchen so she could peek around the corner and see what was going on.

"Aaron, that's too loud," someone yelled over the music.

Kacey doubted he could hear. It was the perfect excuse to interrupt him and his possible ex. She entered the kitchen. Liz leaned in to say something to Aaron, who was looking at his phone. The loud music quickly lowered.

"I left my panties at your place." Liz's loud voice rang through the silence.

Kacey sucked in a breath. There was another gasp to Kacey's right. David's wife, Sandra. One quick glance around proved others had also heard the outburst. Liz's face turned as red as her hair. Aaron cringed, and Kacey fought not to turn and run like the rejected girl in a drama-filled teen movie.

• • •

"Looks like I interrupted you guys." Kacey's voice sounded carefree, but Aaron's blood turned ice-cold.

"Kacey, this isn't..."

Kacey lifted her hands and shrugged. "Isn't what it looks like? Sure." She took a step back. "I'll let you two finish."

She turned and strolled out of the kitchen. Liz groaned and pressed a hand to her temple. "This is a nightmare."

"Tell me about it." Aaron put down his phone and hurried out of the kitchen. He placed his hand on Kacey's arm to keep her from making it to the door. "Let's go somewhere and talk."

She tried to pull away, but he didn't let go. He knew she wasn't one to make a scene, and after one tug of her arm she didn't try to pull away again.

"Fine," she bit out.

The music started again, thankfully. He glanced toward the kitchen to see David come out and give him a head nod. He returned David's nod and took Kacey outside to the front porch. When she jerked her arm, this time he let her go.

"Are you sleeping with her?" she asked.

"No."

"But you were."

"We've slept together. Yes."

"When did she leave her panties at your place?"

Aaron ran his hand over his face. "Last weekend."

Kacey's jaw dropped. "Last weekend."

"She came over. She was drunk."

"So that makes it better."

He pointed to the door. "She was upset about a breakup. She started crying—"

"Let me guess, you comforted her with your *penis*!"

"No!" He took a deep breath. "We didn't have sex. I couldn't send her home in a cab like that. I was going to take her home, but she passed out. When I woke up the next morning, she'd already left."

Kacey crossed her arms. Her foot tapped rapidly on the porch. "Was she there when you called me?"

He wanted to lie, to make this conversation easier, but he wouldn't. There was nothing to hide. "Yes."

"So you had a woman in your bed and you called me for phone sex."

Aaron pulled his hair, then dropped his hands. "Kacey, it wasn't like that. I'm telling you everything that happened. Liz was seeing someone else. We hooked up a few times earlier, and she came over last weekend after she and her guy broke up."

"How convenient for you."

"Nothing happened. She wanted to apologize just now for showing up like that. I knew that wasn't like her. She was really upset, otherwise I wouldn't have let her stay."

Her face twisted with a condescending smirk. "Aren't you just a great friend?"

"Yes, I am a good friend. Liz is my sister's best friend. She was upset and I wanted to make sure she was okay. Would you rather I'd kicked her out, drunk and upset?"

"I'd rather not hear that your ex booty call was in your bed."

Aaron flinched and shifted from foot to foot. Why did this stuff always happen to him?

He closed the space between them, and took Kacey's rigid hands in his. He stared into her eyes. "I never lied about who I was or the things I've done. I could say she's lying. Or tell you that I sent her home the second she arrived drunk trying to hook up."

Kacey scoffed and tried to turn away. He tightened his grip. "But I won't lie to you. I get it, hearing a woman say she left her panties at my place sounds bad." Her scowl grew. "Really bad. But I promise you I wouldn't lie about this."

She glanced away, but not before he saw she was wavering. She shook her head. Aaron knew the argument that was coming next. The *I can't believe you* or the *why should I trust you* accusations. He didn't have good answers for why she should; he only knew he needed her to trust him. Needed her to know he only wanted her. He pulled her close and kissed her. For a second she relaxed, her body trembled, then she jerked away.

"You don't just kiss me and think that makes everything okay."

He grinned and lifted a shoulder. "It was worth a shot, and you liked it." He hoped humor helped; that usually got them out of awkward situations.

She glared and crossed her arms. He grinned wider and raised a brow. She rolled her eyes and shook her head.

"I can't *believe* I believe you." Her voice shook.

Aaron stopped smiling and took a step closer. "I'm telling the truth. Nothing happened with Liz."

She pressed a hand to her forehead and bit her lower lip. "Aaron, if you're lying to me..."

"I'm not. I meant everything I said to you before. I only want you, Kacey."

She massaged her temples. "You're making me crazy." She dropped her hands and glared at him. "I can't do this again. I can't be made a fool of."

"I won't make a fool out of you, Kacey." He took her hands and stared into her eyes. "Trust me."

Her brows drew together. He imagined all of the arguments going through her head. Then, by some miracle, she stiffly nodded. Relief flooded him, and the fear that he was losing her, not the deal, evaporated. Aaron relaxed and pulled Kacey into his arms, but when he kissed her, her body remained stiff.

CHAPTER 26

The blaring sound of a cell phone jerked Kacey awake the next morning. She blinked and glanced around the unfamiliar surroundings before remembering that she was in Aaron's apartment, in his bed. Aaron groaned behind her. He lifted the arm around her waist, rolled to the opposite side of the bed, and lifted his phone.

Aaron looked at the screen. "Umpf."

"Who is it?"

"Nothing," he said.

Kacey rolled onto her back. "Nothing" was not an answer. She got a quick glimpse of the screen before he blacked it out. Denise. She quickly rolled back over, anger rising in her chest as swiftly as the sun. Closing her eyes, Kacey took a deep breath and suppressed the emotion. She'd chosen to believe him last night. Chosen to trust that nothing had happened between him and Liz. That he was only being a good friend.

Monique's voice rang in her head. *Girl, are you crazy?*

Maybe she was, but Aaron had been nothing but honest with her. He made no apologies for his past lifestyle, but he'd said he was falling in love with her.

You've heard that before.

She pushed the thought aside. Aaron was not a predator looking to take advantage of a young girl. He wouldn't lie. She hoped.

His lean arm wrapped around her waist, and he pulled her back against him. The length of his morning erection fit snugly in the crease of her backside. Kacey wanted to wiggle her hips and press backward, but she felt off. They'd come to his place, talked, laughed, eventually had sex, but in the back of her mind she wondered whether that's how he'd been with Liz. Or someone else.

"Mmm, Kacey, I'm trying not to jump your bones first thing in the morning."

"Why?"

"Because I feel like every time I'm near you, I can't wait to sleep with you. I need to detox to make sure the voodoo you've put on me can fade from my system."

Kacey smirked; if anyone was under a spell it was her. "Voodoo?"

"Yes, you're wicked and addictive. And I'm not a guy who's good at self-control."

"Then let me help you." She slipped out of his arms and out of the bed.

"Where are you going?"

"To the bathroom, and then I'm taking a shower. Aren't we supposed to have brunch with your parents at nine?" Kacey pointed to the clock. "It's nearly eight."

Aaron glanced at the clock. "Damn, I'd much rather stay in bed with you all day."

Kacey gathered her hair at the back of her head, then used the band she'd taken out the night before to put it up into a messy ponytail. "Nope, you're not blaming my *voodoo* on you missing brunch at the parents'. I'm showering."

She walked across the room to his bathroom and felt his gaze on her naked body the entire time. Despite the off feeling, her nipples beaded and she wouldn't turn him away if he joined her in the shower. The bathroom was a decent size but, like the rest of the house, it was undecorated. Aaron's place reminded her a lot of the way Reggie had lived before he'd married Camila. Just the basics with no flare or personality. Maybe if she and Aaron stayed together, he'd let her add some touches to the place. It would be their second home when they were away from Resilient.

He doesn't live in Resilient. Monique's voice rang in her head again. *You'd be decorating his apartment where he offers shelter for beautiful, intoxicated female friends of the family.*

"Ugh." Kacey jerked back the shower curtain and turned on the spray. She jumped in before the water had the chance to warm up. She needed the cold hit to clear her brain.

She had to squelch the doubts in her head. Otherwise they'd grow and fester. But she did need answers. She would see what, if anything, she could get out of Janiyah during the brunch today. If Aaron was sleeping with her best friend, she doubted Janiyah would be happy about him bringing another woman around the following weekend. If she was anything like Monique or Ashlei, she would only rat out her brother if he was in the wrong.

After her shower, Kacey got out and grabbed a towel out of the closet in the bathroom. She went into the bedroom to get her toothbrush out of her bag. Aaron wasn't in the room.

She searched every pocket of her bag, but no toothbrush. "Damn. Aaron, do you have an extra toothbrush?" she called out.

He came back into the bedroom. He'd pulled on a pair of shorts and a T-shirt. "Check the drawer on the right of the sink," he said. "I have nothing to make coffee, but there's a place right across the street. I'll be right back, okay?"

"Sure." She went into the bathroom and opened the drawer. There were several extra toothbrushes in the drawer. Along with combs, bands to pull back hair, women's deodorant, perfume, even a pack of panty liners. She frowned. What the hell? Did he have that many women coming through that he had to provide a concierge drawer for their convenience?

Kacey grabbed one of the generic blue toothbrushes. With every second she brushed her teeth, the doubts she'd tried to push aside crept up. While deep down she wanted to believe Aaron, her mind wouldn't let go of the way she'd easily believed every lie Dewayne had told her.

Kacey finished brushing her teeth and slammed down the brush. She jerked the bathroom door open and went to the bed. Lowering to her knees, Kacey scanned beneath it. She didn't know what exactly she was looking for, but when her eyes landed on a pair of lacy pink panties, the tightness in her chest told her she'd found it.

I left my panties at your place. Liz's words rang in her head.

I promise nothing happened. Aaron's voice followed.

Kacey slid back from the bed. She took a deep breath and went over what she knew. He'd admitted Liz came over. Admitted that he let Liz sleep off her hangover in his bed. What he hadn't admitted was how her panties got off and under his bed.

Aaron's cell phone chimed on the nightstand, startling Kacey. She'd expected him to take the phone with him. Not caring that she was being the snooping girlfriend, she picked up his phone. Then clicked on the alert to read the text message from Denise.

GREAT! SEE YOU SOON.

Frowning, Kacey read the previous message from Aaron to her.

GOT YOUR VM. I'LL COME THROUGH.

That was where that particular conversation ended. There were no previous messages with Denise. She checked his other messages—mostly with his brothers and friend Fred. Nothing incriminating, until she saw a conversation with Tara. Flirty on Tara's end, not really on Aaron's, but why was he even answering? She went through his contact list. Mostly women with a range of area codes. Did he have a female in every state of the union?

She clicked on the voice-mail icon. He had visual voice message but she hit the Play button to hear the most recent message from Denise.

"*Hi, Aaron, it's Denise. I know this is out of the blue, but Rocky was on TV and it made me think of you. I hated that movie until we watched it together. Remember that night? Well, now I can't stop thinking about it. Which isn't good because I'm getting married in two months. I'll stop rambling and say, I need to see you. Tell me when you'll be in Texas again, okay? Call me.*"

The door to Aaron's apartment opened. Kacey dropped his phone back on the nightstand and jumped to her feet. Her heart raced and her mind whirled. She hurried over to her bag and searched through the contents for her clothes.

Aaron came into the room. "Hey, I got coffee and a few of those croissants. I know we're eating in a few at my parents', but I couldn't resist."

He crossed the room and wrapped his arm around her, coffee in one hand, a bag that had a delicious smell of pastries in the other. He kissed the side of her neck and she stiffened.

"What's wrong?"

She wanted to yell, scream, push him down. But she didn't do crazy outbursts. Honestly, she didn't know what her next move would be. She'd confront him, but not right now when she was fuming with anger. That would only turn into a drama-filled screaming match that accomplished nothing.

"Nothing," she said. "I'll eat in a second. You need to hurry up and get dressed if we're going to make it to your parents' on time."

Aaron slowly backed away from her. She felt his gaze boring into her back. She clutched her clothes against her chest. They stood there for what seemed like hours. She was too confused to face him. She was sure he wondered what had made her so stiff.

"Okay," he said a second later. "I'll get dressed."

He put the coffee and the bag on the nightstand. Kacey glanced over her shoulder. Aaron frowned down at his cell phone. He glanced up at her and she turned back to her bag. Guilt and anger made her cheeks hot. He had to know she'd gone through it. She waited for him to ask, but a second later the bathroom door opened and closed.

• • •

Laughter and conversation greeted Kacey and Aaron's arrival—a complete contrast to the tension that had hovered between her and Aaron on the ride over. He hadn't said anything or asked her what was wrong while they'd silently gotten dressed and driven over. He'd played as if nothing was wrong by holding her hand and giving her his easygoing smile when they made eye contact. But she knew, deep down she knew, he knew she'd seen the texts.

Kacey sat outside by the pool with Janiyah and Sandra. Aaron and his brothers were huddled around the grill. Roger and Loretta sat with their feet in the pool, and Neecie had volunteered to change the baby's diaper inside, giving Sandra a break.

"Kacey, I need to apologize again," Janiyah blurted out.

"For what?"

Janiyah sighed. "For Liz. Well, more for her outburst. She's mortified that everyone heard. She was in a really bad mood the other weekend, and I thought it would help if she and Aaron...you know." Janiyah shrugged. "But nothing happened and she's so embarrassed that now the entire family knows she tried to seduce Aaron in a drunken attempt to get back at her ex."

Kacey took a deep breath. *Still doesn't explain the underwear.* "Are you sure nothing happened?" Kacey asked. "She left her underwear under his bed."

Sandra cleared her throat and shifted on the chair. Janiyah glanced between the two. "I know that sounds bad, but I trust Liz. And I know Aaron. He's never been a straight-up dog. He wouldn't sleep with her if you two are officially together."

Kacey smiled at Janiyah, whose eyes were bright with sincerity. Kacey hoped Janiyah's trust in her brother wasn't misplaced. "Thank you, Janiyah."

Sandra reached over and patted Kacey's hand. "Aaron is a good guy, and he reminds me a lot of David when we first met back in college. I think he's really into you, but he is still trying to figure out how to come to terms with that. You just trust your instincts and let him know when he steps out of line. Honesty is the easiest route."

Kacey glanced at the guys, all in some deep discussion by the grill. The music playing in the background kept her from hearing what they said. Aaron glanced up her way, and the corner of his mouth lifted in a smile. She smiled back. Trust her instincts. Right now her instincts said to hold on to her heart.

The guys finished grilling, and everyone sat around the long glass patio table by the pool to eat. Conversation flowed around baby preparations and wedding plans for Kareem and his fiancée, Neecie. They'd set a wedding date for the following year. The glow on Loretta's face, along with the hopeful looks she threw Kacey and Aaron's way, made Kacey uncomfortable. She and Aaron had barely made it a few weeks, no way could she guarantee a full year.

Loretta looked at Aaron. "Are you in town for a while, Aaron, or are you staying in Resilient after you take Kacey back?"

Aaron leaned back in his chair and took a sip of his iced tea. "I'll stay in Resilient for a few days, but I've got to make a delivery to Texas."

Kacey stopped chewing the grilled zucchini and her stomach knotted.

Roger leaned his head to the side. "Why do you have to deliver? Now that you and Reggie have consolidated, you've got plenty of drivers. It's time to settle down and run the business instead of gallivanting across the country, son."

Aaron's answer to his dad's scolding was his normal carefree grin. "It's not gallivanting. I'll still take deliveries every once in a while. But I'm going to check in on a friend in Texas who I haven't seen in a while."

Three sets of eyes zeroed in on her: David's, Kareem's, and Fred's. Now she knew what they'd discussed around the grill.

Instead of asking if she'd checked his cell phone, he'd gone to the guys in his family. Kacey swallowed the lump of zucchini, grabbed her glass of tea, and gulped the drink down. Fine, they wanted to see if she'd react, she'd give them a reaction.

"Is the friend Denise?" Kacey asked.

Aaron slowly twisted in his chair and stared into her eyes. "How do you know about Denise?" The false surprise in his voice made her grit her teeth.

"You know how I know. I listened to her voice message. I saw you reply that you were going to see her."

"So you went through my phone?"

"Yes."

He scoffed and shook his head. "I can't believe this."

"Don't try to turn this on me. Why are you texting Tara?"

"Those texts don't mean anything."

"That's what you keep saying, Aaron. The texts don't mean anything. You just have friends who invite you to Hawaii for a week. Women come over when they're upset and *leave underwear at your place.* Everything is no big deal."

"I'm with you. They're just friends. Friends I knew for a long time before we got together. I'm supposed to just ignore them?"

Sandra grunted. "Yes."

Kacey looked to Sandra, who narrowed her eyes at Aaron. David placed a hand on her arm. "Let's stay out of Aaron's business."

Sandra pointed to Aaron. "You should be giving him advice on how not to make mistakes with women."

David closed his eyes and shook his head. "Sandra, let's not go there."

Janiyah sat up. "Well, I'm going there. I stood up for you over what happened with Liz, but I can't if you're going to Texas to see someone else."

Aaron frowned at Janiyah. "Why are you butting in?"

Janiyah's look said she had every right to butt in. "Because I thought you and Liz were becoming serious. Instead you're seeing Kacey, and now you're going off to see that girl you were crazy about a few years ago."

Kacey turned to Aaron. "You were crazy about her?"

Aaron shook his head. "She's just a friend."

Kacey narrowed her eyes. "They're all just friends."

Kareem grunted. "Everyone quit giving Aaron a hard time. He's not engaged to any of these women." He looked at Kacey. "I mean no harm to you, but my brother doesn't owe you anything. You've been together for what, a few weeks?"

Neecie hit Kareem's shoulder. "I can't believe you just said that."

"It's the truth," Kareem said.

Janiyah sucked her teeth. "You guys are disgusting." Fred tried to take her hand, but she shook him off. "You too. I bet you're all cheering Aaron on to be a big ol' player."

The couples started their own arguments around the table. The baby started crying, adding to the various raised voices.

Roger stood. "That's enough!"

Everyone fell silent. Even the baby stopped crying. He glared at each one of his kids. "Aaron's fight with Kacey is not a reason to start problems in your own relationships. Janiyah, David, Kareem, you all had your own issues before you worked things out. Aaron's doing the same now. Stay out of his business."

Roger's hard stare landed on Aaron. "Now, you two need to work this thing out between yourselves."

Aaron watched Kacey and she stared at her plate. She glanced at him. "Why are you going to see her?"

He let out a deep breath; he looked tired of the entire conversation, and that hurt more than the panties at his place. "Because I have to know if this thing I feel for you is real."

"Why wouldn't it be? You said you never felt this way before."

"I lied," he said. Kacey sucked in a breath, and Aaron rubbed a hand over the coils on his head. "I felt this way about Denise, but then I broke up with her and never went back. I was about to do the same thing with you, but..."

Kacey frowned. "But what?"

He lifted his chin. "I didn't want Reggie to break the merger."

The pain in Kacey's chest was terrible. A Mack truck of pain that slammed into her heart and turned the muscle into roadkill. Tears sliced the backs of her eyes. "You said all of that just to save the deal."

For once, his good-natured smile was missing. "I meant what I said about my feelings for you. But keeping the deal alive was a part of it."

Kacey blinked rapidly, trying to keep the tears from falling, but one escaped. She hastily wiped it away and slid her chair back from the table. "Well, good thing you finally signed the papers and the merger falling through is not an issue anymore."

She stood and Aaron jumped up with her. "Kacey, that wasn't the only reason. I do care about you. I just don't know if I'm ready to do the wife and family thing."

"Who's asking you to do the wife and kid thing, Aaron? I'm not ready for that either. I've got school to finish and the second restaurant to open. But I still took the chance on believing we might actually work. Stop using having a family one day as an excuse to avoid a real relationship. You either want to be with someone or you don't. That's all there is. No major switch clicks, or force of nature shifts the universe. It's just that simple, and you've proven that you really don't want to be with me."

She glanced around at his family. "I'm sorry this happened today. You all have been great." She looked at Aaron. "If you'll take me back to your place, I'll get my stuff and rent a car to take home."

The anguish on his face almost mirrored what she felt inside. But she couldn't believe it was anything more than a show put on for his family. "You don't have to do that. I can take you home."

Kacey shook her head. "Sorry, but I don't want to be near you any longer than necessary."

CHAPTER 27

Aaron took Kacey to his place to get her stuff and then to the car rental office. He didn't apologize again, because the words seemed too simple for the amount of pain he saw in her eyes. He didn't say much of anything because he didn't know what to say. Knowing how much he'd hurt her caused him more agony than he expected. He didn't want her to leave, didn't want this to be the end of their relationship. Didn't want to know that when he saw her in the future, the friendly atmosphere between them wouldn't be there.

He wanted her in his life, but the discomfort with the idea of one day becoming the old married man kept him from begging her to stay.

"I won't ruin your and Reggie's business deal over this," she'd said after the rental agent put the keys in her hand. "I'll tell him I broke up with you because I wasn't in love with you."

She hadn't met his eye when she said the last part. Aaron had a sneaking suspicion she might love him, which only made him hurt worse.

"Kacey, we can get through this. We can try."

She shook her heard. "No, I don't want to try. And you're not ready to really try, Aaron. Not yet."

She turned away, got in the rental car, and drove away. Aaron stood in the lot for several minutes after wondering what his next step would be, only to end up back at his parents' house.

His mom was sitting in the den reading a magazine. She glanced up at him when he came in and gave him a sympathetic smile. "He's in the sunroom."

Aaron walked over and kissed his mom's cheek. "Thanks, Mom."

He squeezed her shoulder and then went to the sunroom, where Roger sat staring out at the now empty back porch.

"I kind of ruined brunch, huh?" Aaron said, trying to sound lighthearted.

"I haven't had a tantrum from one of my kids in a while," Roger said. "I guess this one was overdue."

Aaron chuckled and sat in the chair next to Roger. "I wouldn't call that a tantrum."

"I would. All my kids arguing with their spouses over nothing. That's a tantrum."

They were silent for several minutes. Aaron leaned forward resting his arms on his knees, not sure of the exact question he wanted to ask, but knowing he needed advice. That he needed the epiphany Kacey said didn't happen. Was she the one, or not?

"I don't know what to do about Kacey," Aaron said.

"Go see Denise," Roger replied.

Aaron sat up and turned to his dad. "I didn't expect that."

"What did you expect?"

"That you'd tell me Kacey is great. That I should do right by her and that being with her is the right thing."

Roger shrugged. "Okay, I can tell you all of that, but then it's me telling you to settle down with her. You need to decide that for yourself."

"How is seeing Denise going to help?"

"Because Denise was the first woman you really cared about. You need to know if all of that is gone before you settle down with anyone else."

"Why can't I just...I don't know, see a woman and know that's who I want to be with? It happened with Fred, David, even Kareem. It should be that simple."

Roger chuckled and shook his head. "It's never that simple, Aaron. You haven't been able to sit still your entire life. You were always looking for the next thing to do. The next toy to play with. I couldn't understand it, but you found a way to channel that energy into creating a business. And for that I'm proud of you. But you treat women the same."

"I'm not some womanizer, Dad," Aaron said.

"You're not the guy out there looking to take advantage of women, but you're the guy who won't settle down and who also won't let go." Roger looked at Aaron. "Why do you have all the numbers of your ex-girlfriends in your phone? Why do you still text them?"

Aaron shrugged. "We're friends."

"Son, you're holding on without committing. It was the same way when you were younger. You didn't want the things you were tired of, but you didn't want me to throw them away either. Sometimes you have to let go of the old to make room for the new."

Aaron slumped in the chair and rubbed the bridge of his nose. He was getting a headache. "Were you happy, Dad? I mean, really happy, being married and having kids."

"Why would you think I wasn't?"

Aaron dropped his hand and said something he'd never dared to before. "Because of the way you flirted with other women."

Roger sat up in his chair. Aaron shifted and held up a hand. "Wait, before you get mad, I know you never cheated on Mom.

But I saw the way you were with women. I know part of it was being a salesman, but you seemed to turn on a little extra charm with women. And I even saw you check out a few."

"What are you trying to say, Aaron?" Roger asked, his voice heavy with a warning that Aaron was going too far.

"What I'm saying is that you're the most straight-and-narrow guy I know. You're more rigid than I'd like, and the only time that wavered was when you had to deal with beautiful women."

"Looking and enjoying the attention of a beautiful woman is one thing. I would never be unfaithful to your mother."

"How did you know that? How did you know that harmless flirting wouldn't turn into a one-night stand?" Aaron sat up suddenly and tapped his chest. "That's where flirting goes for me."

"I love your mother, Aaron. No matter how much I might flirt, those women weren't worth breaking up my family over. No woman, no matter how long I may have known her, is worth the chance that I might lose your mother."

Aaron nodded and sat back in his chair. He let his dad's words sink in. "It sounds like losing a bit of freedom."

"Maybe it is. That's why some people are forever single. Marriage isn't for everyone. Long-term relationships aren't for some people."

"I still want to be with Kacey."

Roger stood and placed a hand on Aaron's shoulder. "Go see Denise. Then figure out if giving up your ties to the women in your past are worth a lifetime with her."

CHAPTER 28

"I know that look," Monique said when Kacey came in to help with the lunch shift.

She'd just met with her professor and spent the rest of the morning in the campus library working on her thesis project. She couldn't work at home. Being alone gave her too much time to think of Aaron and the debacle of the previous weekend.

"What look?" Kacey dumped her bag on the end of the bar and sat on one of the stools.

"Your *'the professor's ripped me a new one'* look." Monique poured a shot of tequila and slid it across the bar to Kacey.

"It wasn't that bad today." Kacey sipped from the shot.

"Hmm...you sipped instead of telling me to quit wasting the liquor. So that must be your *'I'm still hurt over Aaron'* look."

Kacey scoffed. "I'm not thinking of him." She got up, grabbed her bag, and headed for the kitchen.

"Oh yes, you are," Monique's voice followed.

Kacey pointed to the door. "You can't just leave the bar unattended."

Monique looked to Jamelah, who was talking to one of the cooks. "Hey, Jamelah, watch the bar for me for a second."

Jamelah nodded. "Sure."

Kacey rolled her eyes and went into the office, Monique fast on her heels. "What did he really do?"

"Nothing. I told you, once I went to South Carolina and met his family, I realized I'd rushed into things with him. That's all."

"No, that's what you told Reggie so he wouldn't go down there and break Aaron's arms and legs before withdrawing on a legally binding contract." Monique sat on the edge of the desk. "Tell me what he really did."

Kacey sighed and leaned back in the chair. She had kept this pain to herself too long. Monique might have her secrets, but Kacey could no longer keep her thoughts a secret. "Being with me was about saving the deal."

"He lied."

"He claims he meant what he said, but saving the deal was also a part of it. But that's not the worst." She told Monique about what happened with Liz, the texts, and the phone calls.

"That dog!"

"Should I really be surprised? I mean, we both know when he came in that night that he was looking for a hookup. We heard the stories from Reggie. I knew what I was walking into, and still I fell..." Her words trailed off. She turned away from Monique, and the pain of what she couldn't admit pressed inside her chest.

She had fallen in love. That was why this hurt so much. Why his admission and the jealousy over the women he kept in contact with made her so crazy. She was no smarter than she'd been at seventeen—still falling for a smooth man's lies.

"Kacey, I'm sorry. Aaron is a dick and you're better off without him. I have half a mind to go tell Reggie so that he *can* go break his legs."

"No, we are not telling Reggie. This isn't all Aaron's fault. I saw the warning signs and I chose to ignore them. Besides, despite his personal flaws, he's a good businessman. He and Reggie working together will help them both."

"Yeah, but you'll still have to see him every once in a while. And how will you do that without wanting to kill him?"

"Because he's not worth it. My focus is back on Momma's Kitchen, finishing my degree, and opening the second restaurant. To hell with Aaron Henderson. The best revenge is to do better and move on."

"I still think slashing his tires is pretty good revenge."

"But not worth it." Kacey stood. "I'm pissed, but I'll get over him. Let's just move on and worry about the lunch shift."

Monique sighed and stood. "Wait, I need to tell you something. And after hearing what happened with Aaron, I kind of hate to."

Kacey slowly sat back down. "Why?"

"Because I'm happy about the news, but you may not be." Monique twisted her hands before her.

Oh, God, please don't let this be about Julio. "Just tell me."

Monique took a deep breath, then pulled a sheet of paper out of her apron and handed it to Kacey. "I'm going to culinary school."

If Kacey hadn't been sitting down, she would have fallen over. She scanned the paper, which welcomed Monique to the culinary program at Maryland's School of the Arts, then looked back at her sister.

"Culinary school? In Maryland?"

Monique grinned. "I know, can you believe it?"

"Why didn't you tell me you applied?"

"You know. What if I didn't get in? I didn't want you all to think I was a fool for trying."

"Monique, I'd never think you were a fool."

"Well, you're learning the business side to make the second restaurant a success. I figured I'd learn more about the culinary side to make the Chattanooga restaurant stand apart. I'm good in the kitchen, but I can be a lot better."

"Does Momma know?"

Monique shook her head so hard her long hair swung from side to side. "Not yet. I wanted to tell you first."

"Is this in any way related to those secret phone calls?"

Monique took a deep breath and shook her head. "Yes and no. I was talking to Julio, but only because I remembered him mentioning a cousin in culinary school. He gave me his cousin's number and we've been talking."

Kacey didn't like that Monique had gone to Julio instead of her, but she wasn't in any position to give advice. "Why Maryland?"

"I need to get out of Resilient." Monique held up her hand. "Not forever, mind you, but just for a while. I can go to Maryland, visit D.C. while I'm there. It'll be good. But I hate leaving knowing you're heartbroken."

Kacey jumped up and hugged her sister. "Go and do a great job." She pulled back. "My heart will heal, and this opportunity is more important."

Monique grinned, revealing her deep dimples. "I'm so excited. Thank you for understanding."

Kacey and Monique talked about the school and her ideas for the menu at Momma's Kitchen. She'd never asked Monique for many of her thoughts about running the place. She'd underestimated her sister, something she wouldn't do again.

CHAPTER 29

Aaron had been in Tyler, Texas, a few times since he'd broken up with Denise, but he'd never visited any of the places they'd frequented. As he waited at the bar in the Mexican restaurant they used to go to, he wasn't sure why he'd avoided those places. He felt no sense of loss or remorse being there.

"Aaron?" Denise's voice came from behind.

Aaron put down the beer he'd been nursing and spun on the bar stool. She hadn't changed much. Average height, clear light brown skin, and bright whiskey-colored eyes. Her hair was shorter, framing her face in a small bob instead of the shoulder-length style she'd worn before, and her curvaceous build was even more pronounced by the dark pink jumpsuit.

"Hey, Denise." He stood to greet her. He held out his hand and her face twisted with confusion, so he opened his arms and gave her a hug, which she quickly backed out of.

They stood staring at each other for a second, an awkward silence building despite the mariachi music and conversations going on in the background.

"I saved you a seat." Aaron pointed to the stool next to his.

"Thanks," she said.

He stood back while she slipped into her seat. Her perfume was the same; he used to love lying beside her and breathing in the apple-scented body spray she favored. For the longest time after they split, the smell of apples would get him aroused in a second. Now his body didn't react.

He sat on his stool and gave her his easygoing smile. "Want a beer?"

She nodded and glanced around the place. "Sure."

He motioned to the bartender and ordered a beer for her. There was another long silence while Aaron glanced at the televisions behind the bar. What the hell was he doing here?

"Getting married, huh?" Aaron asked after he couldn't take the silence much longer.

Denise nodded and grabbed the beer the bartender set before her. She lifted it to her mouth and took a sip.

Aaron raised a brow and slowly shook his head. "Are you excited?"

"I am. Anthony is a great guy. I haven't felt this way about anyone since..." She sipped her beer and took a deep breath. "I haven't felt this way about anyone since you."

And that was why he was here. He and Denise were both going through the same thing. "What's different this time?"

"Nothing's different. He's funny, he's smart and successful. We get along well together. I love him. Just like I loved you."

"Then why did you want to see me?"

"Because, Aaron, it's *just* like it was when we were together, but then we just ended abruptly. One day we were happy. The next day you were giving me some excuse about needing space right before you left town."

Aaron turned on the stool to look Denise in the eye. "Did you ask me here for revenge?"

She shook her head. "No, I asked you here because I had to see you. I don't know how to explain it, but the closer I get to my wedding day, the more I think about you. And I wonder..."

She frowned and lowered her eyes. Aaron hesitated before placing his hand on hers. "If it was real or just your imagination."

She lifted her eyes and nodded. "If I imagined everything that happened between us, how will I know if I'm imagining the same thing now? Am I supposed to marry Anthony, or is this just a big delusion and one day I'll wake up and he'll be ready to walk out the door?"

Her outburst made Aaron flinch. He drew his hand back and ran it over his hair. "Denise, don't think like that. I'm sure this guy is great and things will be wonderful."

"Don't tell me what everyone else is telling me. I know a part of this is cold feet, but another part is thinking about how I was so sure we were really falling in love and then you walked out."

"I didn't walk out. I choked," he blurted.

Denise sat up and tilted her head to the side. "You what?"

"I choked. It was real, Denise. I felt everything you felt. I started thinking about marriage and kids and maybe growing old with someone."

"Then what happened? You broke things off as if it was no big deal."

"I wanted to be with you, but I wanted to be single more. I knew that no matter what I felt for you, I wasn't really ready to just tie myself to one person. I'm not a cheater, or a liar, so I broke things off before I ended up doing ether one of those."

"Did you love me?"

"Yeah, I think I did. I just didn't love you enough."

A line formed between her brow and she looked away. Aaron turned back to the television.

"Why did you agree to come see me, Aaron?"

"For the same reason you needed to see me. There's someone new...and I'm feeling some of the same things I felt with you."

"Wow. What's her name?"

"Kacey. Her family owns this restaurant in Tennessee, and she's in graduate school getting her MBA so that she can open a second restaurant and hopefully start a franchise. She works hard, too hard actually, but she can let loose sometimes. She's fun."

"You love her?"

In that second Aaron, sitting there talking to a woman he didn't really want to be with, knew he loved Kacey. He'd probably loved her when he'd made the declaration to Reggie, but he had used the excuse of the business to ignore the emotion.

"Yeah, I do."

"It sounds like things are going well for you two."

"Not really. We broke up last week."

Denise scoffed and rolled her eyes. "Why am I not surprised? Are you determined to end up alone? Or did someone break your heart before and now you're afraid of commitment?"

"I'm not determined to be alone and no one broke my heart. I'm just not going to settle down before I'm ready."

"When will you be ready, Aaron?"

"In the future."

"The future isn't promised to us. Anything can happen to anyone on any day of the week. You let me slip away—are you really ready to do that with someone else you love?"

He frowned at her disgusted tone. "Why are you so angry?"

"Because there's another woman out there going through the same pain you put me through for no reason. There's no telling how many others fell in love with you and you left. Let me guess, you've still got 'friends' all over the country that you call and text. There are still women who drop by your apartment just to see how things are going. You're nothing but a selfish little boy." She jumped up from the stool. "I hope you stay alone!"

She turned and marched out of the restaurant. Aaron pulled out his wallet and tossed some money on the bar before hurrying after her. The bright sunlight temporarily blinded him after the dim interior of the restaurant. He glanced left then right, where Denise continued her angry retreat.

"Denise, hey, wait up." He jogged and caught up with her.

She spun to face him. "What?"

"I'm sorry." She scoffed and tried to turn. Aaron placed a hand on her arm to stop her. "No, I'm really sorry. I know the words don't mean much, and there really is no way for me to make things up to you. We were great together, and we would have been happy, but we both know it wouldn't have been for long. I wasn't ready—you know I wasn't."

Her stiff shoulders relaxed. "I know. I get that, believe me, I do. But to hear that you're still the same, that after all these years you haven't changed... It's kind of sad, Aaron."

"Marriage isn't for everyone."

"No, it's not. But love is rare and hard to come by. I wasn't sure if it would happen for me again after we broke up, but it did. And honestly, it's actually so much better than before. I don't want to run the risk of losing that because there *may* be someone out there that I still might want to sleep with one day. So ask yourself, is losing Kacey worth that?"

He took a step back. No, it wasn't. Keeping in contact with his ex-girlfriends wasn't worth never talking to Kacey again. Sleeping with Liz or any other woman who crossed his path wasn't worth never holding Kacey in his arms again. Having the freedom to visit any place he wanted, or take up any offer to spend a weekend at a friend's beachside condo, wasn't worth never again being allowed through the front door of Kacey's home.

Denise smiled and squeezed his arm. "I didn't think so." She lifted on her toes and pressed a kiss to his cheek. "You take care of yourself, Aaron."

He nodded. "You, too. And congratulations. Anthony is a lucky man."

"Thank you." She turned and walked away.

Aaron pulled his cell phone out of his back pocket. His hands trembled slightly, and he shook them out. He took a deep breath trying to calm his racing heart. What in the world could he possibly say, over the phone no less, that would make her take him back? Nothing. He'd have to show up. Have to prove that he was really ready for this.

Are you really ready?

There it was—the voice that made him bolt after a few weeks with one woman. He ignored it, and thought about what Kacey had said. You're never ready, you just make the step.

He dialed her number. "Pick up, pick up, pick up," he chanted during the ring. He was about to give up hope when she finally answered.

"What?"

Okay, that wasn't promising, but at least she had picked up. "I love you."

"Seriously? You're calling me with this? Save it, Aaron. I didn't tell Reggie anything and you don't have to worry about him trying to break the contract."

"I don't care about the deal. I don't care about the contract. I just want us to try to work things out."

"Whatever. Where are you? Please don't tell me you've had a few drinks and your guilty conscience made you call."

"This is not my guilty conscience, and I'm far from drunk. I'm in Texas. I just saw Denise."

"And that's supposed to make me believe you."

"Yes. Seeing her made me realize I messed up a good thing."

"Not helping, Aaron."

He gripped his hair and paced along the street. "I don't want to mess up again."

"So, I'm your consolation prize because Denise is getting married and you need to avoid the same thing happening with me?"

"No...yes, in a way, but not in the way you're twisting things."

"Sure. 'Bye, Aaron."

"Wait, Kacey, dammit! Girl, I'm crazy about you. I don't want Denise or any other woman. I was way too immature to settle down with Denise, and we both know that. But I'm not that guy anymore. I'm the guy who knows that being with you is more important than being with any other woman out there."

No angry comeback. There was a lot of noise in the background, but he couldn't make out what it was.

"Where are you?" he asked.

"I'm driving home from school."

"What's that noise?"

"It's storming."

"And you're talking to me on the phone. Look, call me when you get home. Let's talk. Better yet, I'll come to you."

"No, no, no, don't. I'm not going to go there with you. I won't let you lure me back in only for you to break my heart later. Or turn into another Brenda, staying with a man who'll force me to put up with his mistakes." Her voice raised with each word. "I'm not getting played by you again."

"I'm not going to play you. Kacey, I love you."

"Stop it, Aaron. Just stop right now, okay? We're over, and we both can just mo—"

Her words abruptly ended. The sickening sound of metal and glass crushing and shattering replaced her words. Aaron's stomach dropped to his knees. His suddenly cold fingers gripped the phone.

"Kacey?" His voice trembled.

Nothing. Aaron's entire body shook. He looked around frantically, refusing to accept what he had just heard.

"Kacey, baby, talk to me." Silence. "Kacey, please, please, Kacey, tell me you're okay."

Silence.

Aaron ran down the street toward his truck. "Kacey!" People stopped and stared. Others got out of his way. The silence on the other end of the phone made Aaron's stomach heave.

The future isn't promised. Anything can happen to anyone on any day of the week.

Denise's prophetic words rang in Aaron's head, bringing panic to his already overwhelmed heart. This couldn't happen. He couldn't lose her. He gripped the phone; tears burned his eyes. "Kacey!"

CHAPTER 30

The door to the hospital room opened, but Kacey kept her eyes closed. Nurses had been coming in checking her vitals almost every hour since they had admitted her the night before. *Thank you, concussion.* The attending physician did say that she would probably go home today. But the sun had barely come up, and Kacey was pretty sure she wouldn't get out of this place until well after noon.

"My vitals haven't changed in an hour. My arm is still broken, and my body still aches but not enough for me to take more pain medicine," Kacey said, even though she knew hoping the nurse would leave without taking her temperature again was a waste of a good wish.

The footsteps didn't come closer. "Thank God, you're alive." Aaron's voice, tired and hopeful, came from the direction of the door.

Kacey's heart raced, and she jerked her eyes open. No, the concussion was not making her hallucinate. He was definitely standing at the door. His blue cotton T-shirt and jeans were wrinkled. Red rimmed his normally carefree eyes, and the curls on his head were askew.

"How did you get here?"

"I drove all night." He rushed across the room to the bed. With a shaky hand he reached for her, then pulled back. "Kacey, I thought... When I heard the sounds through the phone, I thought you'd..." His voice cracked and his eyes turned glossy.

He drove all night? Was he seriously about to cry, over her? Her heart thumped behind her bruised ribs. Warmth spread through her body, something that hadn't happened since she'd been admitted, no matter how many blankets she requested from the nurse. "I'm fine. Thank you for calling Reggie."

When her family was at the hospital the night before, Reggie told her Aaron had called, frantic and half-crazy, to say he'd overheard the accident. The ambulance was already on the scene when Reggie and Camila traced Kacey's route from the house to the school, but they were still worried. Kacey had to pretend the drugs had knocked her out in order to get her family to leave after she was admitted.

"Was it your tires?" Aaron asked. "I bet it was the tires. I told you to change them."

"You're seriously going to lecture me right now?"

"I'm sorry, I just—" He ran a hand through his hair, messing his curly fro up even more. "Everything ran through my head on the way here. Every mile I cursed myself for not changing those tires my damn self."

"It wasn't the tires. Someone ran the red light and hit my passenger side."

His body relaxed. "Thank goodness."

"You're happy someone hit me?"

"I'm happy it wasn't the tires. Shit, Kacey, I'm happy you're alive." He sounded so overjoyed, she nearly melted. She was forgiving him again.

Kacey lowered her eyes to the thin white blanket on the hospital bed. "Thank you for coming, but you've seen I'm okay, and now you can go."

"Oh, no. Hell, no. I'm not leaving."

"Aaron, you're emotional after seeing Denise and overhearing the rather dramatic accident while we were talking."

"Yes, I am emotional, and who wouldn't be? I love you, Kacey Randal. I realized that before your accident, and the second you left my parents' place I knew I'd messed up a chance for a meaningful relationship. I'm not letting you go."

"What if I want you to? I don't want to be the stupid girlfriend always looking over her man's shoulder."

"If you did look, you wouldn't see anything. I won't make you another Brenda. I wouldn't—*couldn't*—do something like that to you. But no matter how messed up that situation is, I can't be mad at your dad, or your mom, because their indiscretion made you. The woman I'm supposed to be with for the rest of my life."

Why did he have to say things like that? It made hating him so damn hard. "Aaron, I'm not sure. I don't know..."

"I know, but I don't give up easily. I love you, Kacey. And even though you haven't said it, I know you love me too."

"Oh, really?" She scoffed to try and hide how right he was.

"Really. You love me, so don't be pigheaded." His carefree smile came back, and damn if she didn't like seeing it.

"Are you serious right now?"

"Hell, yes, I'm serious. We are going to make this work. What happened yesterday proved we can't take anything for granted. Our relationship might have started out as a one-night stand, but, damn it, I want forever. Forever to show you that I love you."

She wanted to smile, wanted to laugh, but forgiving him seemed too easy. He made everything seem so easy. There was so much to overcome. His female "friends" who lived in different states. Though she'd never say the words out loud, she had serious trust issues with him.

"Aaron—"

"Stop, don't turn me down yet. If you love me, you'll tell me to go get you some Laffy Taffy, we'll giggle at the bad jokes, and take things one day at a time. If you don't, then I'll walk out of that door, hurt, but accepting of your decision."

Kacey stared into his handsome face, then down at her arm in the cast. She wanted him to stay, so badly, but she wasn't sure whether she could. She searched her heart, and listened to the voice of reason in her brain, then met Aaron's eyes and said what she had to say.

"Go away."

CHAPTER 31

"Hey, One Arm," Monique called to Kacey behind the bar at Momma's Kitchen. "You've got another customer."

Kacey continued loading dirty glasses into the basin behind the bar. "I'm not taking customers, Monique."

"I'd love to agree that you shouldn't work with a broken arm, but I'm pretty sure this guy is here for you."

Kacey stopped what she was doing and turned to Monique, who nodded her head toward the end of the bar. Aaron pulled up a stool and lifted his hand in an easy wave. Every day in the six weeks since the accident, with the exception of the one week he'd gone home to South Carolina, he had checked in on her. He'd made himself quite at home in Resilient during her recovery. So much so that Kacey was beginning to wonder if he planned to stay. Well, hope actually.

He'd lied—when she told him to leave her alone that day in the hospital, he'd gotten angry and stormed out, but he hadn't let that be the end. He'd returned an hour later with flowers, Laffy Taffy, and a wrestling magazine. They did laugh at the jokes and argued about the greatness of King Rhames, but she didn't say she loved him. She'd tentatively agreed to see if they could make a relationship work.

"I'll deal with him." She pulled the towel off her shoulder and made her way toward Aaron.

Monique took ahold of her arm in the cast, which was thankfully coming off tomorrow morning. Just in time for Kacey to present her thesis project.

"I know this is going to sound crazy coming from me, but I think he may really mean what he's saying."

"We don't know that. He could just be trying to stay on Reggie's good side."

"He told Reggie the truth and took a punch for using you like that. Then he stuck around. Face it, this guy is really crazy about you. Don't mess things up."

Kacey frowned. "*I'll* mess things up?"

Monique shrugged and grinned. "You have a tendency to ignore the obvious. Besides, I need to know you're happy before I leave."

Kacey pulled out of her sister's grip, but gently pressed her side into Monique's. "I'm talking to him, aren't I?"

"Talking is one thing; you need to get laid."

Kacey rolled her eyes and chuckled. "You'll never change." She walked down to the end of the bar. Aaron's smile grew the closer she got to him. Memories of the first night she'd met him, when he'd given her that same smile and dared her to do something a little wild, filled her mind. Even now that smile tempted her to meet him outside and follow him to the nearest hotel room.

"How are you feeling?" Aaron asked when she reached him.

"I'm fine."

"I really wish you would have waited until after the cast came off before working again."

"We went over this already. I can handle office work with one arm." She held up her good arm. "And doing a little behind the bar isn't hard. Stop worrying."

"I can't help it. You know that."

When he'd first come to see her in the hospital, she hadn't let herself believe him. Now he was wearing down her defenses.

"I'm about to take off, anyway. I need to practice the presentation for my project."

"Do you want me to take you tomorrow?"

Her car had been a total loss after the accident. It still gave her chills to think she'd gotten out of all that twisted metal with only a broken arm and a concussion.

"I can find a ride."

"Let me rephrase that. I'd like to take you tomorrow."

Honestly, she wanted him to take her. "Reggie's taking me, but you can pick me up."

He nodded. "Good. Now finish up and I'll give you a ride home."

Kacey wrapped up a few things and then followed Aaron out to the large SUV he'd recently purchased. She was surprised when he'd bought the vehicle shortly after the accident. Even more so when he said he'd need stable transportation a bit smaller than Bertha to get around town.

They pulled up to her house, and Aaron came around to help her out. His warm hand clasped her elbow and he walked with her to the front door. She unlocked the door and faced him.

"Thanks for the ride."

"Anytime."

His inviting smile popped up, and all of the longing she'd suppressed in the past six weeks bubbled to the surface.

"Do you want to come in?" she asked.

Aaron raised a brow. "Oh, so I finally get the invitation into the house."

"You've been in here since the accident."

"Yes, but only because your family let me in or you needed my help to do something. Not at the end of the day when there was no family or chore that requires two arms instead of one to distract us."

Her face heated. "If you're trying to make me beg, forget about it."

"I'm not trying to make you beg. And believe me, Kacey, there's nothing I want more right now than to come inside with you."

"Then why don't you?"

"Because I need to finish up some things at my place."

She glanced at the stairs leading to the upstairs apartment. "What do you need to do up there?"

"That's not my place anymore. I signed a lease on a house across town."

"What? When? Why?"

"What, is I'm renting a place across town. When, is I signed the lease this morning. Why, well, that's more complicated. First of all, I don't need the prying eyes of your brother every time my shadow passes over your door. And second, because everything I want is right here in Resilient, so there's no reason for me not to stay."

She felt the goofy grin starting and tried to summon the thing into submission. Though her lips refused to frown. "Your business is headquartered in South Carolina."

"It was, but now that both owners are in Tennessee, we've moved corporate. The South Carolina location is a satellite office."

"Oh really."

"Really. So tomorrow, after I pick you up, we'll go to my place, okay?"

She nodded and bit her lip to keep the goofy grin under control. "Okay."

He leaned over and gave her a soft, sweet kiss. "Good night, Kacey."

She barely slept that night, her mind too busy going over the revelations that Aaron had just given. He was staying in town now.

Did that mean... Could they really... Did she want to...

Three questions with various endings that ran through her head as she prepared to present her thesis.

Reggie took her to the doctor to have her cast removed. She tried not to look at the pale, wrinkled flesh as another reason to be self-conscious before her presentation. She'd survived the accident with a broken arm and a concussion; withered skin was worth the side effect.

Right before the presentation, she finally wrangled all thoughts of Aaron and put them away. The end of two years of hard work deserved her undivided attention. The idea of being able to go home at night and not study or cram for an exam was exhilarating. Now there would be nothing to prevent her from opening the second restaurant, or taking more time to enjoy herself. Time with Aaron.

Her presentation went better than she could have imagined. Even Angry Professor said she'd done a great job. Kacey hated to admit the push the professor had given her during the semester had streamlined her franchise plans. So she accepted the compliment and hugged the woman for good measure.

Aaron waited for her afterward, dressed casually in an orange button-up shirt and tan slacks. His curly hair, unruly and wild on his head, and the small amount of stubble on his chin made her want to kiss him.

"How did it go?"

"I knocked it out of the park."

He wrapped her into a big hug, then lifted her feet off the ground and swung her around. "That's fantastic."

Slowly he lowered her to the ground. "I knew you could do it."

His eyes were bright and happy, his body was pressed against hers, and she'd just finished school. She went with what she wanted to do and lifted up on her toes to kiss him. His second of hesitation meant she'd surprised him, but that didn't stop his arms from increasing the pressure around her waist. They locked into the first kiss they'd had since before the accident. She was through pretending she wasn't in love with Aaron.

Desire heated his eyes when they finally broke apart. "Are you ready to go to my place?"

"Yes."

He took her hand and led her to his SUV. They talked about her presentation and how things had gone on the short drive. Aaron parked before a brick ranch-style home in a cute single-family subdivision near downtown. Several cars were parked in the drive and along the street.

Kacey looked from the cars to Aaron. "What's going on?"

He shrugged and did a poor job looking innocent. "I have no idea."

They walked through the door and a chorus of "Congratulations!" greeted them. Everyone was there, not only her family, but also Marcus and his grandmother, the families of the kids of Aaron's baseball team—which he was coaching regularly now. Luigi with his awesome cannolis. Even her dad and Brenda. Being around them would always be awkward, but after being hit by a two-ton vehicle going fifty miles an hour, she no longer cared. Her parents' arrangement was their business, not hers.

Her momma and sisters came over to hug her. "Were you surprised?" Ashlei asked.

Kacey nodded. "Definitely."

Sabrina took her hand and squeezed. "Good." She reached for Monique's hand, and then Monique grabbed Ashlei's. "This is the last time all three of my girls will be in the same room together for a while."

Monique rolled her eyes. "I'm going to Maryland, Momma, not Morocco. Don't get all weepy."

They laughed, and Sabrina blinked away the glossiness in her eyes. "I'm proud of all of you." Reggie walked over and took Ashlei's other hand. "So proud of all of you."

Aaron ducked his head over Kacey's shoulder. "This is supposed to be a party, but if you keep up the speeches, I have a feeling there will be crying."

Kacey chuckled and then hugged her momma again. "He's right. Let's have some fun. The speeches can wait."

The next hour was spent talking about her franchise plans, Monique's plans to move to Maryland for school, and how great things were going to be for Momma's Kitchen. There was laughter and music, and Kacey and Monique even sang some of their songs from the restaurant. Then Luigi brought in a karaoke machine so everyone could sing. Kacey sat cheering for Marcus and Lenny singing a cute rendition of "Uptown Funk" when Aaron tapped her on the shoulder and pulled her away from the crush of people, down the hall into an empty room.

Kacey looked around. "What room is this?"

"It's going to be the master bedroom. I'm waiting on my bed to arrive from Columbia. My brothers are bringing my stuff up this weekend."

So he really was moving. Inside she squealed for joy. Outwardly, she walked calmly over to the window and leaned against the sill. "Thank you for my party. You didn't have to do that."

He stood next to her. "Yes, I did. I can't think of anyone who deserves to be celebrated more than you."

"Aaron, there's something I need to say. About us."

"Let me hear it."

"I didn't believe you when you came to town after the accident. I thought you were hyped up because of the accident or feeling guilty because of what happened at your parents' house. I still can't believe you leased this place..."

"Everything that's important to me is here." He slipped a cell phone out of his back pocket. "I did something else." He tossed the silver-cased phone to her. Kacey caught it with both hands.

"What?"

"It's a new phone."

She looked up from the phone to him. "When did you do that?"

"Last week, though you didn't notice. No old numbers are transferred over. The only people in there are my family, your family, and you. No more texts or phone calls from ex-girlfriends. Having contact with them means nothing if I can't talk to the one woman I want to talk with every night before I go to bed."

"You did this for me?"

"For you, but for me, too. It's time to grow up. I've run from responsibility, only built my business to prove to people that I could. I've treated work and relationships like a hobby. No more. I love you, Kacey. You were right; it wasn't one magic flip that made me realize that. It was a slow buildup over time. The more I got to know you, the more time we spent together, the more I wanted to be with you."

He shifted on his feet and rubbed his hands along the sides of his pants. "The only thing left is for you to make your choice. Do you want to see where this takes us?"

For once he didn't wear his carefree smile. He watched her with serious, nervous eyes. Her heart swelled with her love for him. "I love you, too. Yes, I want to see where this takes us."

His shoulders relaxed, his happy smile came back, and he swept her up into his arms for a kiss. Kacey laughed and wrapped her arms around his neck.

"You thought you were getting me only for one night," Aaron said. "But I'm afraid, Kacey Randal, that now that I know you love me, you're stuck with me forever."

Kacey grinned and pressed closer to him. "I think I can live with that."

EPILOGUE

Christmas music played in the background as Roger and Loretta Henderson watched their four kids, their kids' significant others, and their two grandchildren open presents around the large Christmas tree in their family room.

Loretta leaned closer to Roger on the couch. "I think Neecie will be making an announcement soon."

Roger stopped watching his two grandkids wrestle with a discarded bow in a pile of wrapping paper to look at Kareem and Neecie standing beneath the mistletoe. He'd noticed the extra attention Kareem paid to her and the thickening of her waist. "Our third grandchild."

Loretta nodded. "And I overheard Sandra telling Janiyah that she and David were ready to try for their second."

Roger grunted but smiled. "Before long we'll be bankrupt from spoiling all these grandkids."

She chuckled and placed her hand in his. "It's good to see them all happy."

"Mmm-hmm." He pointed to Aaron and Kacey. "You're about to be happy."

"Why?"

"Just watch."

Kacey opened her present, and frowned. "Slippers?"

Aaron grinned and nodded. "Yeah, remember you've complained about your feet getting cold."

Kacey raised a brow and glanced from him to the slippers. "Umm...thank you."

Then Aaron reached into his pocket and pulled out a small jewelry box. "Well, if you don't like them, you can have this."

He opened the box and revealed a bright diamond ring.

Loretta gasped and sat up. She clasped her hands in front of her. "He's asking."

Kacey cried and laughed, then wrapped Aaron in a huge hug. Immediately Janiyah, Freddy, David, Sandra, Kareem, and Neecie were over there congratulating them.

"And I guess that's a yes," Roger said with false surprise.

Loretta turned to him. "You knew."

"I may have," he said with a sly smile.

"All of them married," Loretta said. A small smile came over her face. "Now what do I do?"

Roger slid forward and wrapped an arm around her shoulders. "They're all settled. David's running the business, and I'm perfectly healthy. I think we deserve a vacation. I haven't seen my baby brother in a while, and none of his kids are married. We can visit him and see if some of our blessings will rub off on them."

Loretta looked from her husband, back to her children. They were blessed beyond measure. She took his hand in hers. "I think that's a great idea."

ABOUT THE AUTHOR

Synithia Williams has published over twenty-five novels since 2012. Her novel, A Malibu Kind of Romance was a 2017 RITA® finalist, she is a 2018 and 2019 African American Literary Award Show nominee in Romance. Her books were listed as Amazon Editor's "Best Book of the Month" in Romance. Reviews of Synithia's books can be found in Publisher's Weekly, Library Journal, Woman's Word, Kirkus and Entertainment Weekly. Synithia lives in Columbia, South Carolina with her husband and two kids. You can learn more about Synithia by visiting her website, www.synithiawilliams.com[1].

---

1. http://www.synithiawilliams.com

ALSO BY SYNITHIA WILLIAMS

HENDERSON FAMILY SERIES
Just My Type
Love's Replay
Making it Real
From One Night to Forever

CALDWELL FAMILY SERIES
Show Me How to Love
Love Me as I Am
Trust Me With Your Love

SOUTHERN LOVE SERIES
You Can't Plan Love
Worth the Wait
A Heart to Heal

HARLEQUIN KIMANI TITLES
A New York Kind of Love
Full Court Seduction
Overtime for Love
Guarding His Heart
His Pick for Passion

BOOKS AS NITA BROOKS
Redesigning Happiness
The Essence of Perfection